King's Pawn

'Deal quickly, King. I don't think I can wait much longer. I want to get my hands on this lass now,' a deep sexy voice said.

I could hear the noise of a card game being played, bids being taken and the cursing when someone lost, but I could concentrate only on the finger that probed me. I moved about as much as I could, trying to gain purchase on it, but its owner was far too clever. Every time I gyrated enough to force the finger further in, it moved away, tantalising me.

All these attentions took my mind off my discomfort and, of course, off the card game until I heard a whoop of joy.

'Congratulations, Bishop, the pawn is yours. Choose your game,' I heard Mr King say, with a slight tinge of regret, I like to think.

I had no idea what he was talking about but I knew that it was me he had won. My heart pounded in my chest, and I wondered exactly what rights were now his and what game he would choose. I also wondered what they meant by a pawn and what the choice of games would be.

This, my first book, is dedicated to Foxy, who dominates my heart, body and soul.

King's Pawn
Ruth Fox

BLACK LACE

Black Lace books contain sexual fantasies.
In real life, always practise safe sex.

First published in 2002 by
Black Lace
Thames Wharf Studios
Rainville Road
London W6 9HA

Design by Smith & Gilmour, London
Printed and bound by Mackays of Chatham PLC

ISBN 0 352 33684 6

*All characters in this publication are fictitious and any resemblance
to real persons, living or dead, is purely coincidental.*

1

I glanced up from my magazine, hoping that no one else in the train compartment could see I was becoming very turned on by the article I was reading. It told vivid tales of dominance and submission; of masters whipping helpless women and the women begging for more.

The article was perfect food for my fantasies. I fantasised almost daily about being held down and forced to do unspeakable acts and accept things that were in truth abhorrent to me.

Well ... they were supposed to be abhorrent to me.

It all started for me when, as a younger woman, I had spent an evening on a double date with a close friend and her boyfriend. Halfway through our dinner at a classy restaurant, Catherine – my friend – started to behave strangely. She became slightly petulant and, for want of a better word, naughty. It seemed that everything her partner Andy suggested she argued with. I knew there was some underlying issue at work but, to begin with, I had no idea what.

By mid-evening it became obvious that they were playing out a sexual game, and I have to say that when the exchange between them heated up I became intrigued and watched in awe as their drama unfolded. My partner was forgotten as I devoured every nuance and suggestion that was a part of their act.

It was impossible not to notice that, when she returned from the loo halfway through the meal, her top button was undone, showing the soft curve of her breasts and a deep cleavage. Andy took one look, leaned toward her and hissed through clenched teeth, 'Do it up, now!'

Catherine just smiled sweetly and I missed the answer she gave him. The button stayed undone all evening as the neckline of her dress fell apart, exposing her body, down to the nipples – nipples that stood out rigid and large through the flimsy material of her dress.

Even the sexy young waiter noticed and kept aggravating the situation by simpering over her with no regard for Andy. She spent the evening doing really silly things that were so unlike her, like slurping her food and talking crudely in a voice loud enough to be heard at the next table.

The climax came when, after an hour of messing with her food and behaving like a spoiled child, Catherine made a play for the waiter. She giggled like a three-year-old as he leaned over her. His eyes glued to her near-naked breasts, as he topped up her glass; she giggled and asked him in a pathetic parody of a bimbo, 'Oh, I must be careful. I can't be trusted when I'm squiffy. Do you think I'm getting squiffy, waiter?'

I gasped, I think, probably out loud, but it was lost on my two friends, who were obviously nearing the end of their game. I watched spellbound, sometimes forgetting to eat or pausing with food halfway to my mouth.

The waiter replied that he thought she was delightful and left the table.

Andy grabbed hold of Catherine's wrist and pulled her close. 'One more trick like that, miss, and when we get home you'll get the punishment you deserve.'

My whole body responded to his threat, flushing with a prickly heat as my mind raced and searched for the unknown ingredients. What did he mean? How would he punish her? Did he really mean it? Jesus! My heart was palpitating and my crotch was damp and throbbing.

My gaze, which had been transfixed on Andy's face, snapped to Catherine's to see her reaction. She was smiling knowingly, her pupils dilated and her mouth slightly open in a very provocative way. It was like being part of a tableau in which all the characters showed the wrong reactions.

Andy, having made such a statement, should have looked angry, but he was staring into my friend's eyes, his expression dripping with arousal. Catherine should have been angry and/or scared, but she just gazed at him, sharing the moment. I should have been indignant for her but I think I was more aroused than either of them, and my partner – who should have looked confused, or horny like me – had missed the whole thing. Typical! They both calmed down a little then. It was as if they felt they could relax now the 'game' was out of the way.

I wondered for days about what he had done to her when they had got home. In the end I just *had* to know, so I phoned Catherine and asked her outright.

There was no shyness on her part. She just laughed and explained that they both loved spanking and bondage games and they both found it much more enjoyable if the punishment was for a real misdemeanour. She apologised for dragging us into it.

'We usually keep our games private,' she said, 'but until that night I'd always wanted Andy to take our games up a step and whip me, and I thought if I really showed him up in front of friends then that might do the trick.'

I anticipated her answer with a burning twitch between my legs when I asked, as casually as I could, if her ploy had worked.

She obviously realised how fascinated I was and went into great detail about how he had tied her, spread-eagled and face down, on his bed with her hips raised over a pillow. He spanked her long and hard, then he had whipped her across her back and buttocks with a rubber whip they had bought years before. She told me it had been hanging from a hook in their bedroom, tantalising her ever since its purchase. I must have been so fascinated that I didn't respond, because Catherine explained that it wasn't how it sounded in books. He had started very slowly and gently until the sheer frustration had aroused her to fever pitch. Then he had upped the pressure but keeping the pain level well within her limits.

'But, Cath, doesn't it hurt?' I asked in a suspiciously croaky voice.

'Only when he stops and teases me for hours. Try it. You never know, you might like it.' She chuckled.

I have long since lost touch with Catherine and Andy and I can't even remember the name of my date, but on that night almost ten years ago her fantasy became mine – and I longed to be tied down under threat of punishment.

Until that day on the train, though, I had never had a real need to experience it. I suppose I was too scared.

The carriage was dotted with the last straggling commuters, who ignored each other daily and just read, or conducted intricate business meetings by mobile phone – all oblivious to other travellers.

I found myself wondering which, if any, of these harried people played the sorts of games that were described in minute detail on the pages before me.

The article was full of accounts by women just like me: intelligent, articulate, independent women who fantasise. I was surprised to find that a great deal of them, like me, have deep, dark yearnings that they can hardly admit to themselves.

Reading about other women admitting their need for these so-called 'perversities' opened a door for me, mentally allowing me at least to find out more.

An insistent pressure on my knees disturbed my concentration, so I tore my thoughts away from the submissive woman's description of utter debauchery and looked up.

I was sitting on a bench seat, facing another, with only enough room between for average legs. Mine were average; his were not. The man sitting with his knees pressed against mine was tall, with incredibly long legs. He was fit and lean, with dark wavy hair down to the collar of his black polo shirt. He looked completely embarrassed and tried to shift about to give me more room, muttering an apology.

I have a definite wicked streak and at that moment it was aroused into action by the article I was reading. I smiled seductively at him and, instead of squirming away, I returned the pressure.

His embarrassed gaze turned to disbelief. He was obviously not quite sure whether he was reading me right, so I decided on the spur of the moment that a game with him would break the journey. I lowered my magazine to my lap with the headline emblazoned across the top of the page: WOMEN WHO NEED TO SUBMIT.

He focused on the upside-down words, then looked at my face, then read them again, and a slow grin creased the corners of his very sexy mouth. The pressure on my knees returned. His gaze would not leave mine and I am ashamed to say that I chickened out first and turned my head to look out of the window, but I kept up the pressure on his knees. My eyes met his in the reflection, and this time I had the courage to hang on to the game. While his eyes bored into mine, I felt the pressure of his knees increase and a slight movement outwards. My reflex action was to clamp my legs shut tight but the pressure was insistent.

I frantically looked around me and, to my surprise, found that there was no one else in close proximity to us. I relaxed a little, waiting to see how far he would go, knowing that, if he kept up the assault on my knees, he would certainly get an eyeful.

As the meeting I was going to was rather important, I was dressed in my dark business suit with its stylishly short skirt. Already, just because I was sitting, my skirt was riding up my thighs. His knees broke my thoughts with their firm pressure against my own, which were trembling as his forced them apart until there was at least a six–inch gap between them. The intensity of his burning look in the window swept through my veins, pushing aside all hesitation and flooding me with the anticipation of what he would do next. His eyes left mine and lowered a fraction to glance briefly at my legs, then returned to my shamed gaze and my flushed cheeks. An almost imperceptible grin crinkled the corner of his mouth

I kept my gaze fixedly on the houses rushing past outside, watching snippets of the lives of the people inside, who were oblivious to the progression of our erotically dangerous game. I guessed that, with my legs spread this far apart, my beautiful stranger could probably see the dark welt around the top of my 'barely black' stocking tops and decided he wanted more, because, gradually, my legs were spread further apart. Eventually the suspenders attached to the taut stocking tops, the soft pale flesh of my thighs above the stockings, and, probably, the gusset of my black lace knickers were exposed for his eyes to consume. And consume them he did – with undisguised hunger. He licked his lips nervously as he fed on the picture before him.

Can you believe I actually felt my pussy blush, and my juices respond to the situation by soaking the tight black silk? He just stared. Not once after that did his eyes meet mine; instead, they stared at my crotch and pinned me in place like a butterfly pinned to a board. He took a book from his bag and leaned forward with his elbows on his spread knees, trying to look casual and cover the exciting exchange that was going on between us. I carried on staring out of the window, scared now that he would stop. I was ready to explode.

His hand, when it brushed against my naked thigh, was warm and gentle, making its way upwards, towards my crotch. I instinctively tried to close my legs to stop his exploration, but there was no way he was going to allow that. His knees moved slightly till they were just inside mine, and pushed outwards until I felt the crotch of my wet knickers tighten and the sinews in my thighs stretch. I grabbed my coat from the seat beside me and placed it over our knees. I slid further down in my seat but he would not have it, and grabbed the coat that hid my mounting excitement from his view and threw it on the seat beside him.

The heat that washed through my veins sent a powerful shudder of delight down my spine as his fingers continued where they had left off. They stroked their way up my thighs until they reached the apex, delved under the damp crotch of my knickers and, without a pause, pushed their insistent way between my sticky lips and right into me.

I bit my bottom lip to stop myself crying out with the sheer rudeness of it all – but panted far too loudly as his fingers searched deep within me.

I tore my eyes from the window and watched him, hypnotised by the way his brown eyes gazed at the place between my legs where his hand disappeared from view. I could tell by the rapture on his face and the bulge at his crotch that he was not satisfied with what he already had in his sights. I was therefore not at all surprised when he tossed aside his book and, with it, all pretence that we were on a normal journey. He reached forward and pulled aside the silk of my knickers until my sex was in full view, with his fingers pushed deep inside me. His very experienced thumb found my erect clitoris and manipulated it gently until it was pulsating greedily. It was so difficult not to make a single sound as I rushed towards orgasm, but the necessary silence increased my arousal until I was an absolute wreck.

He looked so pleased with himself as the clutches of my orgasm sucked on his fingers and throbbed through my clit.

The train slowed to pull into a station just as the throes of my orgasm began to subside. The sweat was trickling down my spine and running through my hair as I did my best to pull myself together, my stranger watching my every move with complete fascination. I was desperately trying to think how I could manage to repay the compliment as I adjusted my clothes. The loo was the only option I could come up with but, before I had a chance, he stood up, leaned over me and placed a soft kiss on my lips before turning to leave the train.

I was totally astounded as he walked alongside my window on the platform and, giving me one last enigmatic grin, he put his index finger in his mouth and sucked.

Sadly, I never saw him again.

My imagination was fired. I wanted to know how it felt to be restrained. Just the thought brought me out in goose bumps. I really wanted to know how it felt not only to have my legs forced apart but to be completely tied up, not to be able to move and to be at the mercy of a lover – to be so restrained that I couldn't even respond by wriggling.

In the magazine I was reading one particular woman had written about her sub/dom relationship. She described the utter acceptance she felt as the blindfold went on and she found herself totally helpless at the exquisite mercy of her 'master'. I wasn't quite sure if I could go along with the 'master' bit, but the rest caused a definite stirring in my lower regions. For the rest of my journey, I tried very hard to talk myself out of the idea that was threatening to take hold in my aroused brain. I knew that, if I did choose to go ahead with my crazy scheme, I would have to be very careful whom I chose to 'deflower' me. It could, after all, be very embarrassing, but I knew the time had come to experience restraint at first hand. Thoughts of the danger I was letting myself in for didn't cross my mind for a second.

The ideas of bondage and submission that filled my thoughts were still just wisps of fantasy that floated through my mind and tugged at my nerves.

There was one easy way to find out whether it would all turn me on or not, I decided, as I let myself into my house. I carried out the usual chores with my mind bursting with not only memories of what I had let him do to me on the train home, but the very real feeling of his fingers still inside me. Later that evening, when I could stand the suspense no longer, I lay on my bed feeling very foolish. First, I tried to think of a way to tie myself up, but came up with lots of ideas for my legs and none for my upper torso.

I found two leather belts and first buckled one around my ankles and the other around my knees, pulling them quite tight just to experience the feeling. The tightness and the creaky sound of the leather, the musky smells and the sight of the black against my pale skin were enough to excite me before I had even buckled them.

It wasn't enough; I wanted more. I racked my brain for a way to bind my hands behind my back – but came up with nothing. Whatever ideas I had needed another person to tie and untie me. I reluctantly undid what I had done so far and went down to the shed. After some rummaging about I found an old padlock and key – rather large, but it would do. I tried the key in the lock with my heart pounding, but it was rusty and wouldn't move. I realised then that I didn't have anything to padlock together anyway! My arousal had just got the better of me.

Back to the bedroom. I would just have to imagine I was restrained. I replaced the belts and buckled them tightly, then switched off the light. I lay in the semidarkness with just my thoughts for company. I lay on my hands to try to imagine how it would feel to be completely helpless. My crotch, trapped between my trembling thighs, tightly held by the leather, got hotter and hotter. My legs started trembling and I longed to release my hands to touch myself, but I held out to see where my feelings would go.

I imagined the stranger on the train standing above me, looking at my predicament and cracking a whip through the air, watching me writhing and wriggling in my discomfort. I flushed with excitement at each imagined snap of leather and closed my eyes to add to the thrill. I imagined him waiting until I groaned and begged for him to touch me before he even contemplated putting me out of my misery. I found myself actually groaning out loud as I tried to force my legs apart. But the straps did their job and held me fast.

My poor pussy had never been so frustrated. It longed for attention. Attention of any sort would do. In fact I had no idea what it wanted, or what *I* wanted, for that matter. My hot pussy and I certainly wanted something, badly. After only a few short moments I could stand it no longer. I pulled my hands free and rammed one between my thighs, rubbing and grinding my fist in the sopping wet crotch of my knickers, hoping to satisfy the yearning I had awakened.

My body shook with the small tight orgasm that was forced out of it and I lay on the bed, shuddering in the aftermath, totally unsatisfied and a little frightened at the intensity I had felt. If just five minutes of rushed fantasy could leave me shattered like this, should I really go on to explore further? It then became a matter of *principle* that I explore further. It was so humiliating to remember myself thrashing about on the bed in my own bonds. I was determined at least to find out more about this exciting side of my sexuality. I am basically an independent woman and was certainly not used to being unable to get what I wanted.

Over the next week or two I couldn't get the idea of being helpless out of my mind for more than a few minutes at a time. How would it feel to have a pair of hands and even perhaps a mouth roaming my body at will? Wherever I was, I found myself imagining a lover controlling me. During quiet moments at the office I would stand with my hands clasped behind my back and pretend they were tied, so I knew the time had come to do something positive.

I was so naïve then. I thought it would be easy. At that stage I had no idea of the games people play. I thought it would be as simple as finding someone who was turned on by bondage and having a little try. My world was still reasonably normal.

Those were probably the last few days of near sanity in my life.

I suppose I had always known that for me there had to be more. I would listen to other women talking about their sex lives, and lots of them were bored but craved gentler loving. I longed for the opposite: a bit of intensity.

After the experience on the bed with belts buckled around my legs and the disappointing climax that followed, I knew masturbation was not the answer. The feeling I craved needed to be provided by a second person.

I lay in bed at night imagining all sorts of lurid acts being performed on my helpless body. I imagined that a man clad entirely in leather overpowered me, and that he was raping me. Or, I was in a laboratory being watched by hundreds of students in a gallery above me. I was strapped to a table and next to me was a trolley covered in instruments. I couldn't quite make out each individual instrument, but they excited the hell out of me.

My most recurring dream had me being dominated by a tribe of Amazon women, who kept me as a slave and carried out despicable acts of degradation on my chained body. I enjoyed that one most.

I was obsessed and felt as if I were losing my grip on my life – and certainly on my control. I had become like a teenager again, thinking about sex all day. I couldn't escape it.

I decided that I needed to talk to someone before I lost my marbles completely. I wanted to go over all the things that were playing havoc with my sanity and see what a friendly ear would make of it all.

Ruth, my closest friend, was the natural choice. I knew I could tell her anything. She wouldn't moralise or judge me. In fact I decided she would probably get an erotic kick out of this one. I picked up the phone, holding my breath and desperately hoping she was there. She had been a good friend for years.

'Hi,' she said in a very husky and seductive voice as she picked up the receiver.

'It's only me,' I said, laughing, 'so you can cut the flirty voice.'

I told her that I had a very exciting subject I wanted to talk over with her and invited her for coffee. I knew her terrible curiosity would get the better of her.

'On my way. Put the kettle on and get the digestives out. I should be about half an hour, and then you can tell me all about it.'

As I waited for Ruth to arrive I took stock of my life, wondering whether I was being stupid even contemplating risking changing a lifestyle that worked so well.

After ten years at Adtec Services, I had worked my way up from admin assistant to personnel officer and was really proud of myself. I had everything a single woman could want: a cosy detached cottage in a smallish rural village, where, even though I didn't really join in the usual village activities, I did have a nodding acquaintance with most of its inhabitants. I made sure I went to the gym at least twice a week to keep my body in a reasonable state. To date I had managed to keep my boobs from sagging too much, and my weight at a level that allowed the occasional binge or meal out.

I had two or three men friends with whom I could go to the theatre or up to town for a meal, who if the mood took us were quite happy to stay over after a night on the tiles so that we could satisfy our urges. The only problem with that was that it never did quite seem to satisfy mine. The fantasies persisted.

Tom, one of my men friends, had a way of hinting at the type of sexuality I craved, but he never came across with the goods. He would joke with phrases like 'If you keep doing that I'm going to have to put you across my knee' or 'If you don't stop fidgeting I'll tie you to the chair' if we were perhaps watching a play that he was enjoying and I wasn't. Once I even turned my bottom towards him in bed and coyly squealed, 'Oh, no, please don't spank me.' So he didn't.

Twenty-five minutes after my call Ruth swanned into the kitchen after tapping on the back door. She looked cool and beautiful as ever with her long shapely legs shown off to their best, bare and brown, and her slim body encased in a figure-hugging, short, denim dress showing off her perfect golden tan. Ruth shared my evenings at the gym but never had to exercise because she is one of those sickening women who can eat anything they want – even chocolate – and still stay a perfect size 12. She would languish under the sun lamps perfecting her tan while I huffed and puffed my way to an uncertain size 14.

She is so beautiful with her short, jet-black hair in a sleek bob and big, blue, very expressive eyes that just make you want to tell her your deepest secrets. I have never got used to her beauty. Wherever we go she turned heads. Most people who meet her immediately feel she is a bimbo, but it is just a façade. Under the fluttering lashes and husky voice is an intelligent lady. She runs her own business and can, when necessary, be very strong and determined; but, when she is with me, she is just Ruth, my friend. As teenagers we had shared everything, from gossip and make-up to boyfriends, and I hoped that what I had to tell her wouldn't shock her or taint our close relationship.

'Hi,' she said as she bent to kiss me on the cheek. 'What's up? I'm intrigued. What is it that couldn't possibly wait? I was coming round tomorrow anyway. Oh, don't tell me, I know: it must have something to do with a man. I'm right, aren't I?'

'Sort of,' I replied. I always seemed to be complaining about one man or another not behaving the way I wanted him to and Ruth always had the knack of putting things into perspective. I couldn't help wondering as she sat down opposite me whether she would be able to do that quite so easily this time.

'Well, go on, then, I can't wait. Who is he?' she cajoled.

We were sitting at the kitchen table, as we usually did if we were going to have a gossip, with a plate of biscuits and a pot of coffee in front of us. I plucked up courage and came out with it.

'Do you fantasise, Ruth?'

'Of course I do. Doesn't everyone? Why? What have you been fantasising about that's brought such a sparkle to your eyes? Tell me, for goodness' sake.'

'I don't know how to begin,' I whispered, suddenly feeling very foolish and shy.

She took hold of my hands then and looked in my eyes.

'Come on, silly. You know you can tell me anything. I know, you tell me yours and I'll tell you mine after. And I bet mine will shock you more than yours will shock me.'

She had no idea!

I stumbled a little at first, but, when I realised she wasn't batting an eyelid, I told her everything. I told her about the game I had played on the train with the stranger and my fantasies of bondage and punishment. I added details of the magazine article, and my recent decision to do something about it. I finished by asking for suggestions of how I could meet someone to dominate me and tie me up.

She wasn't fazed at all: 'I suppose first you need to decide exactly how far you want to experiment and what type of person you want to do it with. Then we'll have a better idea of how to go about getting it for you, won't we?' She grinned.

I explained I wasn't quite sure. I knew that the most powerful image I had was of being spread-eagled and tormented, but I also knew that it was just a fantasy. We decided that I should be realistic and that my best bet was to find a man who knew I was a beginner and liked the idea of initiating a novice into his own particular way.

'I know, Cassie. Why don't you get one of those magazines – you know, the top-shelf type with personal ads in – and place an advert? That way you don't have to answer any replies if you don't want to. You can pick and choose and no one will ever know who you are unless you want them to. You can even lie if the mood takes you. Come on, let's do it now before you chicken out. I'll help.'

I got caught up in her enthusiasm and agreed instantly without a single thought for what might lie ahead. While Ruth finished her coffee, I went to slip on my shoes and coat. A lick of lippy and we were set.

At the local shopping centre we browsed the top shelves in at least four different newsagents' trying to pretend we were looking for hairdressing magazines. After that Ruth started to get frustrated, so she grabbed hold of my hand and marched into the next shop. Luckily, there was only the owner in there. The poor Asian man didn't know what hit him. My rather stunning friend walked straight up to the counter, leaned across to him and in a seductive whisper asked if he could help her.

'Yes, miss, I would be pleased to. How can I help?'

'Well, my friend and I are looking for a man and we want one of those magazines that have contacts in them. Do you have any of them?'

'Oh, yes. Come with me.'

He was almost dribbling. I stood back and just let her get on with it. They walked over to the magazine rack and he took down three or four from the far corner and discussed them at length with Ruth, leaning close and sharing something that highly amused them. She flicked through the glossy magazines and, having picked one out, walked over to me, saying far too loudly, 'How about this one, Cassie? Look, it's just what we need.'

The magazine was called *Bound to Meet* and the front cover had a very pretty picture of a naked girl kneeling on a velvet cushion, with her hands tied behind her back and her eyes blindfolded. My crotch responded instantly but I did manage to nod.

'Thanks, we'll take this one. You've been really helpful,' she simpered at the man, who at this stage was almost apoplectic. He grovelled and almost bowed to her as he insisted that she come back if she wanted anything else. He obviously loved every second as she walked over to him, put her hand on his arm and assured him that he would be the first person she would turn to for help.

'You're terrible. That man thought you were flirting with him,' I admonished as we left the shop.

'I think I was. He was rather nice, wasn't he? He kept telling me that he knew lots of men who would be more than happy to meet us if we would like to go down the pub on the corner tonight. How do you fancy it?'

'You're joking!' I exclaimed, shocked – but not for the first time – by her behaviour.

'Course I am, you silly sod. Not about the offer, though, only about going. You and I have much more important things to do. Come on. Let's get home and start on this ad.'

We spent the next hour and a half writing and rewriting an advert for me until there was a pile of screwed-up attempts on the floor. The biscuits we had started earlier had all gone and the coffee pot was cold and empty. Then we finally agreed on a wording:

Cassie, 32-year-old tall attractive brunette with wild fantasies about bondage and domination, would like to meet an imaginative man to teach her the ropes with sensitivity.

When we had finished the advert Ruth got up to leave. We said our goodbyes as usual with a perfunctory kiss on the cheek. But by the time she had got as far as the door I remembered her promise.

'Oh no you don't,' I called. 'You haven't told me your deep dark secret yet. I want to know yours too, now that you know mine.'

She paused at the door, turned, laughed and insisted that she would tell me one day.

2

The following two weeks dragged endlessly. It took that long for my advert to get into the magazine. I was lucky that I'd just met the deadline. If I had been two days later I would have had to wait an extra month. I would probably have gone mad if I'd had to wait that long. I went through countless scenarios in my mind as I waited for any replies I might receive, wondering what the men reading my advert would think and how they would picture me from my carefully crafted words.

I couldn't believe how quickly I received replies. Only ten days after I had seen it in the magazine a large brown envelope arrived with my name on it. I knew immediately it was the one I was waiting for. I ran upstairs, opened the envelope and tipped the contents on to the bed, then ran my hands through the eight envelopes. I shuffled them around trying to decide which to open first. I was beside myself, jumping up and down and squeaking with delight at the bounty spread out before me.

I piled them in categories: brown, white, handwritten, typed, local, distant. But, whichever pile it went into, one caught my attention over and over again. It was a small buff jiffy bag that obviously had more in it than a letter. It was begging to be first. What could I do but comply?

I separated it from the rest, placed it in front of me on the bed and looked at it, trying hard to imagine what it said, what type of person had sent it and, most important, what his speciality was – assuming it was a he. I pictured him just like the man on the train who had shared with me the most debauched half-hour I had ever spent.

With shaking hands and pounding heart, I carefully picked out the staples holding the flap closed, putting off the moment that would be the start of my adventure. I stuck my fingers in the end and was quite disappointed to find only one sheet of paper, folded down the middle. I drew it out telling myself, 'Well, at least it's good quality.' I was convinced it would disappoint me.

Dear Cassandra

I read your advertisement with interest. I am intrigued and couldn't possibly miss the opportunity of teaching an attractive inexperienced lady the delights of bondage and submission at the hands of an experienced Master.

You will find enclosed a sample of the bonds I will use on you. Test them for strength and comfort at your leisure. Try to imagine how you will feel as I tie the last knot, the one that will hold you secure for me.

I would like to offer you the opportunity to 'give' yourself to me for one whole day. Obviously you will be free to leave at any time but if you choose to stay I will expect you to accept anything I want to do to you without question. My sole purpose will be to explore your sexual limits, not abuse them.

If you agree to my terms send me a postcard with one word on it, 'Yes.' When I receive it I will send you instructions that I would ask you to follow implicitly.

I will expect your answer by return of post.

Regards

Mr King

I read the words over and over again until they were committed to memory. They thrilled me to the core. I had always considered myself to be quite a dominant personality but inside me something was melting. He was so arrogant and sure of himself, confident that I would go. I had to keep looking away from his words to compose myself, then go back to them and read them again. It was a few minutes before I realised that there must be something else in the envelope – I was in such a daze.

I tipped up the envelope and a little package wrapped in black tissue fell out. I turned it over and over in my trembling hands, and, putting it to my nose, breathed deeply. Not leather, then, I told myself. The need to open it was like a cold knot in my stomach, but the courage to do so hovered just out of my reach.

I leaned back on the pillows stacked behind me, closed my eyes and took a deep breath. With my eyes still closed I tore open the tissue and shook it out.

The sight as I opened my eyes and the jolt to my senses will stay with me for ever. It was coiled there in front of me like a scarlet silky snake: a length of bright-red shiny rope that gave the illusion of having a life of its own as the light from the window danced along its length. I was stunned. I picked it up and was surprised to find that it was soft to the touch and almost fluid in its movement. I visualised yards of it tied round my limbs, staking me out and holding my body taut and waiting.

Even in my wildest dreams I could not imagine what came next. In my fantasies I never got further than being tied, helpless at the mercy of . . .

So many unfinished thoughts, I told myself. Now was my chance to fill in the missing places, if I had enough courage.

I forced myself to put all thoughts of him aside for a few minutes and opened the rest of the letters, but they were uninteresting compared with the one from Mr King. Only one other held my attention at all.

Two of the letters I relegated to the bin straightaway. They were pornography with no coherent sentences to join the suggestions together. The ideas on one of them turned my stomach and the other writer was probably mentally unstable. That left five and Mr King's. Two were sent by men who were obviously totally uneducated. Not that that mattered in itself – we all crave a bit of rough sometimes – but they were written on scraps of paper torn from notebooks and explained nothing. I wrote back to them briefly thanking them for their trouble but explaining that I had changed my mind. That left three.

The first of these was completely in German, so I binned it. One left me chuckling because it had obviously been forwarded to the wrong advertiser and was from a gay cross-dresser trying to find a male soul mate. I thought that, like me, his chances of finding the perfect one were so limited that I sent it back to the magazine to be sent safely on its way to Delphine of Box No. 924.

When I opened the last I thought it was a mistake, too, because it was from a woman, but, as I read further, I realised that she was very like me. The letter had a small passport-size photo pinned to the top with a very pretty blonde face smiling out with sparkling eyes and full mouth.

Dear Cassie

I know as I write this that you are probably looking for a man to answer your very intriguing advert but I thought I would have a go anyway.

My name is Rebecca but most people call me Becky and just like you I have dreamed for years of being restrained, but more than that I long to restrain a woman. To be totally honest I am not sure if I am gay or not. Although I have had one or two very exciting short-term relationships with women, I have also enjoyed men. My bondage fantasies, however, tend to lie with women.

I suppose I should tell you a little about myself – please don't completely disregard me until you have read more.

I am a little bit younger than you at 29, single, a staff nurse at our local hospital with a wide circle of acquaintances but no one I can tell my thoughts to. I love theatre and sparkling white wine, mountains and tranquil places. I am 5′ 9″ tall and just about the right size for my height. I won't bother describing my looks because you can see the photo. I suppose I should be honest and admit that it is a very good one. If you saw a picture of me when I had just woken up, when my hair looks like a tangled horse's mane and the make-up that I didn't wash off properly the night before is rubbed around my eyes, you would throw it away immediately. Perhaps I shouldn't have told you that but I want to be as honest as possible.

Obviously you might be completely heterosexual and be throwing up as you read this, but if you are open to new ideas and enjoy the idea of a sexual adventure why not give me a ring and we could have a chat? I promise I will put no pressure on you to do anything but chat.

We probably live at opposite ends of the country anyway, but if we are within driving distance and you fancy anything about me at all please ring.

My number is on the back of my photo. I live alone so don't be embarrassed, and I would truly love to hear from you.

My very best wishes

Becky.

23

It was a shame that I had so recently read the letter from Mr King, because I would probably have given Becky more thought. I really liked the sound of her. I had never actually had sex with another female but I was certainly not against trying anything new. I was just so wrapped up in the image of Mr King having his evil way with me. There had been the odd occasion when I had caught a girl's eye in a pub or watched the sensuous mouth of a female colleague without her knowing. I even quite fancied Amanda, my secretary. I would be standing there, wondering how it would feel to kiss her and trying to concentrate on the business at hand. One thing I had fantasised about was the idea of sucking the nipple of a soft female breast, with the breast cradled in my hands and her soft groans filling the air. The only problem was that I had no idea at all what I would do after that.

The card with the one word 'yes' printed in my best handwriting in the centre of the card stuck to my fingers for a fleeting second before fluttering into the postbox. I had wanted to say so much, ask so many questions – questions such as, 'Can I trust you? Are you going to hurt me? If you do hurt me, will I like it?' The one word said so much but so little. A million times over the past few hours I had changed my mind and decided not to answer. I had torn up two postcards with the word 'yes' on them, only to end up writing new ones. But finally I admitted that I had to go for it if only for my own peace of mind. I could always back out if I wanted to. Couldn't I?

He must have done it on purpose. Days went by and I almost gave up hope of getting a reply. I got so fed up waiting.

My thoughts were full of Mr King. I found it quite

strange that he had written about such a sensitive subject but signed only his surname. Then I had to admit that it all added to the anticipation and attraction. What did he look like? How old was he? And why didn't he write, for Christ's sake? What was wrong with me?

Occasionally I managed to convince myself that he would still answer my letter, but I suppose deep down I thought that he had decided I wasn't right, or that I had done something wrong already, or – horror of horrors – that it had all been a wind-up.

One evening, after three weeks of waiting, when I had almost given up hope of ever hearing from Mr King, I found myself curled up in my squidgy sofa with the phone in one hand and the letter from Becky in the other. I had fortified myself with a glass of wine and felt softly mellow. Quite a few times I had found myself thinking about her letter and wondering what she was like. I had really liked the picture that showed such a happy pretty face, with large blue eyes and a generous full mouth. Decidedly kissable.

I dialled the number with my heart pounding in my chest.

'Hi, this is Becky. I'm sorry, but I either can't make it to the phone right now or I am probably doing something far too exciting to want to. Leave me a message and I'll get back to you. Bye.'

She sounded so bubbly and happy that I was disappointed that she wasn't there. I had to make a quick decision about leaving a message and managed to stutter like an idiot.

'Hi, Becky. My name's Cassie and you answered my advert . . .' That was as far as I had got when the phone was snatched up and I heard her breathless husky voice in my ear. Already I felt a shiver run down my spine at the rightness of her voice.

'Cassandra, I'm so glad you decided to ring. I was

beginning to think you weren't going to. It must have taken a lot of courage. Thank you. Hello? Are you still there? Cassandra?'

For the first minute or two I felt shy, but before long we were chatting like old friends and by the end of the twenty-minute conversation we were flirting. I had never actually flirted with a woman before but found that it came as easily as with men, especially if you fancied the person concerned. And I knew without a doubt that I really fancied her. Even without meeting. What made it so special was her female knowledge of all things sexual instead of the mystery that it must be to men.

I found myself telling her about my experience on the train and my letter from Mr King. Becky was just as excited and intrigued as I was, but, when I described sitting with my legs apart in the train carriage with a total stranger's fingers buried inside me, and having not even said one word to him, she called me a dirty girl and my stomach flipped.

We knew instinctively that we would be very good friends and probably lovers, and the conversation reflected that knowledge. Becky didn't actually come out and ask if I would be interested in 'playing' with her to begin with but hinted at how good she thought she could make me feel. I loved her use of the word 'playing' and the horny female in me felt as if I had come home. Becky made a point of describing for me how a woman knows so well just how another woman wants to be treated, and I almost hyperventilated at her words.

'Believe me, Cassie, when you have a woman's soft head between your thighs, with her long hair brushing your skin and her slow, sensual tongue exploring all the folds that she knows about so intimately, you'll finally know what it's like to come the way a woman should come.' Her voice became almost gravelly with arousal as she talked to me, and my body responded admirably. My nipples were aching and my hand had wandered into my knickers with a will of its own.

'Will you do something for me, Cassandra?' she breathed in my ear.

'Of course I will.'

'I want you to strip from the waist down and sit with your legs apart for me. Will you do that?'

I felt almost compelled to obey. I confessed that my hand was already exploring, and Becky laughed. 'Oh, God, we're going to get on just fine, Cassie. I think you're me. Right. Now I want you to slide your index finger just inside your beautiful pussy, then I want you to slip that very wet finger out again, and up through the groove of your sex until it's reached the hardness of your clitoris. It is hard, your clit, isn't it, Cassandra?'

I groaned my answer as I did as she requested and my clit jumped to attention.

'Good. Now I want you to thrust your hips out as far as you can and spread your legs until they hurt. Imagine you're held fast and that the finger on your clit is my tongue. Now stop the pressure of your finger and just lightly touch right on the wet shiny tip, so that you want more and you can just imagine your fingertip is the gossamer brush of my tongue. But you can't stretch any further, Cassandra, because you're completely restrained. Now take your finger away and feel how exquisitely frustrating that is.' Becky paused for a second, then admonished me, correctly.

'No, Cassandra, take the finger away and don't put it back. Just imagine that you can still feel my hot breath cooling your juices and my hair sweeping across your thighs.'

I am not sure at what stage she changed from talking

in general to talking specifically and intimately about us but I wallowed in it. I felt utterly like the dirty girl she accused me of being.

'Now be brave and get dressed again without any more touching. Imagine that your hands are tied behind your back so you're unable to do anything but stew in your arousal and wait. How does that make you feel, Cassandra?'

I forced myself to do as she asked and wriggled back into my soggy knickers with the phone tucked under my ear and her crooning still filling my head. Just at that one touch and her controlling words I was so horny that I felt I would burst if I didn't come.

'Christ, Becky, that was amazing. If you can make me feel like that over the phone I can't begin to imagine the fun we could have playing together.'

'Where do you live, Cassandra? Please don't say Aberdeen or Cornwall – I don't think I could take it.'

'Suffolk'.

'You're joking. How close to the M25?'

'About an hour.'

'Can I come to you now. I know it's late but it's Sunday tomorrow. Please, Cassandra. I won't pressure you into anything, but, let's face it, even if we don't want to play together, we know we'll be good friends. We can at least enjoy swapping stories and you could tell me more about your Mr King. I could be there by ten o'clock. What do you think?'

'I think you should try to get here quicker.'

We both laughed and I gave her explicit instructions to get her right to my door in the fastest possible safe time. I explained that, even though I found our conversation horny, I was also a bit embarrassed and had never 'played' with a woman before.

'Oh, good. If the truth were known this is all a little new to me, too, but already I know we'll be good together. Oh, and by the way, Cassandra, don't even think of touching yourself before I get there. Please indulge me and keep your hands busy doing something else so that I can spend the journey imagining your sexy pussy hot and hungry.'

I was still groaning inwardly as I put down the phone and went into a right tizzy. Without the sound of her voice spurring me on I was convinced that I would be completely put off by the fact that she was a woman and wish I hadn't invited her to stay. At least I had spare rooms I could put her in if necessary. Over the next two hours while I showered and had a quick tidy-up I reminded myself that we had been very easy together and it wouldn't really matter if we ended up just friends. Then I would remember her sexy voice and again I would feel my body oozing in all its most shameful areas.

It was actually two hours and twenty minutes by the time Becky got to me and by then I had decided that she had chickened out. Once or twice I nearly rang to see if she had left, but I liked the thought that she was on her way to me, so I forced myself to be patient. I am not very good at being patient.

When I answered her knock I was so glad that I had chosen not to dress up because Becky stood on my doorstep in just a comfortable pair of jeans and sweat-shirt. Her wonderful blonde hair hung around her face and shoulders like a cloud. Her fringe was too long, so she had to keep flicking her head slightly to look at me properly and for me to get good look at her saucer eyes. I stood back and held the door open as she walked into my hallway, dropped her bag and held her arms open to me.

'Cassie, I feel as if I've known you for ever.' She must have noticed my hesitation because she quickly added,

'If I had to choose I would far rather have you as a friend, so please relax. It's not going to be the end of the world if we just spend all night talking and I go home in the morning. Is it?'

Becky kissed my face tenderly as I returned her hug and I have to admit that I felt a jolt in my groin and a decidedly warm glow where my breasts squashed against hers. It was strange, because I had hugged friends all my life and it was not uncommon for my friend Ruth and me to hug each other for long minutes at a time if one of us was hurting or lonely, but I had never felt anything like I felt in that hallway.

We pulled apart reluctantly but I kept hold of her hand as I showed her into the lounge. I have never known anything to feel so right or to flow so fluidly. Becky and I just melted into each other, our bodies blending and moulding together as if it were meant to be. She showed me just how beautiful it is to have a woman between my legs as very tentatively, with her adventurous tongue, she explored my folds, as she put it. I finally got to realise my fantasy of filling my mouth with a soft breast, two in fact, and a very, very wet pussy. She was hot and steamy between her thighs and I took to the difference like a duck to water. Although I had always revelled in sucking a man's cock, this was new and magical. We weren't very experimental, spending most of the time just holding each other and talking, but I learned enough to know that being with a woman can be just as exciting as with a man.

We lay tangled in each other's arms and legs in the morning not wanting to break the spell, then realised that we had explored none of the restraint or bondage that had brought us together. Both of us agreed that if it was to be it would come naturally, when the time was right.

The joy of Becky and me was the fact that I could talk

to her about my hunger for Mr King, and she felt that I should go, even though it could be dangerous. She even understood that the danger was part of the attraction. We knew by the time she left that we had a long way to go but that we would enjoy every second. I would probably have asked her to stay longer but she had to go for a family tea, so I saw her off with a bit of an ache, a bit of a tear and a devil on my shoulder saying it was too good to be true, and that I would probably never see her again. I desperately hoped the devil was wrong. We promised to ring each other soon.

3

It arrived the following morning, just when I had given up hope of ever getting a reply. I stood at the front door collecting my milk, and the postman was just coming out of the drive next door, so I hung on, drawing my housecoat closer about my body and thinking about Becky and how her tongue had excited me. He walked up to me with a pile of two or three letters in his hand.

'Thanks.' I watched his small tight bum as he walked to the gate. I flicked through the letters and bills in my hand as I had every morning for the past 27 days, not expecting anything different.

Electricity bill, PVC window circular, and an innocent-looking white envelope with my name typed in full on the front. My hopes faded until I read the London postmark. This was it. I hurried inside without taking my eyes off the envelope, racking my brains to think if I knew of anyone else that it could be from.

Dear Cassandra

Follow the route on the enclosed map. You will arrive at the above address at 10 a.m. on Thursday 12th. The front door will be open until 10.05 a.m. After that it will be locked. Inside the hall you will find your next set of instructions. I suggest you follow them implicitly.

You will wear a short black pleated skirt, a sheer white blouse, black seamed stockings, black lace suspender belt and black high-heeled shoes (at least 3in). No underwear!

This is a very brave step you are taking so please be sure!

Regards

Mr King

Even while my brain was shouting, 'Don't be stupid!' I knew deep down that I would go. I reasoned with myself. He could be a maniac, or a murderer. You could arrive to find the house full of dirty old men.

What if I wanted to go home and he wouldn't let me?

Arguments against my going far outweighed the arguments for, but I knew that the one 'for' argument – my hunger to experiment – would always override all others.

And I knew without a doubt I would still go.

Being quite an independent woman with a successful career in my own right and therefore unused to following orders, I felt part of me rebelling against the idea of following his. The arrogance of the man! I knew I wanted to see how it felt to be dominated in the bedroom but I considered the rest a little excessive. The arrival time for example. My feisty side wanted to turn up at 10.06 a.m. just to annoy him. Would the door still be open? I wondered. He obviously wanted this as much as I, or did he? Would he really give up the chance to 'own' a woman for the day just to prove a point, and all over one short minute? After much reflection and rereading his letters, I decided he probably would.

So, Cassie, I told myself, if you are going to go through with it, then for once in your life be on time and do as you are told.

Thursday was a week away but I had so many exciting things to do to prepare myself. Becky phoned that same morning to tell me that she couldn't stop thinking about me but she was on a strange shift pattern for the next ten days and would be unable to get away, so I put thoughts of her to one side and I shopped for a whole day just to find the right clothes. I wandered around clothes shops delighted by the secret I held. I found myself wondering what these fellow shoppers would say if they knew what I wanted this special outfit for. What if one of the assistants asked why the skirt had to be of a certain type and I answered that I had a date with a stranger and he had instructed me to wear just such a skirt.

I gathered five possible skirts together in a very nice little boutique and took them to the changing room. It was fitting that I took off everything to try on the skirts, so I checked the curtain was pulled across properly and stripped off. The whole day was so sexually charged that I was finding it difficult to contain myself.

The first skirt I tried was not really pleated, but just had a pleat or two down the side, so I discarded it. The second almost reached my knees so, that had to go, too.

Every time I bent to pull on a skirt my breasts hung away from my body, delighting me with visions of being instructed to bend in just such a position. Would he expect me to take my clothes off on a first date? I chuckled to myself then at the ridiculous idea of calling it a date. Anyone would think I had agreed to go out to dinner with him, not give myself to him for a day to do with as he pleased! A ripple of delight at that thought brought goose pimples out all over my skin and I shivered involuntarily.

The short pleated skirt that I tried on next was just perfect. Made from heavy chiffon and just about transparent, it swayed with an almost imperceptible fluidity every time I moved. I was transfixed by the image in the mirror of the barest hint of my naked bottom through the sheer fabric, and when I looked at the front view I was thrilled by the wicked glimpse it gave of my sex.

As soon as I had paid for it I had second thoughts, remembering that, whatever I chose to wear, I also had to wear for the journey of a hundred miles or so that I had to make to get there, and perhaps a see-through skirt wasn't quite practical. As usual, my enthusiasm had got the better of me.

I loved the skirt so much – the way it had shimmered around my thighs and caressed my naked bum – so I decided I had to keep it. I then bought a far too expensive lace half-slip to go underneath it, persuading myself that the occasion justified it and, anyway, if all else failed I could wear it for Becky. I had gone back to the changing room and tried the gossamer slip under the skirt and decided that the finished look was almost as sexy as the skirt alone had been. The deep lace at the bottom of the silky slip just reached the bottom of the skirt and, if I stood in front of the light, you could still see through to my bare flesh – just. I couldn't imagine any man being able to resist the chance to look closer.

The blouse was easier. The first one I picked up was cream silk and complemented the skirt to perfection. My breasts were clearly visible through the soft material, and my nipples, hardened by my constant state of arousal, jutted blatantly, breaking the cut of the cloth. Until that moment I had been disappointed that Mr King didn't want me to wear underwear, because I would really have enjoyed picking a set that was raunchy but right. As I stood there, however, with my chosen outfit on, which highlighted rather than hid my disgustingly horny body, I knew he had been right, and that when Thursday came I would feel a million very naughty dollars as I took that drive to London. I only hoped he deserved the effort I was putting into this.

Until I came across a little old-fashioned lingerie shop

down an alleyway in town I had thought the seamed stockings were going to be impossible to find. I also found a darling little lacy suspender belt in the same shop, so that left only the shoes. After trying on pair after pair in numerous shops, I settled on a pair of very plain, black leather court shoes with a five-inch spike heel and a deep shine. I was assured by the wide-eyed male assistant that they looked 'absolutely superb, madam'. He had watched me strut up and down the length of his shop, his forehead glistening with sweat. He had knelt at my feet, slipping shoe after shoe on to my bare feet, taking sideways glances up my skirt until I thought he would burst a blood vessel. I went home exhausted but very happy with my purchases.

I poured myself a glass of cold white wine and sat on my comfy sofa enjoying the goodies I had bought. I slipped my hand into the smooth coolness of the silk and lace and tried hard to imagine what was in store for me. Would Mr King finally administer the spanking I had longed for since Catherine had said those fateful words, 'You never know, you might like it'?

I was determined to keep the clothes without trying them on until the day came that I would wear them for Mr King, but I regret to admit that that determination lasted only one single hour. By six o'clock that evening I was standing in the bedroom in front of my long wall mirror dressed in all my delicious garments.

My first thought was that I looked like a whore but then, as I walked up and down in my five-inch heels, I changed my opinion to classy escort. As I walked I tried to imagine what would happen to me and what Mr King was like. He had become in my mind a sort of fantasy figure, I suppose because of his glamorous name. I didn't for one minute think that Mr King was his real name but I liked the thought that using a pseudonym kept him from being ordinary. I think now on reflection that if his name had been George or something – not that I have anything against the Georges of this world – I wouldn't have gone. Somehow I got through that endless week and I am ashamed to say that, even though Becky and I spoke almost daily and talked in excited anticipation of our next meeting, I didn't tell her about my appointment.

My dreams on Wednesday night were filled with faceless men probing and poking my body, in a room full of thousands of watches and clocks all with their hands stuck at 10.04 and 59 seconds. The second hands whirred noisily, straining to reach the 12 so the minute hand could click to 10.05, but were held in limbo. Three times during the night I dreamed I was bound by red rope from head to toe. Wrapped like a cocoon and hanging from a tree branch, I couldn't get away and just hung there struggling, twisting and turning helplessly until I woke sweating and straining to get out of the blankets that had wrapped themselves tightly around my legs. I wrestled with the bedding until 5 a.m. unable to get more that a few minutes' sleep at a time, then gave up and went downstairs.

I sat at the kitchen table watching the sun come up with a steaming cup of tea held tightly in my hands, having a two-way conversation in my head: my sense of reason on the one side, trying to persuade me to give up this crazy, dangerous idea; my wicked, adventurous voice on the other side, shouting down my sense of reason. It was obviously in cahoots with my body, which was crying out for some excitement.

I was scared rigid. The most adventurous sexual experience – apart from my fantasies – that I had experienced was on the train and my night of exploration with Becky and I knew that most people would have found those just a tad too naughty, but this was a whole new ball game. Not only did I really want to experience this, but I also had a scary feeling that I might never be the same again. I had decided earlier, as my brain went through its turmoil, that I ought at least to let someone know where I was going. Ruth being the obvious choice, I picked up the phone and dialled her number, feeling a little guilty that I hadn't told her about my budding relationship with a female. I wasn't quite sure how she would feel about it.

Luckily, she had already gone to work, or not come home last night, so I left a very cryptic message on her answerphone telling her where I was going and asking her to come and rescue me if I wasn't home in time for breakfast the next morning.

My guilt reasoned with and my duties carried out, I rushed up the stairs ripping off my housecoat. I had worked out a strict schedule to enable me to arrive at my destination with time to compose myself and make any last-minute adjustments. At least two hours would be taken up by the journey, so that left an hour to get myself ready and to prepare myself mentally and physically for whatever was ahead of me.

I soaked up the scalding hot water in the shower, my mind full of sketchy images. As I soaped my full breasts I imagined a pair of rough unknown hands grasping them and was glad they had retained their shape and didn't sag too much. The shower gel was cool and slippery on my hot flesh, setting my body alive with pictures of unfinished obscenities being performed on my naked, restrained body. I spread my legs wide and tried to imagine how it would be to have them held in place by soft red rope while an unseen tongue tantalised my sex with soft gentle licks across my straining clitoris.

I dragged the large fluffy bath towel from the hook and padded back into the bedroom. I was beginning to wish I had at least some experience to draw upon. Even second-hand would do. But I didn't know of anybody who got their kicks from being either restrained or treated like a slave, so how could I even begin to guess what I was letting myself in for? I even racked my brain to see if I could remember where Catherine had said she was moving to.

All the new items I had bought were draped over a hanger tucked in the back of my wardrobe, hidden, just like my fantasies. I laid them all out on the bed and a thrill of apprehension snaked down my naked damp spine.

I sprayed a delicate mist of Clinique Elixir all over my body, then clipped on the suspender belt and adjusted the suspenders. Next came the dark, severe stockings. I balanced my heel on the bed and smoothed the silky nylon over my foot and up my taut calf, taking care to keep the seam as straight as possible. Then I clipped it to the clasps at the top of my thigh. Pairing the seams was almost impossible, but by standing with my back to the full-length mirror, and after a few minor adjustments, I managed a passable display.

I was quite shocked by the eroticism of the vision in the mirror behind me as I bent over to twist a seam. My naked white bottom thrust out, framed by the black suspenders, and my long shapely legs, emphasised by those jet-black seams on a smoky black background, created an image that any woman would be proud of.

The blouse of sheer cream silk with embroidered lace at collar and cuffs slipped over my naked perfumed skin and felt deliciously cool clinging to my nipples and caressing the sensitive contour of my breasts. I slipped on the chiffon skirt that floated round my thighs and exposed a glimmer of white flesh through the thin gossamer pleats. On second thoughts, I wasn't quite sure whether a petticoat qualified as underwear, but decided that, as I spent so much money on it, to hell with Mr

King's orders: I would wear it anyway. I could always plead ignorance, couldn't I?

I stood before the mirror trying to recognise the Cassie I am comfortable with in the image that faced me. My dark hair, which was usually tied back in a band for practicality, was curling softly in waves, just touching my breasts. I had brushed it until my arm ached and it shone with red highlights in the light from the window. My green eyes were sparkling with mischief as they took in the fact that the dark surrounds to my nipples were clearly visible through the creamy silk. My erect nipples were thrusting against the material, causing the line of the blouse to pucker blatantly.

I took my new shoes out of their box and slipped them on my feet. Immediately my posture changed: my back became straighter and my calves tightened as I added five inches to my height. I now stood at six foot one – and most of that seemed to be leg! The black seams appeared to rise for ever before disappearing beneath the skirt, which just covered the welt of my stockings. I felt raunchy and daring as I took one last look and wobbled downstairs. I walked up and down the hall a few times to get the feel of the shoes and to make sure that I could move in them with chin up and back straight.

During that walk my personality changed. I was doing all this because I had been ordered to. I wouldn't dream of dressing like this usually, but it was an order, so it was OK. It felt good. I liked the fact that I was dressed very provocatively and that any man who saw me might think I was available. Oh, God, did I say that?

When it was time to leave for London I was thankfully still excited. The fear didn't hit me until later.

I had enough petrol, so I didn't have to leave the car, but on the busy dual carriageway the lorry drivers had a wonderful time. One of them was particularly persistent and nearly fell out of his window with shock when I flashed my naked thighs to him. He rushed to pass me again, then slowed to a crawl, so I had to overtake him. This went on for a few minutes until I decided to give him a show that would stay with him for years.

I pulled my skirt right up, exposing myself from the waist down, and opened my thighs as wide as I could as I drove slowly past him. He drove with one hand and hung out of the window of his cab from the waist up. I raised my hand and wiggled my fingers at him in mock goodbye, then buried three fingers deep within my cunt, which by now was quite moist. I drove alongside him, taunting him for a few moments until I feared for his safety, then sped up, leaving him drooling in my wake. I could hear his horn blaring for a full minute and his lights were still flashing as he disappeared from my rear-view mirror.

Three times I drove past the house. The first time was to check that the address was right. The second was to check that the address was still right and the third was to try to see if the front door was open. I had forgotten to look the first two times. Yes, it was the right address, and, yes the door was open as promised, so I parked down the street, just within sight of the house, to kill time.

It was 9.54. Six minutes to get through. It was the longest six minutes of my life. I felt sick with nerves, petrified of what he would do to me, but I couldn't bring myself to drive away. I stared at the house, trying to see if he was watching me. It looked normal enough, an average-sized, detached, family home with probably quarter of an acre of garden and a curved drive leading up to that ominous front door, which was still standing open.

A couple of times I almost talked myself into forgetting the whole thing. After all, I had Becky now and I could experiment with her. But at 9.59 I started the engine and drove up the drive with my heart pounding in my chest, parked in front of the door and switched off. I was so terrified that I couldn't get out of the car. I felt light-headed and dizzy and dropped the keys twice trying to put them in my bag; but I pulled myself together, opened the door and, swinging round placed, my five-inch shiny heels on the gravel.

I walked the few steps to the door on shaky legs and stood still. At that moment I would have traded my soul with the devil to know what was behind that very ordinary front door. It wasn't carved oak; it didn't have gargoyles grinning down at me. It was just a regular suburban front door. But it was standing open, and Mr King, or whatever his name was, was behind it. Somewhere!

I knew that if I waited any longer I would change my mind, so I checked my seams, straightened my back, tilted my chin, took a deep breath and grasped the handle. Just as I started to push the door a loud gong sounded from inside the house. I screamed out loud and my hand shot back as if scalded as I shook uncontrollably. A second gong sounded, not quite so loudly, it seemed, from inside. You silly cow, Cassandra! It's a clock striking the hour and that means you're right on time.

When it had finally stopped chiming, before I had a chance to change my mind, I again grabbed the handle, pushed inside, leaned back with my bottom to shut it and leaned on the door, breathing heavily.

I was facing a large hall with the guilty grandfather clock trying to look innocent in the far corner, a picture of a fighter plane on one wall and two closed doors. The stairs that curled up to my right disappeared into oblivion, luxurious in their deep red carpeting. The only furniture was a small occasional table at the bottom of the stairs. There was a clutter of things on the table but the lighting was quite subdued after the bright sunlight so I left the comparative safety of the front door and moved over to it.

Even in my wildest fantasies I hadn't guessed how this moment would feel as I looked down at the group of things on that table. I hadn't thought beyond the letter. Mr King had warned me that there would be new instructions behind the door but this blew my head away. My heart crashed scarily.

They were laid out so neatly. A black leather collar with silver studs at regular intervals along its length; a pair of shiny, silver handcuffs, a black leather blindfold, a tiny gold bell and a list.

I felt my nipples harden and prickle against the silk of my shirt just at the sight of them and the implications that thumped through my intoxicated brain. With shaking hands I picked up the list and read it.

CASSANDRA

1 Lock the front door.
2 Fasten the collar around your neck.
3 Stand with your feet at least two foot apart.
4 Put on the leather blindfold.
5 Pick up the bell. This is your safety call. If you want to go home at any time just drop the bell. There will be no discussion – you will go home, never to be invited back. If you want to stay, hang on to it tightly.
6 Lock the handcuff on to one wrist, put your hands behind your back and lock the other cuff on to other wrist.
7 WAIT!

With these terrifying words scrambling around in my brain, I leaned against the far wall trembling violently from head to toe. Trying to hold the paper still enough to reread it.

I had to act quickly in case I chickened out, so I moved to the front door and locked it. Once I had made that move I think my mind and body switched on to automatic and I went to my tasks like a robot. I picked up the collar and held it to my nose, my senses reeling as I breathed deeply of the pungent smell.

I was so aroused already I could feel the moistness between my thighs. Just reading the next instruction had my stomach in knots. Stand with your feet at least two foot apart. Why did it make me feel more vulnerable than all the others put together? I suppose it was the absence of knickers, thus exposing my sex to anything.

Although it was quite difficult to keep my balance in the high heels, I soon settled into it and found the exposure very exciting. My thighs were now separate from my very aroused pussy.

Next on the list was the blindfold. The leather was soft and supple and moulded comfortably to my face, settling into my eye sockets as if custom-made. With the blindfold resting across my nose, I could smell the leather with each trembling breath I took, filling my senses with the heady smell and causing the tiny hairs on the back of my neck to stand on end.

I was in a dark, silent world of anticipation and expectant fear.

I fumbled for the handcuffs. The noise of the chain as I picked them up seemed deafening in the silence and I frantically clutched them with both hands to quieten them.

I realised with a jolt that I should have put the first cuff on before the blindfold. I wasn't going to admit I had done it wrong and start again so I played with them until I found a break in the circle and pushed my wrist against it hopefully. As if by magic the cold hard steel clamped around my wrist.

This is it, Cassie! I stood with my cuffed wrist dangling by my side for precious minutes before I could go on. I have no idea how long I stood there in the silence. I had heard no sound since entering the house and I was panic-stricken. My legs were trembling so hard I stumbled a few times, losing my bearings completely. I was almost reduced to tears and couldn't seem to pull myself together.

It's simple, I told myself: just do it. You only have to snap on that last cuff and the rest is out of your hands. Go on, do it.

I groaned deeply, groped around for the bell, picked it up and, putting my hand behind my back as ordered, snapped on the remaining cuff.

It was easier to relax once I was helpless, although I was still trembling vigorously and panting, trying to regain control of my ragged breathing.

I realised with horror I couldn't remember the last instruction. I knew there were seven so I ran through them in my mind. Lock door, collar, feet, blindfold, bell, cuffs and ... *What else?* my mind screamed. I went over and over it, counting each move I had made since I had walked through that door until now. It seemed like hours ago. Nothing! Again my panic rose like bile in my throat. Then it hit me. Wait! That was it: wait!

So I waited, trying to imagine how I would look to Mr King as he came into the hall. Because I was helpless, my instinct was to protect my body by curling inwards. This was virtually impossible because my legs were spread apart and the cuffs on my wrists thrust my breasts forward. They strained against the silk, rising and falling with each of my laboured breaths.

I gained a little comfort by rounding my shoulders and resting my chin on my chest but it wasn't really worth it. I really wished he would come. The silence was deafening and anything would be preferable to this horrible waiting.

I shifted my balance from left to right, straining my ears to hear a sound, but still jumped a mile when a creak filled the empty silence. Every muscle in my body tightened and I caught my lip in my teeth to stop myself from crying out. I began to lose my bearings, forgetting where the doors were, therefore having no idea which area would produce the sound I craved.

He could be creeping down the stairs this minute, I told myself, but I knew I would hear that, so I ruled out the possibility and tried to concentrate on where I thought the doors were.

Every other aspect of my life had been left outside the front door. I was just Cassie, awaiting the discovery of her sexuality. Nothing else mattered, just the smell of the leather, the cold steel that was biting deliciously into the tender skin of my wrists, the darkness, the silence, the still-cool silk against my hard nipples and the hot aching throb of my waiting pussy.

I waited.

4

All my nerve endings danced to attention as I heard what could only have been a door opening behind me. This time I had no doubt of what I was hearing. All the silly flutterings of noise that had made me jump over the last few minutes paled into insignificance. My knees tried to buckle and I think I actually whimpered. Tears burned my eyelids.

In those few seconds I would have done anything not to be there.

My pulse pounded in my ears so hard I thought I would faint if he didn't say something or do something. Anything!

I held my breath so I could hear every move, and realised he was standing right behind me. I don't know how I knew. He made no noise, nor did he touch me, but I knew. Then I felt the faintest breath on the side of my neck and I smelled him, not too strong, just a whiff of a heady, musky aftershave that filled my head.

I couldn't believe how aroused I was. I had never been so aroused by anything in my life. Everything – every move, every sound and touch of his breath – aimed straight for my crotch. I could smell him and feel him with my sex and I felt my pussy blossom like a flower opening its petals in response to his presence. I couldn't imagine I would ever want anything more than I wanted him to touch me right at that moment.

I had no idea who this man was, what he enjoyed or what he disliked. His looks and personality were totally irrelevant at that moment. He was to be the instrument of my submission, I was his plaything and that was all that mattered.

He walked slowly around me, just close enough to brush my clothes lightly in passing. I wanted to talk to him and beg him to touch me, but, even though I had never played these kinds of games before, I knew instinctively that if I spoke without permission I would be breaking the rules and therefore the spell.

As he walked around me a second time I felt myself leaning towards him, begging him with my body to touch me, consumed by a compulsive need that at that time I was still unable to identify clearly. He stopped in front of me, so close I could feel the hairs on my face bristle. My skin was alive, each nerve ending clamouring to be the first to gain his attention.

A warm finger hooked itself under my chin and raised my face to a jauntier angle, but, as soon as it was released, my chin again sank down to my chest. He patiently repeated this movement three times until I had the courage to hold my head up without knowing what was in front of it.

He then put his finger lightly to my lip, which was still caught between my teeth, persuading me to let it go. He clasped my shoulders firmly and I realised I had been shaking almost uncontrollably. I took a deep, shuddering breath and relaxed the best I could.

I felt his hands on the top button of my blouse and just the occasional brush of his warm hand against my flesh as he undid it to the waist. He ran his finger from my chin, down my neck, sliding deliciously between my breasts and down to the waistband of my skirt. I shuddered from head to toe.

The atmosphere was electric with tension. Even though I could sense calm vibes from him there was an almost imperceptible quiver to those warm, dry, tantalising fingers. Was he as nervous as I was? Had he ever done this sort of thing before?

He grasped each side of my blouse front and, in one smooth movement, slipped it off my shoulders and down to my waist, baring my breasts. The shirt slithered down my arms and caught on the handcuffs at my wrists and hung there.

At that stage I was finding it very difficult not to go completely to pieces. Each tortured breath rasped in my lungs; my naked breasts heaved dramatically and I felt light-headed and sick.

What was to come? Why was I standing there letting this complete stranger gaze at my nakedness? I knew that I had made an unconscious decision at some stage in the proceedings to allow this man total use of my willing body, to do with as he pleased, but I had no idea why. I didn't really know what it was I craved. Not at that point, anyway.

Once again he gave me time to calm down, and my breathing returned almost to normal. All he did was put one finger delicately to the end of my right nipple and I groaned deep in my throat, thrusting my breasts out, wantonly begging for more. He obliged and touched the other straining nipple just as tenderly. He then moved on and, taking each nipple between finger and thumb, rolled them gently. The pleasure shot like arrows from nipples to crotch.

The soft waves of pleasure were short-lived as his grip became harder and harder. He increased the pressure very slowly, taking me through the usual waves of intense feeling to the edge of pain. I could feel the sweat beading on my brow as he continued to squeeze my throbbing nipples.

'Owww!' I cried. Something made me stand there and wait for his next move, even though he had hurt me.

I opened my mouth to complain but immediately felt his hand, gentle again, between my spread thighs slowly making its way up to the top of my stockings. I gulped and whimpered, swallowing my unspoken words as his hand caressed the bare flesh at the top of my legs. Already I had forgotten the punishment as the residual pain mingled sweetly with the pleasure of his probing hands.

Occasionally his hand innocently brushed against my pussy, which was already oozing shamelessly in anticipation of what was to come. The throbbing pain in my breasts was forgotten as his finger slipped between my sex lips and buried itself deep inside me. Again my knees buckled, but I had learned my lesson and immediately stood again as upright as possible. I was beginning to understand the rules of this game.

Obedience, pure and simple, that was what he expected from me. He could do what he liked but if I complained or refused to obey I got punished.

My breathing was coming in strangled gasps as his finger continued on its exploration. I don't know how I stayed on my feet, for each time he wiggled his finger my legs instinctively closed, but he sharply slapped the tender part of my thigh just above the dark welt of my stocking. Again I learned the intoxicating lesson.

He slowly let his finger slip out of my wetness and my body followed it as if hypnotised until I almost lost my balance. I was making pleading, sobbing noises in the back of my throat, trying to convey how empty I felt without his inquisitive finger. He put a finger to my mouth and I expected him to say 'Ssh', but he didn't. I had no doubts what he meant and gritted my teeth and obeyed the unspoken order. I realised with shock that the finger against my mouth was wet and sticky. The smell of my own sex filled my nostrils but he still managed to shock me when he slipped that wet finger between my lips for me to taste. It had never occurred to me to taste my own juices before, and I was quite surprised to find it erotic and not at all unpleasant. Becky flitted through my thoughts. In fact I latched on to that finger and sucked it deep in my mouth like a baby with its dummy.

I felt quite close to him for those few moments but I'm sure he sensed that the added intimacy made me feel more at ease. As soon as I began to relax with my pacifier he pulled it free quite roughly, hooked his thumbs in the waistband of my skirt and slowly lowered it until it was a heap around my spread ankles. He had evidently crouched down in front of me, because I felt him grasp my right ankle, and then my left, as he slipped the crumpled skirt from under me. I nearly toppled over but just managed to regain my balance.

I felt so vulnerable with my shirt round my wrists baring my naked breasts and only a petticoat to cover my lower half. Thank goodness I had decided to wear the petticoat. He paused for a moment and I could imagine him admiring the intricate lacy garment that, although quite flimsy, still left something to the imagination.

I had no idea how I would come to regret that simple decision.

Then, still crouched before me, he once more grasped my ankles, and removed my shoes. Then my petticoat was raised to my waist and my stockings unclasped then rolled down my thighs and off my feet. The shoes were immediately replaced before he reached behind me and removed my suspender belt, then tucked my petticoat more firmly around the elastic at the waist.

My body blushed from head to feet as I sensed that he remained still, gazing at my sex, so open and exposed. My pussy lips, which had been stuck together with my secretions until then, slowly swelled with my arousal. I was aware of each single blood vessel as it became engorged with blood. The swollen flesh hung open, wanton and begging before his gaze. He brushed his fingers lightly across the crinkled darker flesh of my lips, then ran one finger down the exposed channel between them, slick with need.

The air whooshed through my gritted teeth as I tried to contain myself. I had never felt like this before, so helpless and alive. I had always been turned on if I read of damsels being captured, then used and abused, in romantic novels. When I read of women being intimately examined while exposed, my heart always fluttered and my pulse raced, but this unbelievable experience was worth any price I might end up having to pay.

If he sent me home now it would have been worth it just to discover that my body could feel like this. If all he dished out for the rest of my stay were pain it would still have been worth it. This exquisite pleasure that pounded through my spread, exposed body was everything.

He moved behind me and replaced the unyielding handcuffs with what felt like buckled leather cuffs, allowing my trapped silk blouse to slip to the floor at my feet.

What he did next confused me long enough to catch me off guard. My petticoat was rolled down to my feet and he indicated with a gentle push for me to step out of it. Then he held the bunched-up garment over my mouth and nose. I could smell my perfume on it. Just as it became difficult for me to breathe, he removed it and placed it in my hands, which were still clutched behind me. By now I realised that he was trying to impart a message of some sort and began to panic a little when it didn't make sense. He took it from my hands and rubbed it again in my face, quite roughly. *What?* my head shouted in its confusion. I was scared to ask.

I felt the silky material over the palm of his hand as he placed it in the middle of my back and pushed me forward until I was bent over. My breasts hung free from my body, and my legs, still spread open, exposed my sex even more.

Like an idiot I still hadn't caught on when he balled the petticoat into my fist and squeezed, indicating for me to keep hold of it. He grasped both of my hands in his large ones and moved them up to the small of my back. At last it clicked: I realised with horror that he was about to spank me. Before I had a chance to decide how I felt about this or whether I was ready – I had never been spanked in my life – the first stinging blow landed on my right buttock, nearly pushing me over. I gasped at the intensity of the pain but this had no effect on him at all and, without lessening the strength, in spite of my reaction, he landed the next blow just as hard on the other cheek. My buttocks throbbed with heat. I realised, probably for the first time, that this man was not joking. Again he surprised me. He took the petticoat out of my hands and rubbed the soft silky material over my burning bum until the pain abated a little. I couldn't believe the pain was so easy to forget with just a small offering of pleasure, but it was. So, when again he placed the balled-up petticoat in my hands, I was wriggling my bottom sensuously.

The pain of the next smack landed squarely on top of the last, exploded right down my legs, and I fell to my knees and cowered, expecting to be hit again. He did nothing. I was left kneeling on the floor, feeling slightly ridiculous trying to guess what I should do next. I realised that I had overreacted and he was waiting for me to accept that. I could only imagine he wanted me to stand up and resume the position he had put me in to take the rest of the punishment. I was trembling. I didn't know whether I could take much more.

Perhaps I should struggle to my feet and try my hardest to accept whatever he decided I deserved for the unforgivable mistake of wearing a petticoat. My arrogant inner self was still rebelling as my submissive side struggled to take over and help me to my feet. I couldn't give up now. He had already shown me pleasures I hadn't believed possible. Why had I worn the stupid thing, anyway? I asked myself. Hadn't I known deep down that his orders excluded any underwear? Had I hoped for just this sort of treatment? I still hadn't decided the answer to any of these questions when I was again standing in the punishment position of spread legs and bent back.

I vowed to myself that I would never again wear a petticoat as long as I lived. What turned out to be the last bout of my punishment fell on the tender flesh where the underside of my bottom met my thighs and sent pain right to my nerve ends. But even as I absorbed the pain I could already feel the heat rushing through my groin. I waited for what seemed like ages but then relaxed in the knowledge that it was over. At least for the time being. I wasn't totally sure I wanted it to be over.

So that was the spanking I had longed for. Funny how, while it was happening, I hated Mr King with everything in me. When he paused between blows I found myself hoping there was more but dreading the intensity of it and, as soon as he stopped, I craved more spanking, more intensity and more pain.

5

My shoulders were grasped gently but firmly as Mr King helped me into a standing position from behind. As he leaned against my back I ground back on to him thrilling at the contact. I could feel his hardness pressing against my bound hands, so I raised them and made contact with the burning flesh of my bottom. Just for a second he responded and I felt him begin to melt against my nakedness. But almost before I realised what he was doing he pulled away, then led me, guiding me with small steps, forward.

Although I felt quite secure in his grasp I had begun to feel safe in the confines of the hall, and, when my toes came in contact with the riser of the first stair, the fear slammed back into my brain. I couldn't move. I was totally rigid, but he held me firmly until I relaxed a little and we proceeded one by one up the stairs. When we turned the corner at the top I panicked again, and again he waited while I calmed down before he nudged me forward and upward.

When we reached the top of the stairs Mr King gently pushed me to the left and after about two steps stopped me in my tracks. My heart started pounding afresh. He was obviously going to start the second part of his agenda. Well, I told myself, even though it hurt like hell I had become aroused more than I believed possible by his treatment of me in the hall, so this could be good, too. Even as I thought it my pulse quickened to an alarming rate with the fear that threatened to choke me, and I prepared myself to drop the bell.

As I stood still, terrified but excited beyond belief at what was to come next, Mr King unclipped my wrists and refastened them to something high above my head, each arm pulled upward until my muscles stretched, and outward until my breasts lifted with the strain. The feeling of helpless exposure was exquisite until he tied rope around my ankles and spread my legs apart until I grunted with the strain. My sex was stretched so far apart it felt as if it gaped open, inflamed and swollen with need. I could feel the stickiness of my juices suction my lips together for a moment, then give up its hold to allow them to separate shamefully, exposing the part of me that even I rarely saw: the sopping wet hole that longed for his attention.

When I felt his finger touch my inner lips I jumped and mewled with need as I thrust myself forward for his attentions. He took hold of one of my lips in each hand and pulled them in a downward movement that thrilled through me and tugged on my clitoris until I felt the rages of orgasm building in my guts. He stopped and again my needs were thwarted.

'Nooooo! Please don't stop!' I wailed in desperation.

I should have learned my lesson downstairs. He makes the rules and does what he wants. If it happens to be what I want as well, then great, but, if not, tough luck, Cassie. I was his toy to play with as he chose.

In response to my pleas he again took hold of my lips, but I knew that this time it was with a purpose, and a chill ran down my spine. He pulled each lip downward until I had to lower myself to relieve the pain; but, as soon as I had lowered an inch or two, the cuffs around my wrists stopped me, and I could bend only as far as the restraints would allow. Of course his fingers were under no such restraint and they just pulled further, down and outwards until I thought the delicate membranes would split. I gasped with pain and arousal at the image in my brain of the picture I must make to Mr King, who was bent over in front of me, looking, I assumed at the stretched-open, spread-apart, soaking, gaping maw that was my sex.

My wails turned to a continuous moan as he stretched, then released, stretched, then released. Never had I been used like this. What I experienced then was completely different from the shame, humiliation and then acceptance I had felt at his attentions downstairs. This was so intimate and personal. Usually a man would stroke and rub a woman's genitals either gently or roughly according to who he was, but never had I been examined and looked at so intimately. Even when being sucked by a lover, I don't think I had ever been looked at and explored so closely. Perhaps the week before with Becky – but that was different in a way.

I squirmed with intense delight as I experienced flood after flood of my juices oozing from me. I had always taken for granted that if I was aroused I would self-lubricate, but this man had the ability to make my shameful sex positively drip. Being held open like that focused every feeling I had to that one exposed, ravished place. I became just a basic, hungry sexual organ with its insides on show and its protective cover stripped bare, and available for any diabolical deed he felt like carrying out. I was dizzy with excitement.

He stopped what he was doing; it was as if he were reading my mind, but he was probably just reading my body. I wanted more, therefore he stopped.

He stood, then, in front of me and brushed his shirt against my naked breasts and the seam down the front rasped across my nipples and sent another flood south-wards. His warm hands stroked my breasts with a sensuous knowledge that explained why I was so wound up. He knew exactly what aroused me, when to hurt and when to please, what my body meant when it quivered and shook in response to his ministrations.

Gently he took hold of my nipples and pulled my breasts up until the strain on them made me gasp, then he shook them almost imperceptibly so just a delicious tremor filled me with anticipation. He released one breast and, still holding the other away from my straining body, he started to slap the tender flesh gently, around the fleshy undercurve and over every inch, until I could feel the heat burning through me, desperate for more. This time he obliged by doing the same with the other breast, then he released it, leaving my chest heaving and my punished flesh tingling sharply from the onslaught.

He then started slapping a little harder and because he wasn't holding my breasts as before my bust jiggled and swayed in response, sending waves of humiliation washing over me. I am not sure why, but just the thought of him watching, and of course instigating their excessive movement, was very embarrassing and I cringed in shame as my pussy dribbled some more. I was beginning to realise that humiliation and shame also had a very definite place in my arousal process.

I dragged ragged breaths in through my parched throat, trying hard to hold on to the sweet feeling his punishment of my breasts had produced. As before, just as the pain threatened to consume me, he changed his tack and ran a finger through the wet channel of my cunt. Without any preliminaries or warning, he pushed upwards into me until his fingers were buried deep up inside my hole, pushing and forcing their way further in until the pain in my breasts was forgotten and I was scrabbling on tiptoe to relieve the forceful pressure deep inside my sex. His invading hand stretched the entrance to my burning interior apart until I could feel the tension of my tortured lips as they tried to accommodate the intruder.

I was exhausted by the constant roller coaster of feelings he was putting me through. One second I was so aroused by his tender explorations that I thought he was going to let me come, but the next I would be deluged with exquisite pain that, even though it thrilled me, would never take me to the release I craved. It was a confused wreck that he finally released and allowed to sit on the floor.

I sat with my back to the wall and my arms hugged around my knees, weak with arousal and shaking with need. I was totally oblivious to his presence; I just wallowed in the dark, in the throbbing ache of my beaten breasts and the still-full feeling between my trembling thighs. I decided I had had enough. The strength of feeling he had wrenched from me was terrifying and in my pathetic state I felt I couldn't take any more.

I opened my mouth to try to explain but before I could begin he took hold of my hand and pulled me to my feet. He stood behind me and his hands, gentle now, caressed my body with a sensitivity that left me in awe of him yet again. And yet again he had read me like a book and realised I needed encouragement to carry on. He softly massaged my tender nipples and stroked his hands down my body and over my hips and wrapped them around me, holding me close until my breathing eased and my trembling stopped. I think on reflection he knew before I did that I was ready to go on.

He manoeuvred me round to face back to the stairs and pushed me forward until I stepped on to a different carpet, so I knew we were in a room. He took me a few steps further and turned me to face him, and locked the cuffs in front of me. He moved closer to me until I could feel the roughness of his clothes on my skin and his face next to mine breathing on my neck and filling my senses with his smell.

Without any ceremony or finesse, he removed my ludicrously high shoes until I was standing in front of him stark naked apart from the cuffs and the blindfold. I liked the image that created in my mind's eye: me all helpless and restrained again and him still fully clothed.

He moved closer to me until I was being forced backward and stumbled. I hit an object with the back of my knees that, just before I fell into its softness, I realised was a bed.

Without wasting any time he stretched my bound wrists above my head until I thought they would come out of their sockets and fastened them in place. With my arms secured so firmly in position it was difficult to resist when he spread my ankles, then took them in his hands and fastened what felt like a deep cuff on to each one. I was so naked I could almost feel his gaze burning into my skin.

My right ankle was tugged sharply to the right and tied very tightly to the bed leg. Once the same had been done to the left my legs were spread so wide that the muscles in my inner thighs were straining painfully, so I wriggled and murmured my annoyance. In response he undid the knots and pulled them just a little tighter.

'Bastard!' I muttered very quietly under my breath and regretted it instantly, as he stood up and I heard the buckle of his belt jingle and the whoosh as the leather was pulled at speed from its loops. I tried my hardest to recoil into the softness of the bed and draw my legs together to protect my most vulnerable place, but I could hardly twitch, I was tied so tight.

I tensed my muscles and held my breath to prepare myself for the pain that I knew was to come, but nothing could have prepared me for the explosion of fire as the belt landed across the fronts of my thighs. It took a split second for the intensity to send its message to my brain. Just as it did so, and my mouth stretched to scream, his lips clamped down on my sex with such sweet pressure the shock to my system was electrifying.

I gasped and drowned in the swallowed scream trying to catch my breath but it was impossible. My body hadn't got a clue what was happening. My pussy flooded into his sucking mouth as my torso still bucked in response to the pain. My insides melted and flowed out of control as he continued to suck deeply from me. My scream turned to a strangled moan.

As quickly as his mouth had latched on to me it was taken away, leaving me straining upwards for more, the space between my stretched thighs a gaping abyss.

He left me for a minute or two as he fiddled about in the room. My mind worked overtime trying to imagine what he was doing. It was impossible. I had no idea even how big the room was, let alone what was in it. My imagination certainly didn't stretch to what he might do next. Surprisingly I found the anticipation exquisite, every inch of me alive and begging for the next experience.

He sat beside me on the bed and fastened something around the crown of my head and under my chin. I could picture a harness, but, as I had no idea what it could be for, I began to get quite scared and clutched my bell for dear life. More than anything I wanted to ask him what it was but I didn't want to risk incurring his wrath if I broke the unspoken rules. He hadn't said one word to me yet but had managed to make himself quite clear and left me in no doubt that he would be displeased if I spoke.

He let me settle into it before he made his next move. Then, lying beside me on the bed, he cradled my head in the crook of his arm and waited for me to relax. I felt his finger on my mouth tracing the outline of my lips and wriggling its way between them. I sucked on this offering greedily and made soft noises of pleasure in the back of my throat until he removed his finger and teased me with it, brushing it across my hungry grabbing lips. I stretched up for it, enjoying this game of cat and mouse, completely forgetting the harness. Each time he removed his finger I opened my mouth and strained even harder to regain the comfort of it. Each time, I opened my mouth wider and wider, falling so easily into his trap.

The leather dildo was pushed between my unsuspecting jaws and deep into my mouth and I tried to reject it as he buckled it swiftly behind my head. The straps were tightened around my head until I was well and truly gagged.

I was so angry. He had tricked me. Even worse than that, I had fallen for it, fallen for the softly-softly routine. The more I thought about it the more furious I became and I bucked and twisted in my bonds, grunting my anger, twisting my torso rapidly. It wasn't until I was completely exhausted that I took in the fact that he was ignoring my tantrum and as far as I knew had left the room.

Slowly I calmed down by reminding myself that I had chosen to be here, so, unless he did something that was beyond my limits and I dropped the bell, I would continue to be at his mercy. I had to see this through for my peace of mind. This was, for me, my chance to meet my sexuality face to face and discover what the missing ingredient was. So far this unseen man had taken me to heights of passion I had never dared dream of. He had shown me that pain, at the right time, for the right reason and with the right amount of pleasure, could be mind-blowing. He had dangled the elusive orgasm just out of my reach like a rabbit with a carrot and convinced me I was prepared to experiment with anything to taste the thrill of the unknown and my new-found joy of submission.

I awaited his next move with a quiet acceptance of my fate, only to be shocked again when I heard the rasp of a match on a box followed by the flare of a match head, and detected the smell of a candle being lit. My whole being tensed, every muscle screwed up and scrunched into itself with tension, waiting.

I nearly jumped out of my skin as his hand touched my breast and my head whipped round to face him, still very frightened even though his soft touch was raising my blood pressure again. He stroked me from head to toe. Brushing my face with the backs of his fingers, caressing the corners of my mouth as they strained around the gag and almost worshipping my helplessness. Running the flat of his hand over my torso, over my breasts and down again to my spread thighs, he explored my responses. My restrained body quivered at his touch and responded to his every caress, following his hand to prolong the feeling.

I found myself beginning to enjoy the feel of my bonds: the firmness of the leather cuffs cutting into my wrists and ankles, the blindfold making everything anonymous. I could almost believe this was just a fantasy and I was willing everything to happen.

I experienced complete submissive acceptance. My body was his to do with as he wished and until he chose to release me I would strive to please him in every way he asked of me. The gag took away all responsibility. I almost hoped he would want me to prove my acceptance by pushing me beyond my limits. I wanted him to test me.

He placed a coil of rope in my hand for a second. I could picture it curled in my palm as if my blindfold had been removed. The last time I had held it in my hand had been a million years before in my bedroom, when all this had still been a game. I could feel the redness of it.

He tied one end of that soft slinky rope around my knee, looped it under the bed and pulled it tight. Then, fastening it to the other knee, he pulled on the rope and managed to stretch my already taut limbs another inch or two apart. He repeated the procedure with my elbows, then fastened the buckles on the head harness to the bed, immobilising my head.

I was stretched so tight that every breath was an effort and the only parts of me that moved at all were my hands, and they could only flail about ineffectually.

I was staked out at his mercy. For a few seconds panic tried to overtake me, but I told myself it was just instinct. The real feeling that was bubbling up inside me was one of pure arousal. It started somewhere deep within my guts and spread out in waves of pleasure, filling my breasts until I felt them swell, filling my loins with an indescribable heat.

I needed no hands to touch me, no cock thrusting deep inside me. I was slowly reaching my goal without any help. I felt the flush start over my skin and the pulses deep in my belly quicken. My fists were clenching and unclenching rhythmically as my mouth sucked and bit the gag tight between my teeth. I moaned constantly. Just as I was about to ride into my first spasm, he gripped my nipples between his fingers and thumbs and twisted viciously until my mounting passion subsided and I attempted to wriggle away and relieve the pressure on my tortured breasts. The 'Arggh' that I groaned into my gag was lost.

After a few seconds of silent waiting, angry with him but accepting his decisions, my body still twitched as I felt the first drop of hot wax drip between my breasts. I gasped. The second drop and the third drop moved closer to my nipple. While the drips of wax surrounded my nipple with beautiful horny fire, his other hand was placed firmly on the mound of my sex. One finger played lazily with my moist lips and curled in my pubic hair. I strained at my bonds until the strain was too much, trying to reach the hand that tormented me and force it inside me.

The need to be penetrated blotted out all other feelings until my whole being was centred on that one sexy probing digit. He teased me mercilessly, keeping the ball of his hand pressed firmly on my mound, restricting my already severely limited thrusts.

Just when I thought I would go mad if he didn't answer my needs, his finger slipped inside me to the first knuckle and I thought I would explode with tension. The searing heat of the wax continued to drip remorselessly on to my breasts. Closer and closer it moved to my nipple, getting hotter as he obviously held the candle nearer my quivering flesh. He played me like an instrument, regulating the intensity of the pain of the wax with the probing and teasing of my begging pussy.

Not once did he alter the gentle rhythm of penetration. It was enough to keep me boiling on the verge of orgasm but not enough to tip me over the edge. He resisted the natural desire to speed up when faced with heated arousal and kept up the slow insistent probing. I was desperate for his finger to be deeper inside me, but he merely let it tantalise me just inside my now sopping entrance.

By the time he changed his tactics I was pouring with sweat, grunting loudly into the gag and writhing with pleasure-filled agony. The wax was being dropped directly on to my burning nipple. It was exquisite torture and the most intense feeling of pleasure imaginable.

He removed his finger and I swear I would have

killed for the return of it. The wax kept dripping. Without the passion induced by his finger the pain was
becoming unbearable. I tried to cower away from the
relentless drops, but he managed to find a new sensitive
spot of flesh with each new drip. I was just beginning
to get frightened when he placed a thumb and forefinger between my pussy lips and spread them apart,
exposing my hard aching clitoris, which throbbed and
pulsated so close to coming, no longer safe beneath its
protective hood.

Slowly the drops of heat fell closer and closer, down
my torso, inch by agonising inch, giving my brain time
to grasp the concept of what was about to happen. The
pain became almost too much when not softened by the
warm flood of pleasure, but somehow still delicious
because his hand was holding me open, exposing me,
waiting for the ultimate test of my need to know my
limits.

Almost as though a switch had activated in my brain,
the pain became an intense glow. I would still have to
describe it as pain, but I was no longer on that plateau
that was going nowhere. The wax had reached my pubic
hair and was hovering, like a beast about to pounce,
waiting for me to beg. I stretched upwards as far as my
ropes would allow, but they still held me firmly in place.
His hand still exposed my throbbing clitoris, which
pounded and twitched with greed.

The need to come shrieked from every pore in my
body until I thought I would explode into a million
pieces. I had no more movement to beg with and my
need roared in my brain. I gathered up one last effort
and jerked my body upwards to welcome the pain. Still
the wax dripped on the edge of my sex. My insides were
pulsating, building my impending orgasm, waiting for
the trigger. I felt my clitoris grow and throb like a tiny
cock exposed to raw, urgent need.

The drip of scalding wax ripped through me.

His fingers slipped inside me, burying in me to the hilt and spreading me apart, stretching me, stuffing me until I thought I would burst apart. My body bucked and pounded and arced against the soft red rope that until that moment had held me like a vice.

As the wax cooled on my poor abused flesh the sobs of deliverance that racked my body bubbled from my gagged mouth, filling the silent room as the pumping spasms of exquisite bittersweet agony pulsed through my dripping exhausted cunt.

6

Once my orgasm started to fade I felt very strange and more than a little silly. Here I was, helpless, covered in candle wax that had gone hard and clung to my flesh, pulling the fine hairs and holding the creases in place.

I was acutely aware of how quickly passion and need could disappear after a climax and found myself wishing I could be at home and not have to go through the embarrassment of the next bit.

I tried to imagine how we would be with each other. Would he untie me, then offer me a cup of tea so we could talk about what had just happened – or would he start again?

What about his pleasure? I wondered. Did he orgasm, and, if so, how and when? I tried hard to imagine what was going on around me but found it impossible because I had no idea what the room, or he for that matter, looked like.

I could feel his presence still, and a slight pressure on my right-hand side suggested to me that he was just standing watching me. It was funny but even that small contact, and even in my cold post-orgasm state, I started getting a warm twitch between my legs and wriggled invitingly. Well, I *think* it must have been invitingly, because I felt his warm hand on my inner thigh inexorably moving upwards. I strained up to meet it like the slut I was becoming and grunted my approval, but the hand moved onwards and roamed my spread-eagled body at will, almost absent-mindedly.

Then I realised what was happening: he was standing

next to me, gazing at my restrained limbs, at my heaving breasts and my very exposed sex, and he was wanking. I had a rush of very mixed emotions at that moment. I was excited by the image in my mind of him standing over me with his naked cock in his hand, gently stroking along the length of the shaft while his hungry eyes searched his captive, his possession, his prize. Me!

In the almost total silence of the room I could hear the gentle movement of his hand, his breathing becoming more and more ragged and insistent, and I held my breath to savour the sounds, trying to imagine his face. I wished so much at that moment that I could watch his pleasure and perform the honour of supplying it, but I realised with a jolt that, if this sort of encounter was his way of making love, I was probably providing all the pleasure he needed just by lying there and wriggling

My confused thoughts were answered then when I felt his burning hot sperm spray over my skin. The sticky fluid spurted over my legs and mound, then up to my belly and breasts, cooling rapidly and leaving us again at that stalemate.

As with everything else that day, he handled it perfectly. Slowly but carefully, he wiped the sticky globules of come from my body, which again shamelessly wriggled and writhed at his touch. For the first time I heard him make a noise – a deep-throated chuckle – and I felt ashamed at my wantonness. Then he picked the dried wax piece by piece from my skin and generally cleaned me up.

It felt so peculiar just to lie there while this totally unknown man ministered to my needs. He untied the ropes around my ankles and then my wrists, and, releasing the restraints to my thighs, he grasped my hands and pulled me from the bed. I started to put my hands up to the blindfold so I could finally see, but his hands stopped me and firmly placed mine back at my sides. I suppose I could have forced the issue but I was quite happy in my ignorance. It would have been so awful to go through all that only to find that my captor was in his nineties and ugly. I knew he was tall and of slim-mish build from when he had stood behind me and held my naked body against his chest for a second or two, but that was all I did know.

He walked around me, bent down and tapped my ankle. I automatically lifted my foot, expecting some sort of restraint, but he slipped something soft over my foot and then did the same with the other. My hopes crashed when I realised he was dressing me. He even took the trouble to replace my stockings and suspender belt, turning me round to adjust the seams.

Why did he want me to go? I wanted to ask. Had I displeased him in some way? With my thoughts churn-ing away inside, I was led down the stairs to the hall where it had all begun and handed my keys. He turned me around and I felt a soft kiss on my forehead, a mere touch of his lips that belied the torture he had put me through. I was turned again and recoiled when I heard the front door open in front of me. I cowered back away from the noises and the cool breeze, petrified that he was going to send me out still unable to see and fully gagged.

I was totally disorientated and felt a moment of sheer panic, convinced for some inexplicable reason that I would be unable to function outside that door. Could I remember how to drive the car or how to get home?

I broke the rules and clutched at him, still standing behind me, surprised but unbelievably pleased when I felt an unmistakable erection forcing the front of his trousers. The trousers were leather and felt sensuous and tactile under my searching fingers. He tutted and pulled away.

I felt his hand unbuckling the harness that had

encased my head and my will for what seemed like a lifetime, but as he slid the dildo from my mouth and I started to speak his hand immediately silenced me. With one hand across my mouth like this, his other hand loosened the blindfold and held my head like a vice so I was unable to turn around.

I was completely blinded and unable to respond in the usual way. Because I had spent so long unable to move, see or react to anything that happened to me, I didn't resist when I was gently but firmly pushed out of the door with the little bell still clutched tightly in my palm. I just did what was expected of me as I had since I had first walked up the drive earlier that day, a completely different person.

After a few moments my sight cleared and I turned around only to see the front door shut and the inside of the house closed to my gaze.

The house had returned to its innocent suburban persona. No one would have any idea from looking at that façade that anything but the simplest, ordinary, everyday things went on behind the closed door.

I stood for a few minutes transfixed by everything, hardly able to believe what had just happened to me – or, I should say, what I had *allowed* to happen to me. I wondered if he was standing just out of sight watching my bewilderment, and, if so, what was he thinking? Had it just been another game for him? Had he forgotten about me already?

I knew I had to move but felt that if I did the spell would be broken and I would never be able to convince myself that it had happened. One thing I knew for certain was that I would never be the same again.

I drove home in a daze, still able to feel the ropes around my wrists and his fingers inside me. I was acutely aware of the spanking he had given me and how it had hurt; but, funnily enough, I had already forgotten the pain that had made me want to scream and that memory had been replaced with the burning pleasure it had induced.

I experience so many mixed emotions on that journey home. One minute I wanted to go back and stay and beg him to let me live in his bonds for ever, the next I convinced myself that somehow he had drugged me and what had happened had constituted abuse, pure and simple. I jumped between anger and complete surrender to the alien feelings he had evoked in me.

When I got home I stood in my hallway in a daze, not knowing what to do next. I felt lost and exhausted. I almost crawled up the stairs in a trance and lay down on the bed still fully clothed, pulled the quilt up over my shoulder and slept.

I slept for twelve hours and when I woke I lay warm and snug in bed running over everything that had happened since I got up the morning before. I longed to tell Becky or even Ruth what had happened, but I wasn't ready for that, and I was convinced either would think I was making it up to excite her.

The more I thought about it the more I knew that all this was meant to happen. I knew that even if I never met Mr King again I had changed and I could never go back to the Cassie that I was a few weeks before.

I was still wearing the miniskirt and high heels and I remembered how it felt to stand in Mr King's hall. I had no idea where the courage had come from actually to restrain myself and then stand and wait for a stranger to decide what he wanted to do to me. Just the memory of those few minutes and how excited but petrified I had been succeeded in setting me off again.

I searched through my bedside table and found the length of red rope that Mr King had originally sent to tempt me and tied it around my stockinged ankles. The brilliance of the scarlet rope against the dusky black of my stockings created an image that oozed naughty and I found myself imagining the picture I must have made, staked out on Mr King's bed with my pussy forced open and exposed and my breasts helpless.

Again I tried to think of ways to restrain myself, and of course there were many, but none of the ideas included how to get free again. I ripped the rope off again in disgust and frustration, leaving the intense burning sensation between my thighs. So ... I would have to improvise.

I remembered a sleep mask that I had bought the year before for a particularly long holiday flight I had taken, and searched the cupboards until I found it.

I lay stretched out on the bed, still with my clothes and shoes on, and raised my knees up until I could place my feet flat on the bed. The spike heels made delicious indents in the quilt. I then slowly let my knees drop apart so the heels of my shoes met flat on the bed and my pussy lay exposed and uncovered waiting for my next move. My whole cunt was alive with the memory of my experience with Mr King, so I patted it and whispered, 'Hang on a minute, I'm thinking.' As I patted it I winced, realising that there were tender places on my thighs and the soft padded flesh of my pussy, so I sat up to take a look. Across the front of my thighs there was a thin, faint, red welt from the belt. I unbuttoned the silk shirt until my wanton breasts were naked and saw that, down the length of my torso from breasts to thighs, there were dozens of tiny red marks that I assumed were the aftermath of the hot wax. Most of the marks were spaced around the soft flesh of my breasts, getting closer and closer until, around the nipples, which stood erect and swollen, the red blended to form a blush of colour that covered my nipples and half my breasts.

I was completely transfixed by this proof of my surrender and gently stroked the little kisses of red, burning with shame and excitement at the memory they evoked. How could I possibly have let that happen to me?

The power of the memory alone excited me beyond anything I had felt before I visited Mr King. At that moment I would have gladly returned to London and thrown myself on his mercy and begged to stay for ever as his sex slave.

Again I wondered what he looked like and how old he was. I desperately wanted to imagine him so he could assist my masturbation, but found that the physical memories were enough.

I lay down again with my hands feverishly roaming over my body, searching out all the tender places that fuelled my memories. As I writhed on the bed I caught the image of myself in the mirror on the wardrobe door beside the bed and was shocked to find that I looked like a sex-crazed slut. My clothes were all over the place, my five-inch heels digging into the bed and my hand thrust between my sticky thighs. My bottom was thrust upwards off the bed as if it were desperate to get closer to the hand that fed its need. I needed more.

I stopped in mid-flow and placed the sleep mask over my eyes. It didn't have quite the same effect as the black leather blindfold had in Mr King's hall but it served its purpose. It blocked out the light and helped me fantasise that I was back in his house, silent in the darkness waiting to discover my sexuality.

I allowed myself to relive every feeling that had racked my body over those hours I had been with Mr King – the pain, the pleasure, the excruciating fear of the unknown – but uppermost in my thoughts was the total and utter acceptance of my submission to a man I didn't know.

Behind the sleep mask I could be what I wanted. I could be the sex-crazed slut that I resembled if I chose. I writhed on the bed in the darkness, pinching my nipples until they hurt and thrusting my fingers deep into my pussy, trying hard to re-create the feelings I had experienced earlier. My flailing hand grasped the rope that lay beneath me where it had been discarded and I passed it between my hot thighs and pulled it tight up between the lips of my sex so it crushed my clitoris and almost slit me in two. As I approached my goal, the rope buried far up the canyon of my cunt, I remembered the exquisite rush of shame and ecstasy I felt when Mr King discovered my petticoat and bent me over to spank me like a child. My goal was in sight. The pain of the spanking crashed through my thoughts as the rope almost cut me in half and the waves of pleasure and torment blew me away.

I collapsed back exhausted and drained, the rope, slimy with my juices, still clutched in my twitching hands and my breasts heaving in response.

I slept again, this time the sleep of the sexually satiated, dreamless and deep.

7

I was in complete turmoil in the days that followed. I wanted to forget that it had happened and go back to being me, but I wanted even more for him to knock on my door, pick me up in his arms and carry me away to his house for more.

I tried not to leave the house just in case he tried to contact me, and when I did go out I saw Mr King in every man I passed.

For days I tried to avoid thinking about Mr King but failed at least once a minute. I wanted to get into my car and go to him, but I knew I couldn't go back again. Anyway, he obviously hadn't wanted to repeat the experience or else he would have asked me before I left. I did find myself waiting for the postman every morning and snatching up the phone every time it rang, hoping it was Mr King. It never was. Most of the time it was Becky pleading with me to tell her what had happened and trying to tempt me to lunch or coffee or bed. She was desperate to know the sordid details and I was not ready to tell her, not yet, anyway. I couldn't explain even to myself why I had responded so readily to Mr King's summons, so how could I possibly explain it to anyone else? She seemed to accept that eventually I would be ready to tell her, and waited patiently.

Work became a chore instead of the satisfying career it had been, and I even found myself refusing the offers of dinner from my colleagues. One colleague was particularly insistent. He would watch me every time I walked past him, follow me to the coffee machine and just drool. I tried very hard to avoid his advances but it was difficult. The corridor to my office passed his door and one lunchtime he cornered me, pressed me up against the wall and pushed his hard bulge against my crotch. I only just managed to wriggle away before my baser instincts took over. I began to worry that he could see through me.

The last straw was when a young girl from the factory came to me for advice because her relationship had collapsed. After a lot of encouragement she explained that her boyfriend had no idea how to please her sexually and when she had tried to explain to him he had walked out, leaving her alone with a four-month-old baby. I almost risked my job by telling her to make sure that the sexuality she craved with him was the right one for her. It wasn't until she looked at me with a peculiar puzzlement that I realised she thought I was coming on to her. As soon as that thought crossed my mind I waffled on, trying to put her mind at rest and help her with some constructive advice, but when she got up to leave the room I watched her bottom sway provocatively and wondered whether she had ever been spanked. I knew I was not behaving in a professional way, so I decided I needed to get away to think and to pull myself together. Luckily I had some leave owing to me.

I couldn't bear the thought of going anywhere on my own because I suspected that, if I packed a case and got in my car, it would automatically head for London and Mr King. Quite often over the preceding few days I had thought of Becky. I wished I could get Mr King out of my mind to allow me to concentrate more on the possible relationship with my new-found friend. On the spur of the moment I phoned her and suggested we take off for a few days, saying the break would give us a chance to get to know each other better. She was quite surprised, as I hadn't spoken to her for a week or two, but she agreed readily. I needed to tell someone.

Becky's family had a small holiday cottage in Snowdonia, and even though it was still a bit cold we decided we could have long nights in front of a log fire, curled up reading and talking and getting to know each other properly. I knew I was being cruel not having told Becky the story yet, but I still wasn't sure how I *would* tell her, and the problem I had was that it still felt like a story.

I couldn't believe I had been so daring. Perhaps if he had been in contact since, I might have found it all easier, but, as it was, everything that had happened that day with Mr King felt like a dream.

Becky checked with her mum and found that the cottage would be free the following week, so we both made the necessary arrangements to have time away from work and made plans to travel to Wales on the Saturday. I still had no idea how I would tell Becky the extent to which I had let Mr King control me, or if indeed I would be able to share *any* of it with her, but I did know that whatever I decided she would be OK about it.

The morning we were due to go I sat on the edge of my bed with my case packed and my thoughts in turmoil wondering what our little sojourn would hold. Becky had rung to make the final arrangements for the journey and just before she hung up she played with me a little, casually asking if I minded that there was only one bedroom with one large king-size bed.

Until that moment my thoughts had been totally on Mr King but she brought me back to reality. 'I hope you're not so wrapped up in your fantasy man that you won't be able to enjoy our time together in the peace and tranquillity of the mountains, Cassie. Just think, no one to bother us and only the sheep to see what we get up to,' she said innocently, but I knew she was hinting. I longed to see her and we made arrangements for her to pick me up.

For an hour or so in the car we chatted about everyday matters. Becky told me about a problem she was having at work and we discussed at great length whether or not she should have her long hair cut short for the summer. Trivial, girlie things mostly. We both knew we were killing time and that eventually I would give in and explain to her not only why I urgently needed a holiday, but also why I had been avoiding her since my visit to Mr King.

Then, in a long period of silence, Becky blurted out, 'Oh, for God's sake, Cassie, it can't be *that* bad! Anyway, you promised last night that you'd share every detail with me.'

That was probably the opening I needed. As soon as I realised that Becky thought I was angry with her, I knew I had to cough up.

'Right,' I started, and, just so I didn't have to look at her, my eyes searched the hard shoulder as if it held the wonders of the universe. 'Well, you know the day I went to London ...'

'I know all that, Cassie. Just get on with the juicy bits. Come on, tell me what he was like –'

I interrupted before she had a chance to ask too many questions.

'I'm sorry, Becky, but you're just going to have to listen or I don't know how I'll even begin to tell you anything. I'm still finding it amazingly hard to admit to myself what happened. Becky, I love you to bits, but will you please shut up and let me talk?'

'Sorry, go on, I promise I won't say another word until you've finished.'

I knew that would be impossible, but I started anyway.

I reminded her about the red rope and how I had felt when I opened the package and how I imagined it would feel restraining my limbs. She gasped. Then I quoted the letter he sent me word for word, not quite knowing how to explain the feeling of rightness I felt at the abruptness of it. My heart raced at the memory. I went on to tell her every sordid exciting detail from how the clock chiming frightened the life out of me, and how warm his sperm felt as it sprayed over my helpless body to how devastated I had felt afterwards when he didn't ask me to visit again. I explained how debauched I felt one minute and how exhilarated the next.

It took about two hours to tell. I poured out every last detail as we left the A14 and moved on to the M6, with Becky moving with the flow of the traffic and me oblivious to anyone else on the road. I tried to make her understand everything I had experienced during that long day and, to give Becky her due, she hardly spoke once. She gawked at me periodically and gasped with shock in all the right places. She was trying to keep both eyes on the road but she looked at me intently. It was as if she were looking for something behind my face when I told her I had followed his orders and restrained myself, then waited for him to decide what he wanted to do to me. Funny, that: I had done that myself in the mirror. It was as if I were searching for a completely separate person, the one who gave herself to Mr King unconditionally.

When I described the results of the petticoat saga, Becky gasped and groaned in turn and I could tell from how often she swallowed and fidgeted that my description was getting to her. Her hands clutched and released the wheel rhythmically. Then, seconds later, she would glance sideways at me, totally incredulous.

Occasionally she would start to say something in response to a particularly scary bit, such as when I described in minute detail how the gag had sealed my acceptance and how the striking of the match had petrified me beyond anything I had ever experienced before.

She did explode a couple of times, especially at moments like that, punctuating my story with intelligent comments like 'Fuck!' and 'You didn't!' and 'Why didn't you drop the bell?' but I found it best to ignore them.

Eventually, when we got to the border of Wales and I had exhausted every detail and every emotion and every self-recriminating doubt I had experienced since, I stopped talking, took a deep breath and exhaled slowly.

'Well, go on, then. Tell me how stupid I am. Tell me that you're disgusted with me and I'll tell you that I know I *am* stupid and I'm probably more disgusted with myself than you could ever comprehend.'

Becky shocked me then, almost as much as I had shocked myself three weeks before.

She drove in silence for a few minutes, then pulled into the first lay-by we came to, stopped the car, switched off the engine, swivelled round in her seat and stared at me with such an intense look on her face that I had no idea what she was thinking.

'You have *got* to be joking! Yes, I think you *are* stupid, but, believe me, I'm far from disgusted. The only thing that disgusts me is the shameful reaction my body's been experiencing,' she exclaimed incredulously. 'That is the most amazing story I have ever heard. I have to admire your sense of adventure, however scary it was, and I wish I could have seen you on that bed so badly I can taste it. I've always been slightly ashamed of my fantasies until I met you, which is a bit surprising as the most recurring one I have now involves you.' My heart thudded in my chest cavity. 'And, strangely enough, it also involves one of the things Mr King did to you. See, even though you've shared with me all the details of your amazing day submitting to Mr King, I can still only talk in shorthand. I still can't actually say the words. I want to pour out every feeling I experienced as you talked to me but I don't know how.'

'Don't you be stupid now, Becky,' I admonished. 'If I can tell you the story I've just told you, then do you really think any fantasy you have is going to shock me?' I took hold of her hand as it hung from the back of her seat and squeezed it encouragingly.

'Oh, sod it! Here goes, then, Cassie. Part of me knows that I'm a normal heterosexual female. Whatever "normal" means! Basically I love a good shag as well as the next girl, but the fantasies I've had since our first meeting I'm finding it difficult to handle. I imagine us doing things to each other just as debauched as what Mr King did to you.'

Becky was blushing prettily and looking at me with an intensity that I found very disconcerting. I knew that, if I didn't stop this conversation then, we would never get to the cottage. So I suggested to Becky that we save the rest until we got there and then just take one step at a time. The rest of the journey to Llanberris only took an hour.

I was enchanted with the cottage. It stood a mile or so from any other property and nestled on the side of a mountain with a waterfall at the bottom of the surrounding field and sheep in the garden. Just the place to take my mind off Mr King and help me concentrate on the promises that were sizzling between Becky and me.

We kept busy for the first few hours settling in and getting the place warm, so it wasn't until later that evening as we sat on the rug in front of a roaring log fire that we spoke about it all again.

'Weren't you absolutely petrified, Cassie?' Becky asked for probably the third time.

'Of course I was, but haven't you ever done something exhilarating that ended up horny?'

'Yes, I answered an advert and found you, but he could have been anyone!'

I leaned forward and poked the logs on the fire, then turned to look at Becky in the flickering firelight. She sat next to me on the sheepskin rug, legs crossed, exposing her lean thighs, her nightshirt bunched around her hips.

'Look at yourself,' I said. 'You question me but your eyes are shining with excitement and after what you said in the car earlier it's obvious that what I did has really aroused you too, hasn't it?'

'Yes, but I still find it so hard to believe that you let a total stranger, who could have been a mad axeman, undress you and spank you like a kid and then pour fucking hot wax over you while you were tied helpless on his bed. You let him silence you, then put his fingers inside your fanny and wiggle them about like he owned you. You must have been out of your mind. What were you thinking of?'

'What was I *thinking* of? Exactly the same as you're thinking now, Becky. How it would feel to allow someone else to control you. To control your pleasure! To completely own you and your feelings for as long as they chose to. To give yourself over to pure adrenaline just once in your life and bugger the consequences. And, anyway, I had the bell.

'You've admitted that you have some steamy fantasies, just like me,' I continued. 'Are you telling me that you wouldn't want the chance to act them out?' When I asked

83

this last question I rather unfairly looked her straight in the eye. She must have known I was referring to the conversation we had earlier. Again, as she had earlier, Becky wriggled and fidgeted with embarrassment.

'Yes but –'

'No buts, Becky, cut the crap. Are you or are you not wondering what it felt like? Be honest with yourself, even if you can't be honest with me. You're just going through the motions of telling me how silly I've been because you think you should. But I bet you're dying to ask more questions, aren't you?'

Becky was silent for a few minutes, so I took the opportunity to fill our wineglasses. I was beginning to feel decidedly mellow and I noticed as I bent and topped up Becky's glass that her cheeks were flushed. Was that the wine, I wondered, or the conversation?

I wandered into the kitchen, my feet cold on the stone floor. I thought that if I went to get some nibbles it would give her time to think about what I had said. I was right: no sooner had I tucked the crisps and biscuits under my arms than I heard, 'Come back, Cassie. You're right: I have a million questions I want to ask. I want to know how it felt, what you were thinking and what happens next.'

I smiled to myself, pleased that I had read her right, and returned to the comfort of the fire. Instead of sitting next to Becky, I sat, like her, cross-legged and faced her on the rug, and we munched and drank our wine as we talked.

'Here's to adventures!' I laughed as I clinked my glass on hers. 'What do you want to know first?'

'I want to know lots of things but I don't know how to ask,' she said.

'But we've talked loads about sex and it's never bothered you before, has it?'

'Well, no, but this is different. Before, we've always

discussed more normal sex, things that everyone does, so to speak, and now you've moved into a league of your own. You've experienced things that some of us mere mortals are scared to even fantasise about and, to be quite honest, I didn't think anyone actually *did* some of them. I'll never be able to look at another candle without thinking of you.'

'Is that the bit that excited you most, when he slowly dripped burning wax over my tortured ravished naked breasts?' I teased, caressing my breasts in a parody of the story, fascinated to know if Becky shared my fantasies of submission.

'Noooo ... the bit when you arrived,' Becky finally managed to squeeze out, still not able to put her own deep dark thoughts into words.

'What, the bit where I waited in the hall for him?' I knew exactly what she meant but found myself getting very horny making her squirm.

'No, the petticoat bit.'

I drew out my next question, teasing her. 'Becky. Do you mean you want to know how it feels to be bent over naked, with your bottom thrust up in the air and then to be spanked mercilessly by a big strong manly hand?'

I asked this with my face up close to her flushed one, and my eyes locked on to hers. There was not a trace left in me of the submission I had experienced with Mr King. I actually found myself wanting to show Becky, who was usually the one teasing me, just how it felt to be thoroughly spanked. She really shocked me with her answer.

She lowered her eyes, shifted her bottom about as if she were sitting on an ants' nest and giggled. 'I think I'm probably a bit tipsy but I don't care whose hand it is.' And with that Becky raised her eyes again and gave me a very timid, little-girl smile.

We just gazed at each other, both knowing what we wanted but not knowing how to start. I tried to tell myself just to do it, but I couldn't. For at least another ten minutes we sat facing each other in front of that romantic log fire with our knees almost touching, both waffling on about nothing.

We talked about how nice the wine was and how the wind was howling outside and wasn't it a good thing we weren't out in it? We laughed falsely at the end of almost every sentence until I thought I would scream. Becky looked just as uncomfortable as I felt.

She picked up the bottle of wine, filled our glasses to the brim and challenged me to down mine in one. By then we both knew it was an excuse. We both tipped at the same time and gulped the whole glass together. Then she looked at me and whispered softly, 'Please, Cassie.'

I needed no further encouragement. I grabbed her wrist and stood up, dragging her with me, sat down on the settee and pulled her in front of me. I had no real idea how her specific fantasy went, so I had to trust the one that had almost filled my thoughts since we had talked in the lay-by.

'Stand up straight, Becky. I'm going to explain what I want you to do.'

Without a second's hesitation Becky shuffled into an upright position and waited. She looked a little ludicrous standing to attention in her short nightie covered in teddies, but luckily my hunger was blind.

'I want you to lie across my lap and touch the floor with your hands in front and your toes on the floor behind.' Then, as I imagined how it would feel to be the one following the instructions and looking her straight in the eye, I added, 'That will raise your bottom for me. Come on, then, get on with it.' I was a little cruel then because I gave her no help at all, but I based my decision on the fact that when Mr King had humiliated me I had loved it, in a funny sort of way. I knew I was cheating slightly by using all the instructions and expressions that burned my crotch and kept me awake at night imagining.

Becky shifted about, not knowing which end to put over my lap first. She flushed deep red, making strange little horny whimpering noises in her throat, and lowered her eyes. I was thrilled at her reaction and even began to appreciate what it was Mr King had enjoyed about our encounter.

Up until that moment I had no idea how to go about spanking someone, but she eventually managed to obey my commands and her soft body yielded to my instructions. She draped herself over my lap, carefully making sure she touched the floor with her fingertips in front of her and her toes behind her. Her legs were taut and straight – a very pretty sight. Her nightshirt had managed to ride up a little so I could just make out the lower curve of her bottom. Becky broke my trance by putting a hand behind her and trying to cover herself with the hem of her nightshirt.

I smacked her hand away and tutted loudly, knowing that when Mr King sharply punished me like that I was desperate for more. 'Tsk, tsk, naughty girl! Touch the floor, please, and don't move your hands again. Do you understand?'

Becky nodded feebly and her pretty hair dropped to the floor either side of her head, reminding me of the silly conversation we had had in the car about her getting it cut. I grasped a handful and held her head still for a minute, enjoying the feeling of control it gave me.

I knew that in the few books I had read where someone was spanked the spanker would have made the poor person being spanked say something silly like 'Yes, mistress'. But I wasn't her mistress: I was her friend and hopefully lover and she looked so sexy bent over me like that, and anyway the relationship I had shared with Mr King hadn't needed silly titles to make it horny.

I stroked every inch of her back and thighs through the soft material, carefully avoiding her bottom to increase her anticipation and mine. Then, when I couldn't wait any longer, and Becky was wriggling fit to burst and emitting a continuous moan, with her unfettered breasts jiggling about in her nightshirt, I knew it was time to move on.

I took hold of the hem of her nightshirt with both hands and I tantalisingly, slowly, folded it up until it was laid across her shoulders and her bottom and lower back were exposed totally.

Her bottom was beautiful. A perfectly symmetrical round shape, tapering down to her thighs with just a glimpse of blonde fuzz in the V where her thighs met. I laid the flat of my right hand across the cheeks of her bottom and my left hand I gently but firmly laid in the middle of her back. The globes of her buttocks were pure white in the shape of a very brief bikini line, surrounded by slightly tanned flesh that made the white area look ruder than I would ever have imagined.

Becky groaned out loud and raised one of her legs – I assumed to try to cover her shame – but I slapped it sharply and she obediently put it down again. I was really beginning to enjoy this. Thoughts of wanting to be in her position were fading and a need to control was taking over my libido.

I was shocked at how aroused I felt just looking at Becky's naked bottom and having it laid out before me in all its glory. I think she felt the same way because, when she realised I was just looking at her, she twitched and wriggled and murmured sweet little kitten noises until I had to put her out of her misery.

When I raised my hand the first time, Becky gasped

and the flesh of her buttocks clenched tightly to ward off the sting that she knew was imminent.

To begin with I spanked her quite playfully until her cheeks were glowing, then concentrated on her thighs until they too were rosy and hot. Then I gradually spanked harder and harder until Becky was groaning loudly and yelping occasionally. I found the yelping made me as horny as hell and I wished I had worn something more substantial than the nightdress I had on. It had ridden up as soon as I sat down, so I could feel every inch of her naked torso, and it was sending me crazy. I could feel the velvety skin of her breasts dangling against my legs, and her soft belly on my bare flesh was sending me to distraction.

I didn't think I would be able to go on much longer without some direct stimulation and longed to masturbate, but then got wrapped up again in what I was doing. As Mr King had been with me, I was in total control of this sexy lady and wanted to see what pleasure I was capable of giving her.

I wasn't sure that Becky was ready for more obvious sex play yet, so I decided that the best way to get her to allow me to move this on to a more intimate level was to raise the amount of pain until it was almost unbearable. Hopefully, then she would be desperate for any bit of pleasure she could get, so I did just that. I spanked harder and harder, all over her now burning cheeks, on the soft underside of her buttocks and down her thighs to her knees until her flesh was boiling to the touch, and poor Becky was actually pleading with me to stop. I stopped suddenly and bent down close to her ear. 'Open your legs for me, Becky,' I cajoled. The need to be in her position pounded through my brain, intoxicating and encouraging me onward.

'I can't,' she whimpered, 'it's too embarrassing.'

I started the spanking again in earnest, knowing from

my own experience that very soon she would do anything to stop the pain and transfer it into the pleasure that she knew lurked under the confusion she was feeling.

Eventually, when her sobs had increased to wails, she capitulated. I felt cruel pushing her like that, but as she had the option to stop me at any time I carried on, assuming she was enjoying it – at some level, anyway.

Tentatively, her thighs worked their way apart until there was a gap between them of about six inches, and I could see the excitement glistening on the blonde downy hair between her legs.

'More, Becky, spread them wide for me, until the muscles in your thighs feel as if they'll tear. I want to see you open. I want to be able to feel you.'

At that Becky cried out loud, 'For fuck's sake, Cassie, what are you doing to me?'

She snivelled and sniffed and moaned as I encouraged her by spanking some more, right on the tenderest part of her fleshy mounds. But she obeyed and did as I had asked. She stretched her legs apart until I could see the tendons tight as piano wire in her inner thighs. Between those exquisite thighs her pretty pussy lay there all blonde and pink and sticky. The tiny pinkish inner lips peeped from between the pale fluff, open and inviting. I just had to touch her.

Keeping my hand on her back to hold her in place, I ran my right hand down between the heat of her thighs until I felt the wetness of her lips on my fingers. I stroked the petals of her pussy until they opened further, begging me to invade the inner sanctum. The slipperiness of her drew me in like a Venus flytrap attracting its prey, but before I gave in to temptation I gently tapped her cunt with my fingers to see what the reaction would be. Sure enough, just like me, she loved it, so I increased the pressure. As I gently spanked between her legs the guttural groans that came from Becky's pretty mouth shocked even me.

The feelings she was experiencing obviously became incredibly intense, because she squirmed and tried her best to avoid each individual slap. I held her tightly in place and continued until she was finding it difficult to breathe and her juices were dripping off the swollen hood of her clitoris on to the fireside rug, forming a distinct pool.

Mr King had shown me the animal I have inside me when he dripped burning hot wax on my exposed clitoris, and now it was my turn with Becky. I spanked her in that private place until she was soaking wet and obviously very tender. I thought she would come just from that, so I varied my attack and alternately slapped and stroked until I thought she would go crazy.

I teased her, dipping just one finger in and out in a slight twisting motion, knowing it would send her mad. Sure enough, her hips lifted off my lap and stretched upwards, trying desperately to reach my hand, but again I made her wait. Each time I removed my finger, she was forcing herself up to me, so I let my finger, which was slick with her wetness, brush gently across her clitoris.

'Cassie, please,' she begged.

I gave in and added another finger to the equation. They slipped in so smoothly that it was as if they were meant to be there. The hot silky wetness of her was like nothing I had ever dreamed of. It sucked at my fingers, begging me to invade further. Becky was panting and arching her back, then thrusting her steamy bottom up for more, not caring for one moment how debauched she looked.

'Oh, please, Cassie, please, oh, fuck, please!' she begged.

I wasn't ready to let her come yet, so again I ignored

her pleas and started a new assault on her bright-red seat. I paddled away at her cheeks until my arm ached and I knew Becky was reaching her pain threshold, but then her next cry brought me back to earth.

My sweet captive was sobbing uncontrollably, wriggling and twisting to get away from the onslaught. She turned her face up to plead with me and I was horrified by what I had done. Poor Becky! Her eyes were screwed up tight and the tears streamed down her face. I couldn't believe I had been so insensitive to her reactions. I had been convinced that I was reading her right.

I lowered her gently on to the floor in front of me, on to the deep sheepskin rug, convinced I had overstepped the mark. I knelt astride her with my knees either side of her hips and, with my arms astride her head, I looked down at her ravaged face and begged her forgiveness.

'Becky, I am so sorry. Look at me,' I pleaded

She slowly opened her eyes and gazed at me in total surprise. Then in between sniffs she asked, 'What did you stop for? I'm so horny, Cassie, I think I'm going to explode.' And with that she stretched up and bit one of my nipples, which thrust, erect, against the material of my nightie. She bit really hard, with a purpose.

'You little cow!' I screeched, and promptly turned her over again. I grabbed a cushion off the settee behind us and pushed it under her hips to raise her bottom for the real punishment she now truly deserved, and I really laid into her.

This time I sat astride her legs, facing her upraised bum, and, as I slapped the deep scarlet buttocks, she must have realised that this time I meant business. She stood the pain as long as she could but in the end she yelled, 'OK, I'm sorry,' and wriggled free until she was on her back underneath me.

I immediately knew what I wanted to do: I wanted to taste that poor crushed place between her now trembling thighs. Becky obviously read my mind, because she very half-heartedly tried to close her thighs and with a little whimper whispered, 'Cassie.' But all I did was smile at her and raise my eyebrows and her thighs dropped apart.

She groaned deep in her throat as I gripped the hem of my nightie and, kneeling up in front of her, I pulled it up over my head.

I became hypnotised by that magical place between her thighs and, as I lowered my head to explore fully what I had had a taste of on our first night, I paused and looked deep into her eyes, which smouldered with hunger.

'I'm going to worship you with my mouth, Becky. I'm going to take away all the pain and I intend to tease you until you beg me to let you orgasm. Then when you can't stand any more, you are going to fill my mouth with your essence.'

Becky just whimpered again and nodded.

Her musky smell sent me wild and I buried my whole face in her. I nibbled those sexy little lips, puffy with arousal, and dipped my tongue into her wetness until she writhed about the floor and gripped my hair in her hands, forcing me deeper. Her legs wrapped tightly around my head until I could hear nothing, see nothing and smell nothing but sex, and I fucked her with my tongue while she bucked her hips in response.

Still clutched tight by her thighs, I explored further until I felt the hard nub of her clitoris nudging my lip. I forced her to drop her thighs wide apart for me and, bunching the fingers of one hand, I rammed them knuckle deep inside her. With the other hand I exposed the shiny tight pink button for my attentions and sucked at it with my hot open mouth until I heard Becky wailing like an animal, still pleading with me. I spread my fingers inside her to fill her completely and

93

held her clitoris imprisoned with my lips, sucking it deeply into my mouth, and then flicking the end mercilessly with my tongue.

'Now, Cassie! I'm coming *now*!' she screamed. Her hips pounded against the floor and her thighs trembled and spasmed as her sex throbbed and danced to my tune, filling my mouth as promised with her sweet essence. I sucked her dry until her clitoris retreated to its safe haven, back in the secret folds between her lithe shapely legs.

Becky lay in my arms for long minutes, gently sobbing and clutching me as if she were afraid to let go. I just gazed at her in wonder.

8

For one brief moment I felt embarrassed and slightly ashamed of what I had done. I think it must have been a preconditioned response, though, because, when I tried to analyse it later, I realised I didn't care what anyone else thought: it was none of their business and I had loved every minute of it.

We lay on the hearthrug with the logs spitting and crackling for what seemed like hours, wrapped in each other's arms. Becky cuddled into my side like a child, her skin sweaty and glowing in the flickering light from the fire. Eventually, I tried to worm my way from under her to get some more wine, but Becky looked so sleepy that I led her up the stairs and we snuggled together for at least two minutes before we fell asleep.

We woke to the chill of early morning on the mountain, shivering and covered in goose pimples, but Becky was not to be deterred. She leaped out of bed and told me to stay where I was. She brought us breakfast in bed and spoiled me completely. Later, after we had finished, Becky suggested we go into the village and explore for the day. She seemed a little subdued, so I asked if she was having regrets.

'No, Cassie, far from it. I'm feeling ... well, a bit overwhelmed, I suppose, by the intensity of my feelings for you. I'm hoping a day out might calm me down a bit. It was probably the wine. Come on, get up.' She threw my jeans at me.

* * *

The village was so pretty, surrounded by mountains and filled with cute cottages, made of large, pale stone bricks, that didn't even look big enough to swing a cat in. At first we couldn't find anywhere to park, but then we noticed a sign that pointed down a side street. The street was so narrow I think we actually breathed in as we made our way to the car park. The locals were obviously used to the roads, because they would pass us in spaces so narrow you could have shaken hands through the window. The tiny streets were filled with walkers, some in just shorts and backpacks but some in the full regalia of equipment necessary to attempt the climb up to Snowdon's snowy peak.

'I've always wanted to see the mountains,' I told Becky, 'and I've never had the chance.' I was totally in awe of the majestic landscape surrounding us. 'Can we at least attempt a small one before we have to leave?'

'The peak we scaled last night was enough for me,' she laughed. 'Sorry, I was only joking. Yes, of course we can. There's a lovely mountainous walk quite close to the cottage. I'll show you tomorrow, perhaps. But if you really enjoy this sort of thing I want to take you somewhere. It's the most magical place I've ever seen. I've been coming here since I was a child and I've always wanted to share it with someone, but the time's never been right. Come on,' she added as she turned the car around.

Only a mile or two away she stopped the car on a little dirt track and we got out. Then we followed a tiny path whose sign told us it led to the 'Fairy Glen'. I couldn't believe there was even a place with such a pretty name, but the sight before me after we had navigated the rocky path took my breath away. We were in a rocky gorge with outcrops towering above us. A raging torrent of water cascaded down through the break in the rocks either side. The sun tried its best to pierce the mystical darkness through the gorge but managed only one corridor of amazing brightness. The shaft of light filtered through the trees and sparkled on the water that spun off the dripping ferns clinging on to the surrounding rocks with a brilliance that left me speechless. I fell in love with the place and I think a little in love with Becky in the Fairy Glen.

We sat for probably an hour on one of the rocks just enjoying the peace and beauty around us. Becky reached out and took my hand, sealing the bond that had been created the night before in front of the fire.

We spent the rest of the day wandering around the village, and topped off the day with a wonderful meal in a Welsh Indian restaurant. Surreal but very enjoyable!

When we returned to the cottage in the pitch black it was freezing, so we lit a fire and sat on the edge of the sofa, leaning towards the flames until the room warmed up a little.

Becky got up and deliberately stood in front of me and stripped off until she looked, in the flickering light from the fire, like a marble statue covered in goose bumps standing on tiptoe to keep her feet off the cold stone tiles. I watched her, mesmerised.

'Come on, get your things off. I want to play,' she giggled.

While I obeyed – it was getting to become a habit – Becky darted about like a loon, naked as the day she was born.

First she ran into the kitchen and put the kettle on, and then, without pausing for breath, she put fresh logs on the fire. I watched, amused and delighted by her fervour to please me. As she bent over the fire in front of me I couldn't help but notice a small reddish blue mark on her buttock.

I reached out and gently stroked the mark. 'Did I hurt you too much?' I questioned, my hand slipping between her thighs.

She grasped my hand with hers and forced it deeply up into the cleft, where I could feel her juices bubbling already. 'What do you think?' she replied, pulling abruptly away and darting upstairs.

I couldn't believe how comfortable I felt in the aftermath of the night before. There was none of the strangeness I had felt with Mr King. The embarrassment had disappeared completely, leaving me with just a very satisfied warm feeling and a definite twitch between my legs. I remembered then that I hadn't orgasmed the night before. No wonder I was still feeling very horny.

I had to laugh when I heard the most almighty row coming from the stairs, with Becky huffing and puffing and swearing just as the whistle on the kettle decided to make itself heard. 'What happened to the silence of a mountain?' I shouted up to her as I hurried to the kitchen to pour water into the teapot.

'Argh! Quick, Cassie, help!' came the muffled screech from the stairwell.

I opened the door to the stairs to find Becky in a very undignified heap at the bottom, wrapped up in the very large feather bed. It was an old cottage and the turning space at the bottom of the stairs, where it was closed off by the latched door into the living room, was very tiny and Becky had managed to get herself trapped in the corner, unable to do anything. One of her legs was sticking up at a very silly angle and her bottom was surrounded by feather bed and just stuck out like a separate entity, totally unrelated to the arms and legs that protruded elsewhere. I couldn't see her head at all – it was buried somewhere under the tangle.

'Oh, what have we here? A very pretty bottom indeed!' I teased, probing the cleft that was rather rudely exposed to me. She wriggled and twisted, trying her best to get up, but I leaned on her to keep her in that position and touched the little bud of her anus.

I actually hadn't really thought of bottoms as being erotic until I met Mr King, but, since I had spent my day with him, my own bum had taken a very prominent part in my fantasies. After being forced to bend over in front of him and display my naked bottom, I often imagined Mr King probing my cheeks and what lay between them until the shame of it washed over me in waves and I had to stop. I couldn't imagine anyone else thought of such disgusting things. How naïve I still was!

As Becky protested loudly and tried her best to get up, I played with her, just gently probing and searching, watching her cunt tighten and then release. I kept her body tightly enclosed with my legs, mercilessly teasing that tiny bud. I was fascinated by the way it reacted to stimulation, the automatic reaction obviously being to close against intruders, but the more I tormented it the more relaxed and open it became.

I managed to swing around and sit on the bottom stair. This allowed me to pull the door shut, trapping Becky in the tight space in her very exposed position. Then I did something I would never have dreamed of a month before. I pushed apart the cheeks of her bottom with one hand, which put pressure on her tight little sphincter muscle to relax and, wetting the index finger of my other hand, I pushed it against that tiny tight opening, wriggling it and trying to worm it in.

Becky screeched, 'Don't you *dare* do that, Cassie. I mean it! Don't be so disgusting. Cassie, stop it!' All this was said in a very breathless husky voice that made a lie of the words. Her pussy, tightly gripped between her thighs, oozed enough of her arousal to prove to me that she was ashamed of how she felt. So I persevered. I kept softly teasing and invading until her breathing became ragged and I detected the occasional, now familiar grunt.

I gazed, hypnotised, as the tight muscle relaxed slightly and responded to my gentle caresses. The stickiness from Becky's sex trickled down her thigh and I scooped some up to help my entrance. I spread her cheeks further apart, still slightly marked from the night before, and her previously unassailable anus became soft and yielding instead of hard and tight and allowed my finger entry.

I was scared at first and only dipped my finger just inside, but the tightness and heat of her excited me to fever pitch and I just had to go for it. At this stage Becky was forcing herself up to grip hold of me and wailing as she had the night before.

'Oh, no, stop, please stop. I can't bear it any more,' she mumbled into the feather bed.

When I tried to stop in response to her request her hips pumped and she shouted, 'Don't stop now. Please!' And I was more than happy to oblige her.

The wetness I had transferred from her other greedy little hole did the trick, and my finger slipped in until my hand was tight against her, my fist bunched in the hollow between her cheeks. This had the effect of arousing her even more, if that were possible, and she became almost frenzied in her need. Surprisingly enough, her cry then was a new one.

'More, Cassie, I need more. Fuck me with it.'

I kept teasing for a few minutes more, plunging my finger in until it was so deep that my hand pushed against her body, then twisting it slightly on the way out until just the tip kept the way open for me. Before long I found that I didn't need to keep my finger in there to make the hole available, because Becky's anus had bloomed and lay before me open and ready and pleading for more.

I couldn't tease her any more. I bunched my hand into the best penis shape I could manage, with my thumb tucked into my palm, and very gently pushed it against the open entrance. I was convinced at first that I was expecting too much but I had an unexplainable need to violate her. Just as I had felt last night, I wanted to wrench out of her the very best reactions I could. I wanted her to roar and shudder and sob, just as I had for Mr King.

Becky obliged tenfold. As I forced the makeshift penis deeper into her, she expanded and sucked at my fist with those muscles that ten minutes before wouldn't allow the entry of one searching finger. I saw her small hand snake between her legs and rub furiously at her clit and, almost immediately, I felt the exquisite spasms of her orgasm wrapped around my hand, clutching and dragging me deeper while her mouth poured out obscenities.

In the aftermath of our joint introduction into mind-blowing anal sex, I untangled Becky from her soft bonds and cradled her in my arms. We were still perched on the bottom stair in the semidarkness but it didn't matter at all. Again, Becky felt like a child in my arms and I relished the comfort it gave both of us. The experiences we had shared in the last twelve hours had shocked us into silence, neither of us knowing how to talk about it or even put it into words.

Eventually we pulled each other up and dragged the feather bed into the small sitting room, now warm from the fire.

I went and made us large mugs of tea while Becky made us a cosy bed in front of the fire. I don't think either of us was ready to abandon our exploration.

'I can't believe you just did that, Cassie,' Becky whispered as we sat gazing into the flames and sipping our tea.

'I know. I feel the same way, but I enjoyed it and I think, if you're honest, you did, too.'

'I suppose I did in a way,' she admitted but then added, 'in a deliciously wicked sort of way.' She glanced sideways at me sheepishly.

'Since I spent my day with Mr King I want to explore my sexuality more. We're not teenagers any more, Becky. We're adults, and as long as we're not hurting anyone else why shouldn't we try anything that feels good?' I was hoping she would agree. I had a burning between my legs that had started the night before and hadn't eased off apart from when I slept. I had an image in my mind that I couldn't dismiss of Becky's arsehole, open and begging, stuck between my knees.

'I wish you could have seen yourself in the hall, Becky. Your bottom was the prettiest sight I've ever seen. Your bumhole gaped open like a fish's mouth begging to be invaded.' I knew what I said would shame her, so I looked for her reaction.

Becky picked up a cushion and bashed me round the head with it. She squealed, 'You bitch! How *could* you? That is so *shameful*!'

With that we had a classic textbook rough-and-tumble on the made-up bed. We bashed each other and wrestled naked until I found myself on my back with Becky's soft hair spread out between my legs. I gazed down in wonder and gasped as her hot wet tongue tentatively touched my sex. To my horror I behaved like a slut yet again and raised my hips up to her face. Becky seemed to get a taste for me then, because she pushed my hips back to the floor and made love to me with her mouth. She licked and sucked every inch of me, drawing in my lips until I could feel the tug in my loins, then nibbling gently at my clitoris. Her hands roamed up my writhing body to cup my breasts, rolling the nipples between thumb and forefinger.

The way Becky loved me was indescribable, unlike anything I had ever experienced. She was so gentle as she explored every crevice and fold with her darting tongue. Then she prised my lips apart with her teeth, spreading me open for her, and explored the inner core of me. I wanted to weep with the sweetness of it all but just lay back and let her love me. When I felt her tongue slide into me the warmth of it was so overwhelming that I wanted to see her between my thighs, so I bunched a cushion behind my head and watched as she pleasured me.

Occasionally she would glance up and grin as she probed my wetness, licking her lips with a lascivious smirk before dipping again to her task. God, she looked amazing like that with her swollen mouth glistening with my juices, her eyes sparkling and her tousled golden hair so blonde against my skin. I felt my arousal build until I was gripping her hair to make sure she didn't stop what she was doing and, just as she had done, I pleaded with her to make me come.

I didn't give a damn if this was acceptable practice or not, and not once did I think of Mr King as Becky listened to my pleas and started nibbling harder, alternating the sweet pain of the nips with the pleasure of her soft mouth. Her fingers gripped my nipples and squeezed hard, causing my belly to lurch and my hips again to strain upward. This time she let me writhe, sucking the whole of my sex into her hot hungry mouth and tipping me over the brink. The waves of pleasure racked my body as I held her tightly between my straining thighs.

9

We spent three more days of unbridled debauchery playing silly games such as schoolteacher and naughty pupil and doctor and patient, any excuse to spank each other or explore the passion we had discovered on that first night, I suppose.

Then, on the day before we were due to leave, we went for the long walk we had promised ourselves. At lunchtime we spread out our picnic blanket in the most remote area we could find with nothing but sheep and the occasional bird of prey to disturb us. We had become quite open with each other by that time and felt no shame discussing our relationship or the things we enjoyed doing to each other.

'I want to make love to you one more time up here on the mountain,' Becky told me as she laid out our lunch and I had to admit that I had been thinking about the same thing only moments before.

After we had eaten our fill we stood up and had a good look all around us and decided that as far as the eye could see there were no other people, so we laughed like a couple of schoolgirls as we raced to get our clothes off. It was exhilarating to be naked out in the open like that and I'm sure that was what sparked our enthusiasm.

'Race you to that tree,' I shouted as I took off, running as fast as I could to get there first. When I reached the tree, puffing and wheezing, I turned to watch Becky trying to catch me up with her wild hair flying behind her and her breasts, with their rose-pink tips, bouncing and jiggling in time to her strides. The sun caught the blonde fuzz between her legs, turning it into a golden halo around her sex, and my breath caught at her beauty. Time stood still for that moment. The picture Becky made racing across a mountain towards me was exquisite. The clear mountain air, the sun and the memory of the few days that led up to that one minute in time quite overwhelmed me and I know it will stay with me for ever.

When she reached me, the spell was broken as we both stood bent over with our hands on our knees to catch our breath, our breasts heaving, and our nipples hard, cooled by the slight chill of the air.

'You looked magnificent running across there, Cassie. I couldn't take my eyes off your arse, bobbing up and down like that.' A week before, I would have died of shame if she had said that, but I just laughed and grinned at her. She reached across and cupped my dangling breasts in her hands and tugged on the nipples. I grunted my response.

Becky had become far too knowledgeable about what excited me, and I suppose I had with her, too. I knew for instance that, like me, she enjoyed taking orders, but enjoyed giving them more. She liked a little pain but mainly from spanking, and she didn't like being tied up much. My one attempt to restrain her had ended in disaster, but we didn't care. Who was I to complain? Over the past few days, our roles had almost imperceptibly reversed to the stage where, after she had thoroughly ravished me, we settled into a routine of her being dominant and my being submissive – and I loved it.

I stood up and reached up to put my arms around her neck but she squeezed my nipples tighter and admonished me: 'Oh, no, you don't. I think we'll have you back on the blanket.' With that she picked up a twig from the ground and whacked me across the backside with it. I yelped and dashed back to the blanket with her hot on my heels and her twig hot on my bum.

When I reached the blanket I collapsed on to hands and knees, desperately trying to catch my breath, but Becky had other ideas.

She dived on the blanket and wriggled her way underneath me, feet first, until her gorgeous blonde pussy was in my face and her mouth was lined up under my crotch. I could feel myself dribbling down my thighs already. Of course Becky noticed straightaway and told me what a dirty girl I was. What exquisite humiliation!

We fell on each other and rolled about, mouths latched on to each other as if we had discovered the sixty-nine position ourselves. I gripped hold of her cheeks and pulled her hard into my face and she did likewise with me, and it rapidly became a game of follow-my-leader. First she curled upwards from under-neath me and bit me on the bum, so I retaliated by biting her sex. She slapped my arse and I retaliated again. We became more frenzied by the minute, our sweat mingling with our copious juices and spreading all over our hot bodies and dripping on to the blanket as our antics got more and more bizarre, turning into a contest. We rolled and wrestled, trying our best to get the other to submit.

Once, Becky nearly gave in when I played a little unfairly. When she was above me I looped my arms tightly over her lower back and pulled her to down to me, then buried my tongue as far into her as I could get it, then jabbed it in and out. Her breathing went shallow and her whole body melted, her knees buckling. But she completely surprised me when she suddenly pulled away and I realised she had been pretending to submit. Right, I thought. I got hold of Becky's sex lips with my mouth and sucked them in as hard as I could. I could feel the flesh pull away from her body but I didn't let up: I just tugged harder. I thought Becky would give up the game then, because she couldn't pull away without hurting herself, but she did the same to me – with her teeth! I knew I couldn't let go and use my teeth, because she would then escape, so I knew I was beaten. I released her and tried to put my hands down to my pussy to get her off but she wouldn't let me.

'Ow, ow, let go!' I begged. 'I give in, you win.'

She went back to sucking me, pleased with my submission, so I continued my quest between her thighs and that was all it took. We both came together, rocking and stifling our laughter as we did so.

We lay beside each other on the damp blanket in the weak late-spring sunshine panting and exhausted. We must have looked a pretty picture to the soaring kestrels above our heads. Becky with her lithe, pink and blonde body, her pussy pale and fluffy with the tiny, slightly darker pink lips just peeking from the neat folds and me with my rather obvious voluptuous body, all curves and breasts with my masses of long, dark reddish curls. As I lay beside her and looked down I could see clearly the distinct contrast between her sex and mine, with its profusion of dark hair that was completely unable to hide my plum-coloured rudeness, which not so much peeped as exploded from the fleshy outer lips.

The close intimate feeling we experienced at the cottage had filled our days and nights for almost a week. We had slept together, waking to the bright morning sun falling on the feather bed that had started it all. We had romped and played like children but made love like adults. We had done unspeakable things to each other and thoroughly enjoyed every minute, but it was time to go back to reality.

All through the journey home I knew I was being unfair to Becky. But I just sat quietly with so many thoughts running through my head that I wanted to scream. We pretended everything was normal until we neared home, when Becky looked at me with a confused, hurt expression and asked the question that had been on my mind for hours.

'What now, Cassie? What do we do now? Do we just pretend none of it happened, pretend that it meant nothing to either of us?' There was a catch in her voice.

I wanted to take her in my arms and take the pain from her voice but I knew I owed it to her to be totally honest. Yes, there was a very important part of me that wanted no more than to live with Becky and continue the fun and sexual adventure that we had started, but I still couldn't get thoughts of Mr King from my mind.

I couldn't decipher why I was still obsessed with him. I knew that, all in all, not only was the sex I had experienced with Becky more satisfying, but I was growing to love Becky and it made sense that that was the more practical relationship.

I couldn't stop fantasising about another visit to Mr King, though. Perhaps it was the unknown that made the prospect so delicious. Whatever it was, thoughts of Mr King filled my head and my sex.

'Oh, Becky, I'm sorry but I don't know how I feel. If you'd asked me in the cottage I'd have agreed to anything. In fact at the time I could think of no better proposition than to carry on what we've started in a home that we shared, but now the spell's been broken and I can't stop thinking of Mr King.' I felt really cruel but knew I had to carry on. 'There was something about the fact that I didn't know him or see him that made the experience so wicked that it excites me to distraction every time I think of it. So it would be unfair of me to commit myself to a relationship with you.'

'Well I'm not quite sure why you automatically think I want to move in with you and play happy families,' Becky snapped, obviously quite annoyed at my presumption.

I put my hand on her thigh. 'Sorry, Becky. Why don't you tell me what you would like to happen and we can take it from there?' Her thigh was taut under the dress she was wearing and I could feel the warmth of her flesh under the soft material. Becky's legs were spread slightly in the driving position so I slipped my hand down the gap between them and drew it slowly up to her crotch.

How my fickle thoughts had changed. Mr King was banished in seconds and all I could think of was this beautiful woman next to me and her increasingly damp crotch. She flashed her head round to me with a mixture of emotions filling her gaze. She tried to shut her thighs but I just kept my hand where it was, cupped around her cunt, and squeezed gently and rhythmically.

'Bitch!' She hissed through clenched teeth, but her thighs obeyed my call and dropped open, making her available to me. The crotch of her knickers was damp and sticky with her ready arousal, so I had no need to build her up. Like me, she had been in a continuous state of readiness since that first night on the feather bed.

I took my hand away from her and quickly slipped off my own knickers and, pulling my skirt up to my waist, let my own thighs drop apart like hers.

The whole situation felt so naughty. There we were, hurtling down the motorway, I with myself on show for any passing motorist and Becky trying to look normal but with her skirt raised to the point where you could just catch a glimpse of her scarlet knickers with the dark, inviting damp patch.

'Nice choice, Becky,' I crooned as I replaced my right

hand on her sex. 'Did you know you were going to be a scarlet woman for me today?'

She groaned and slipped a little further down in her seat so she could open her legs a bit more, and I pulled the crotch of her knickers aside and wormed my hand into that humid sexy pocket.

There was no way I could manipulate her and masturbate myself with my left hand, so I turned slightly in my seat and tried to get at her properly. It was so frustrating. I could almost get what I wanted but her knickers were in the way. I rummaged about in my handbag until I could find the nail scissors I was looking for.

'Trust me,' I begged when Becky's eyes widened with a flicker of fear. I cut through the tiny side ribbon and, holding my hand between the material and her mound, I cut across the front until they lay underneath her, flat.

Becky gasped in horror. 'I don't believe you just did that, Cassie. I put them on especially for you, and you know they're my favourites.'

'Shut up, Becky, and lift your bum or I'll gag you with them.'

'Ooh, that's an idea,' she chuckled as she sheepishly lifted her bottom. I dragged the scrap of red silk out and held it up to my nose, breathing deeply of her musky smell.

'Cassandra, for God's sake, stop it,' she said, grabbing the offending article and chucking it over into the back seat, where it landed spread out perfectly – just like a pair of damp, scarlet, silk knickers, discarded to allow for immoral practices!

I turned again in my seat and kissed her neck where her beautiful honey-blonde hair dropped past her shoulders. I slipped my hand inside the front buttons of her dress and cupped her breast in my hand, weighing the size of it and manipulating the aroused flesh. Her nipple was hard and crinkly under my fingers and I longed to suck her and make love to her properly, but I knew I had to make do with the possibilities that were available.

I removed my hand and again made that journey up her thighs just as she changed gear, so I could feel the muscles ripple under the taut flesh.

I don't know about her, but I couldn't wait any longer, so I slipped my fingers between her thighs. A trickle of her juice, until that moment trapped by the sticky heat, dribbled down into the crease of her bottom and disappeared. I ran the tip of my index finger down into the wet groove and then drew it slowly from her bottom up to her entrance, which I circled, tantalising her.

When she could stand it no longer and lifted her hips to help its entrance, I moved it upward to her tiny pee hole and tormented that little hive of nerve endings, knowing that she would be feeling a prickly sensation that was nice but irritating both at once. I think I must have been right, because Becky wriggled in her seat and moaned a little. By this time her whole pussy was flooding. Her thighs were wet and my fingers were covered in her creamy lubrication. This made the swollen channel slippery, so when my finger explored further to find her clitoris it wasn't hard to locate.

I ran my wet fingertip around the hard nub that had pushed its way out of its protective hood and stood to attention. I bent forward to try to see her in this aroused state, but the restrictions of the car wouldn't allow it.

'Pull over, Becky. I want to get at you properly,' I persuaded with my finger tickling the exposed tip of her clit.

'I can't,' she cried. 'It's too late. Do me now.'

Forgetting totally that we were on a motorway hurtling along at sixty miles an hour, I manipulated my body until I could get my right hand in position to play with her clit, and buried two fingers of my left hand into her pussy. I pumped them in and out to create maximum impact.

Becky was hanging on to the wheel for grim death and forcing her hot body on to my fingers, grinding and thrusting her hips until I thought she would lose control or break my fingers.

Her eyes stared straight ahead, fixed on the road in front of us, but her bottom half was a cauldron of activity. She twisted and turned, trying her best to get to the position that would trigger her orgasm, but it seemed elusive. I pushed as hard as I could into her depths and rubbed harder on her erect clitoris, hoping it would help, but it wasn't until I took it between finger and thumb and squeezed slightly that she grunted and her release pounded through her. She opened her mouth wide in a grin and yelled at the top of her voice, '*Yeess! Oh yes, oh, oh!*' getting quieter and stiller until she was at rest and the only sign of her debauchery was her dress still up round her hips and her ragged breathing. Oh, and of course the grin that was spread across her face and her scarlet discarded knickers on the back seat.

I couldn't wait any longer, so I pushed my hand into my crotch and rubbed like mad, trying to ease the burning need playing with her had ignited. Becky was totally composed by this time and, steering with one hand, she slapped my hand away and with her arm laid down the length of my body she gently spanked my fleshy mound. She carried on with this gentle torture until we reached some services and she pulled the car over into the near-side lane and drove into the car park. I tried to stop what she was doing but I was powerless against the hunger that gnawed away inside me.

Becky, probably because she was in a state of disarray

too, swung the car around and drove into the farthest corner of the car park under some trees.

We weren't completely safe but just enough to make the idea of someone catching us thrilling. I slid down in my seat until I could see only the heads of people going about their business, but I hoped that to them I looked as if I were snoozing. This position made me even more vulnerable with my bottom hanging off the seat, open and available.

With hardly a pause to pull on the handbrake, the relentless spanking continued. The pressure built to fever pitch as she alternated tapping on my aroused clitoris and harder slaps on to my whole cunt until I thought I would explode. I was moaning and groaning with excitement. Each time the slaps got harder I retreated into the seat. But when I pulled myself down, away from her punishing attention, she quite firmly instructed, 'Bring it up to me, Cassandra,' until I tentatively raised my hips again, my thighs still spread open wide.

She played this game until the fleshy outer lips were hot and throbbing and the inner lips tingled madly.

As with Mr King, the pain was taking me to a new level and I think Becky clocked this because she increased the sharpness of the spanking until I was gasping and my hands were fluttering around hers, almost stopping her but not quite.

'Put your hands behind you, Cassandra. Open your thighs as far as you can and raise your hips. If you lower them again I'll spank you harder.'

Again, the use of my full name and the total control in her voice as she issued her order triggered obedience in me and I sank into the almost trancelike submissive state that I had reached when Mr King had dominated me.

'So, you think you can't manage without your Mr

King, do you? Well we'll have to see what I can do about that, won't we?' And with that she pounded on my vulva, punctuating each blow with a word: 'Am ... I ... good ... enough ... now ... Cassandra? Well, am I?'

I didn't realise I was supposed to answer, so I just groaned my usual response.

'Answer me,' she snapped, and she slapped right on my tender bruised clitoris. I quickly replied, 'Oh, yes.' That seemed to satisfy her for the moment.

'Take your clothes off for me, Cassandra,' she ordered, totally oblivious to the crowds of travellers who were a mere stone's throw away. That shows the extent of my submission because I didn't even hesitate. I did slid further down in the seat, though, as I quickly slipped my dress off over my head and my knickers off my feet. I unclasped my bra from behind and dropped it on the floor in the foot well.

'Hands, Cassandra.'

By this time I was hers to do with as she would. I would have jumped out of the car and run around the car park if she had just said in that horny controlling voice, 'Cassandra, I want you to run around the car park for me.' But luckily she didn't. She just said, 'Hands, Cassandra.' And I immediately pushed them into the small of my back.

I lay there like the wanton slut that I am, naked and sweaty with my breasts thrust out because of my hands clasped behind my back. My thighs were splayed, exposing to the elements my bruised flesh. Even though her punishment had hurt I really wanted her to start again. Perhaps part of me wanted to be punished and I am sure at that stage Becky really wanted to punish me. I knew I had hurt her and this was her retribution.

I pushed my torso upwards to her. Becky wound an arm around my neck and dangled her hand on to my breast, teasing the nipple, then with the other hand she returned to her task. Slowly again, she started slapping and tapping until once more I was grunting and heaving, trying to keep my thighs as far apart as I could, but dying to shut them to stop the intensity that she was creating. Did I really want to stop it? Then, when I really thought I couldn't take much more, she issued one last devastating order.

'Cassandra, I am going to slap your dirty little cunt for you ten times. Each one will get harder and you will count them for me. On the tenth slap you will come. Is that clear?'

I couldn't believe how incredibly dominant she had become. The exquisite rush of heat that flooded from my 'dirty little cunt' as she said those three devastating words will be understood only by a true submissive. I melted inside, my guts turned to mush and I drowned in her control.

'Yes, Becky, I understand,' I answered, my voice croaky and wobbly. I had no idea if I would be able to come to order, but I doubted it. I assumed that if I didn't obey there would be worse punishment, but I didn't care.

Even the first slap caused a tear to form in the corner of my eye but I dutifully counted it out loud, and, as the next six fell and increased in strength, I clenched my teeth and did the same. The passion rose just like the pain, steadily and remorselessly. When the eighth fell I gasped loudly but the level of my arousal grew out of all proportion and Becky gripped hold of my nipple and squeezed. The electric current sizzled from nipple to clit. The last two rapid almighty slaps took me completely by surprise, whooshed the air from my lungs and conveyed all her pain and anger at me, but, combined, they caused the catalyst that ripped my orgasm from me, almost against my will.

I lay exhausted, hanging from the car seat trying to

recover myself. I was entirely mesmerised by Becky, not being able to believe that not only had she come out with such amazing control, but also I had responded to it. Totally!

She stroked my poor sex with a soft tenderness that made a joke of what had gone before. I purred my pleasure and wriggled to show my appreciation.

10

We talked for the rest of the way home about what options were open to us. We decided that the best thing was for each of us to go to our own homes for the night, then meet in a day or two when we had both had time to think, and then we would talk over any suggestions we had come up with.

I was completely thrown when I got home to find another postcard from Mr King. I really had given up hope of ever hearing from him again. I knew I was perhaps being unfair to Becky, but I thought it would finally set me straight on just how I felt about him. So I decided to comply.

Cassandra

I will arrive at your house at 7 p.m. on Thursday 10th. If you want me to explore your submission further you will leave your front door on the latch. I want you to be sitting on a hard-backed chair just inside the front door. You will be naked.

You will have a scarf tied around your eyes and your legs will be tied to the legs of the chair with the red rope I sent you.

This is a test, Cassandra. If you pass the test then this is just the beginning. If you fail the test this will be our last meeting.

Don't let me down, Cassandra.

Mr King

I read and reread every word over and over. Just like the time before, the adrenalin pumped through my veins as I tried to catch my breath. I had longed for just this moment – but that was before I met Becky. Now I didn't know how I felt. One minute I was determined not to do what he asked then the next minute I couldn't wait for Thursday – which was some days away – to arrive.

You all know what I did, of course, and you're right: I just had to.

I toyed with the idea of not even telling Becky, but I knew that that would be an awful way to start our life together. I rang her to explain, after convincing myself that if she said no then I wouldn't accept this next lesson. But, true to form, Becky was as excited as I was and urged me to do it. She reasoned that the more experiences I had the more I could share with her. 'And, anyway,' she said, 'it will give me something to punish you for. Not that I need an excuse.'

Thursday at 7 p.m. finally came around and there I was sitting stark naked in the hall on a hard-backed kitchen chair. I had put the door on the latch, hoping that nobody came to visit. The slight breeze from the letterbox ruffled the tiny hairs on my skin and hardened my nipples. I had managed to tie my ankles to the legs of the chair after cutting the piece of slinky red rope in half. My hands had trembled as I tied the red silk scarf around my eyes to block out all sight. I could actually see shadows through the silk but I wasn't going to admit that.

I was quite relaxed knowing that he couldn't do anything more abominable than the time before. Remembering what happened before still blew me away every time I allowed myself to dwell on it. So I sat and waited, just as I had before.

This time I didn't have to wait so long before I heard

the catch of the front door snap from its home. I looked straight ahead, trying very hard not to flinch as he held the door open for at least twenty seconds. I knew that I was totally visible to the whole street but, to be honest, by that time I didn't care.

I saw his shadow: a tall silhouette against the light from the street, but I gasped out loud when I saw a second shape follow him into the hall in front of me. Instinctively I lurched forward and plunged my hands between my stretched thighs to cover my nakedness.

The first shadow moved closer until he was standing just in front of me with his legs brushing mine. Mr King's finger crooked under my chin and raised my head to the proud angle he had coaxed out of me in his hall all those weeks before. Already I was prepared to do anything, and already I had forgotten the second shadow.

Mr King walked around behind my chair and picked it up with the help of the other shadow. As the mystery shape bent over me I just knew it was a man, too, because of the musky smell emanating from him.

They carried me into my lounge and placed me in the middle of the room then proceeded to walk around me. Mr King – who was still behind me – took hold of my hands and, pulling them behind the chair, tied them in place. I was helpless. I was completely lost; prepared to do anything asked of me.

Mr King's partner still stood in front of me but, when he moved closer until he was pressing between my thighs, I knew something was about to happen. Mr King held my head and slipped two fingers into my mouth, just as he had when I was tied to his bed, so I guessed it was a trick of some kind. this time I was ready for him. I sucked on his fingers as he teased my mouth with them. I went with the game as he put more and more in my mouth until it was stretched wide, full of his fingers. I felt the ring slip behind my teeth before I could respond, and I was left with my mouth stretched wider than I would have thought possible. Without a pause, a strap was buckled behind my head to hold it in place. I felt so open and vulnerable. I groaned into the ring but it just came out as a mumble.

I knew I was dribbling but I was beginning to get used to enjoying a little humiliation. Again Mr King held my head, this time by grasping my hair in his hands. I could smell my arousal all around me as a cock rested on the edge of the ring. I waggled my tongue about, trying to tempt it into my mouth, but it was held slightly out of reach. It was so frustrating being unable to suck it and having to just sit there with my mouth an open receptacle. I felt as if I had no worth at all – just a hole to use for any purpose required. Oh dear, that thought flipped in my stomach and I frantically tried to take the hard cock further in.

Mr King didn't even have the courtesy to allow his friend to fuck my mouth. What they actually did was so shameful. The cock on the perimeter of my mouth stayed in the same place and Mr King used my mouth to bring his friend off, by holding and controlling the moves with his hands wrapped in my hair. It must have been very horny for them both because it only took a minute or two for the cock to spurt its load deep into my throat. I knew I was sinking further into submission when I moaned my gratitude. I swallowed fast.

Mr King's friend moved away and Mr King took his place in front of me. Without any preamble he hunkered down in front of me and slipped one finger in the gaping hole that was my mouth and one hand between my spread legs. I could see the shape of his broad shoulders between my knees and I wriggled my invite. Mr King took pity on me and stuffed me full with his hand. He pushed hard until his knuckles rasped into my tender flesh and his force almost tipped the chair over. His partner caught the chair and held it tipped back so I felt unsafe and on the brink of falling.

I tried hard to take control but I was so tightly restrained that all I could do was accept anything he wanted to do. I am sure that was the lesson he wanted me to learn. His finger left my mouth and immediately took hold of one of my nipples. He squeezed and twisted it quite gently while his fingers explored my dripping pussy – just to show me that it had my destiny in his control. Just like before, he played me like a musical instrument until I was a sweating writhing heap. One or two times I would have fallen over, chair and all, if they hadn't prevented it. Mr King's sidekick kept rocking the chair backwards and forwards until I was disorientated and pleading through my gaping mouth for release.

Just as suddenly as they had arrived, they departed, and I was left sitting in the middle of my room with my mouth still stretched open and my legs stretched wide. I couldn't believe it. I sat for a moment or two, totally stunned and still very desperate for a climax to the proceedings. I waited for what seemed like hours before I admitted to myself that they weren't coming back. I cursed them with grunts. I stamped my feet like a child.

Once I had calmed down a little I explored my bonds and found that the rope holding my wrists was very loose. It still took me a while to get free but at least they hadn't left me completely helpless. As soon as I was loose my hands flew to my clitoris to finish what they had started. I think it took me about ten seconds to find the right combination but it was a very unsatisfactory end to an incredibly horny experience. Again Mr King had left me very confused and definitely wanting more – a lot more.

A note on the hall table said just this:

Soon, Cassandra, you can have more of the same.

I rang Becky and told her what has happened and I could tell that she was just as turned on as I was by the whole thing. I wished desperately that she were there with me. I needed a serious seeing to.

Within a day or two I had almost regained my equilibrium. One minute I was thinking about Mr King but then my thoughts kept returning to the rude episode at the bottom of the cottage stairs, when I had explored Becky's bottom, and the journey home from Wales and the very intense punishment I had undergone. I thought Becky could be everything I wanted; I only hoped I could be the same to her. What was it she wanted, I wondered to myself?

She apparently enjoyed being equally submissive and dominant, and I reminded myself to ask her to be honest about her preferences. I rang Ruth and told her everything. Well, nearly everything! She was so pleased for me. There wasn't even the slightest hesitation when I said I was thinking of asking Becky to move in with me. She gave me her blessing and said she would like to meet her one day. I knew I was doing the right thing.

'What do you reckon, then, Cassie?' Becky asked when we finally met again. We both agreed we should give it a go: live together and enjoy ourselves and sod the rest of the world.

'I have the two spare rooms. There's plenty of space available for us to do anything we want with this house. Why don't you move in here? You rent your house, anyway, and if we share the bills here we'll have loads left over to play with. Please say yes, Becky. I know I messed you about a bit but I really do want this. As we are still a little shy we can tell people we're sharing to halve the bills. Then we don't need to make any major decisions until we have experimented some more,' I added, catching her eye and grinning knowingly.

'I like the idea of the experimenting bit,' she laughed. 'OK, you're on. When?'

Neither of us mentioned my second meeting with Mr King and his kinky shadow.

'Well, there's no time like the present. Can you get a few more days' holiday?' I asked. But she had already jumped up to get a pen and paper.

We wrote a list of the things we had to do. It went a bit like this:

Phone house agent to give notice
Play
Move Becky's things
Buy sex toys
Do up the attic as a playroom
Try it out.

Anyway, I'm sure you get the gist of our next few days. By the end of that week Becky was living in my house with her own bedroom but sharing my bed every night and looking for a job in the area. We hadn't really talked much about our individual needs because we were having so much fun playing house.

We couldn't wait to have a place where we could explore our sex play in comfort, so we tackled the attic first. It was perfect as a playroom, with a high ceiling down the centre of the room that tapered down to gables at the ends. It was big enough to house anything that took our fancy.

As the attic had no window, we fixed red candle sconces along each long wall and covered the whole of each short wall with mirror tiles. We painted the walls and ceiling black and the paintwork red – a little predictable, I know, but very effective and also very atmospheric.

'What are we going to put in it, now that it's finished?' Becky asked as we stood back and looked at the finished room, with its vast space and dark corners.

We decided to pool our money and take a visit to the shops in London we had seen advertised. Neither of us had really looked at sexy mags before we met but in the last few days we had bought a stack of porn and fetish magazines. We were both hungry for information and knowledge about our new-found sexuality and the ideas and suggestions we read about would have kept us busy for at least thirty years.

Neither of us could believe that so many people, who looked quite ordinary when you saw them on the street, actually spent their evenings playing games and doing such rude and exciting things to each other – and some very scary things. To begin with we were both very tentative with suggestions in case our ideas of what was horny differed greatly, but we soon relaxed.

The only problem was that each time one of us read a sexy idea to the other we always ended up rushing upstairs to the bedroom to satisfy our hunger. We would sit either side of the kitchen table, drooling over magazines with a cup of coffee each to the exclamations of 'Oh, God, listen to this' or 'Oh, yes, we must have a go at that.'

The magazines had the most amazing pictures of helpless women tied in the most outrageous positions, with all their genitals exposed and available for attention. These weren't models but people like me and Becky, just playing.

Husband-and-wife teams sent picture stories of the games they played with each other, sometimes hard and punishing games but always consensual. These lucky captives hung from ceilings and walls like ornaments, with the most beautiful of all 'jewellery' attached to their bound bodies: clamps, clips, weights, straps and chains.

One very pretty dark-haired girl with firm, pert breasts and very long legs was even decorated like a pony. She had black and purple leather harnesses on with shiny buckles that accentuated her beautiful body. She had blinkers for her eyes and a bit between her teeth. From the top of her head harness rose a tall purple plume that had been caught by the breeze and streamed out behind her. I was captivated by her arrogance. How could she be submissive enough to let her mistress dress her like that and still have that arrogant air about her?

The front views of her trotting down a country lane pulling a little buggy with a dominant-looking lady sitting proudly in the seat completely hypnotised me. Then, as I read further about her life as a pony girl, I saw the side view and realised she had some sort of attachment to her bottom that gave her an exquisite, long, swishy pony's tail sticking out from between her cheeks. The sight of it left me speechless. I read as quickly as I could, needing to know all the details of why she did it and what it was that the tail was attached to.

I couldn't believe it when I read that she loved being a pony-girl and enjoyed the games they played. The fact that the tail was part of a dildo that was buried deep in her bum shocked and delighted me. It was held in place by the bulb-like shape of the dildo – a butt plug she called it. I found myself squeezing my cheeks together just at the thought of what she must be feeling.

Her mistress, the lady in the buggy, apparently put her through her paces as often as possible, pushing her to her limits of endurance and pain. She strutted down those country lanes naked apart from the harnessing, with her head held high, her tail swishing in the breeze and her impossibly long legs pounding away. Her feet were padlocked into a sexy pair of lace-up, very high-heeled ankle boots that didn't seem to hinder her at all.

I had known for years that I was fascinated by and definitely attracted to these types of wicked games but had always believed that I was almost alone in my needs. When I had occasionally read a book or seen an article on bondage or S&M, the submissive had always been portrayed as being forced into a life of servitude and punishment, locked away somewhere in a dark uncomfortable dungeon and flogged every five minutes. Now don't get me wrong: those stories I read always managed to excite me and had ultimately led to my visit to Mr King, but they didn't relate to me, or to what I wanted.

We both agreed that reading about other people's games excited us both immensely. It was as if we were being given permission to explore our own feelings and needs.

Within a week Becky had been taken on at the local hospital and we were both thrilled with her new blue and white uniform. I guessed that before long we would be playing in it.

One evening just before we were going to bed, we were again engrossed in our magazines when Becky got up without a word and went up into the bedroom. When she came down she had in her hands a bundle of scarves. I sat open-mouthed as she cleared our junk off the kitchen table, then explained her intentions. 'Get up here on the table, Cassie. I've just got to try tying you up properly. I've been dying to do it since we went to Wales and I can't wait any longer.' Who was I to argue?

I thought my head would explode with the rush of anticipation; my heart pounded and my hands trembled as I climbed on to the table.

Becky pushed me gently down on to my back and

wrapped the first of the scarves around my wrist. My head was buzzing so hard I almost didn't notice her tying the other scarves to my other wrist and ankles. My head was hanging partly off the end of the table and my legs dangled over the other end as she began to tie my limbs to the table legs. Memories of being tied to the bed at Mr King's flooded my mind and I knew I was going to enjoy this experiment.

The position was uncomfortable but it didn't matter at all as Becky ran her hand down the front of my blouse, flicking the buttons open on the way. There was none of the tenderness we had experienced up until then as she pulled the bottom of my bra up over my breasts and, grabbing each globe separately, pulled them from their cups.

I gasped as she pulled and twisted the nipples until they were rigid and hard, then made her way downwards. Becky grabbed the hem of my skirt and tugged and wrenched until it was bunched up around my hips. There was no delicacy involved, just the exposing of the bits she wanted to get at, and I wriggled about in delight at her attentions.

The feeling of helplessness worked its magic on me as Becky ran her hands up and down my spread thighs, teasing my crotch through the gusset of my knickers until I thought I would scream. She kept tantalising me, flicking my nipples, rubbing my clitoris through my knickers and pushing her fingers into me, taking the wet garment with them.

In a space of only two or three minutes I was begging her to make me come. I thrust my lower half up to her hands, pleading with my torso for more attention, but she teased me for what seemed like ages, until I shouted out, 'Please, Becky. Please let me come.'

She bent forward and I felt her whole mouth latch on to my crotch and bite gently. Then she pulled away. I tried to draw in my knees in response to the intense feeling but the scarves stopped me from shutting my thighs.

Just the impossible attempt to protect myself excited us both even more, and Becky pulled the crotch of my knickers aside to expose my wet cunt. 'All mine,' she commented as the coolness of the air tickled my mound. I felt little electric shivers run through me and then one burning stab of heat as she touched the tip of her tongue to the hood of my cooled clitoris. I begged then, my need and frustration pouring out.

When I was at my sexual peak and desperate to come, Becky stopped what she was doing and covered me over again with the crotch of my knickers. She came to the top of the table and, cradling her hand under my head, kissed me.

Her soft mouth for the first time really made love to mine. I could smell my arousal on her face as she drew my mouth into hers just as she had with my pussy, and sucked my lips. She nibbled at my bottom lip and explored my mouth with her tongue, darting hers inside to entice mine out to play. Then, as my tongue followed hers, we devoured each other.

This was the first time we had kissed properly and it was more like making love than kissing. As she drew me into her spell with her mouth, her hand again returned to my crotch and she laid the flat of her palm over my whole sex.

The wet material stretched between my legs and was pressed against me as she started a delicate circular movement, with her fingers splayed out and the heel of her hand gently grinding against my partly exposed clitoris. Every so often as her tongue dipped into my mouth her middle finger would press into me. Meanwhile, the heel of her hand carried on the effortless, rhythmical swirling around my clit.

The build-up of pressure was perfectly exquisite and I involuntarily stopped all movement so I could languish in her attention. I just lay there with my clothes all over the place and my legs splayed and restrained. I felt no need to reciprocate and even when I occasionally struggled, wanting to put my arms around her, I would easily accept defeat and relax again. Just as I calmed to a mere throb with her gentleness she again enticed my tongue into her mouth and, as I responded, her sharp teeth bit hold of my tongue and held it tight. What exquisite restraint that was! It succeeded in totally immobilising me with one small move. I couldn't move anything for fear of ripping my tongue. I couldn't protest and any sound I did make was muffled and garbled, but my arousal soared to a new level at this new game.

My orgasm, when it came, spread from my belly in ripples, shivering across my breasts and exploding in my head. It was one of the sweetest, most devastating I had ever experienced. The waves of pleasure rolled over my body and soul, capturing me in Becky's spell.

11

We decided after that experiment that we wanted the playroom as soon as possible, so we planned to shop together in London for furniture and then choose some toys and clothes with which to surprise each other. I had no idea what I would get but felt sure that inspiration would come to me in the right setting.

The day before our planned trip to London, we dragged a couple of floor cushions up to the playroom to get a feel of the room with games in mind; after all we intended to spend a lot of time in there. We sat down on the floor and swigged from a bottle of wine as we talked by candlelight. We had filled the candle sconces with black candles and the dramatic glow from these warmed the room and chased the shadows into the corners. The whole room had a spooky, sexy look about it and I shivered as I imagined playing the sorts of games here that I had played with Mr King, but with Becky controlling me.

'Do you fancy a game of truths?' Becky asked when we had polished off the first bottle of wine. I guessed by the look on her face that she was using this as a way to tell me something, so I played along, intrigued.

'OK,' I agreed.

'Me first,' she whispered. 'Would you like to be spanked the way you spanked me in Wales?'

'You know I would, Becky.'

'Just checking. Is there anything you wouldn't want to experiment with?'

'Well, I know I was a bit rude with your bottom and I

really loved it but I'm not sure about the other way round. I mean, you doing it to me. I've always been a bit sensitive about my bottom.'

Becky had a scary gleam in her eye as she answered.

'But if we did reverse our games would you trust me to stop if I did anything you really hated? We could even use the bell that Mr King gave you. You allow me to do anything I like but if you drop the bell I promise to stop immediately. How does that sound?'

'Yeah, OK. I think.' I had a suspicious feeling that I had just consented to a prearranged game in Becky's head and, I have to be honest, the thought thrilled me to the core.

'One last question, Cassie: how important is it for you to dominate me? Because most of the time you were carrying out your diabolical acts on my more than willing body, all I could think of was doing them to you. I have such a need these days to put you through your paces, so to speak. I long to explore every facet of our sexuality, to push you to your limits and create some new ones. I think some of those magazine stories, and the things you did with Mr King, have gone to my head. How would you feel about that?'

Her eyes were locked on mine and even in the flickering candlelight she must have seen my dilated pupils and flaring nostrils. My chest was pounding to the thrill of her words and all they suggested.

'Oh, God, Becky, that would be perfect for me. I really enjoyed playing with your body but, if we're being honest, most of the time I longed to be in the position you were in. I'd be happy swapping roles for the rest of our lives but this would be beyond my wildest dreams and expectations. I can't wait to explore my role as your submissive to its fullest extent. I'd need all this to stay in the playroom, because I know that the submissive side of me is only sexual. Would you be happy with that?'

'This really is too good to be true. That would be perfect for me, too. I couldn't bear it if you lost your dominant character. It's that person that I want to dominate. It's when you're at your most powerful that I want to make you wriggle and pant. I want to reduce you to a begging, pleading heap that lives for my every touch and has no idea whether that touch will be pain or pleasure, and begs for both.'

'Ooohhh,' I groaned. 'I think you'd better pinch me. This is too good to be true.'

She did pinch me. Right on the end of my nipple, sending a delicious wave of pain shuddering through me. I yelped and jumped to my feet, staggering a bit because of the wine, waved my arms in the air and did a type of tribal dance. My drunken impression of a tribal dance, all the while shouting, 'Fuck off, Mr King!'

Becky dragged me towards the door, breaking the spell. 'Come on, we've got a long day ahead of us in London.'

'But I didn't get a chance to ask any questions,' I whined, the drink slurring my words. Becky just laughed and ran down the stairs ahead of me. 'I know,' she called back. 'It's what's known as being in charge.'

The day in London was a revelation. We went to rubber shops, bondage shops, fetish shops, markets and a large fetish-furniture warehouse that had every item we could possibly have wanted and more.

We had pored over the magazines for hours and decided that the first thing we wanted was a bondage bed. The one we had seen in the magazine was a high cotlike affair with a padded leather top and straps and hooks and buckles to hold each other captive.

Pete, the man in the shop, told us that for a modest fee they would design our 'dungeon' for us, deliver it and erect anything that needed erecting. We all exchanged glances at the 'erecting' bit and giggled. How childish!

We went and had a coffee and talked it over and agreed that, with what we would be saving on rent and living expenses, we could easily afford whatever we needed to get started at least. After all, we agreed, we would be spending a lot of time in the playroom from now on.

We returned to the shop grinning from ear to ear and, when we heard the total price after two hours of decision making and swapping around, I am sure Pete was grinning equally widely.

We made arrangements for them to come the following week and install our 'dungeon'. The final layout incorporated a bondage bed just like the one we had seen in the catalogue, a frame that had rings and bolts attached for suspension, and other framelike activities. Pete assured us that it was a necessity but at that stage we had no idea just how important it would become to our games. It had crossbars that were removable and it was very sturdy and looked imposing – a bit like a scaffold, I thought later.

The only other large item we bought was a chair. It was large and Gothic-looking, made out of black wood. At first I thought it was for the dominant to sit on and look dominant, but, as we examined it at closer quarters, we discovered that it had an entirely different purpose. When we found it had a lift-up seat with a bowl sunk in the hole I was absolutely flabbergasted.

'What on earth is that for?' I asked in all innocence, then realised immediately.

Pete laughed out loud at my naïveté, put his arm around our shoulders and whispered, 'I take it you're new at all this. Never mind, girls, you'll soon get the hang of it, I promise you'.

Like all the other items, the chair had bolts and rings and hooks all over it.

The heat flooded my face and I was very glad that Pete, who by now was really beginning to enjoy himself, had moved away.

As we left the shop, he held the door open and said, 'Well, girls, if you need any other help please let me know.' We looked at each other, knowing we needed no one else.

We moved on from that shop to a fetish clothing shop, where Becky insisted that we buy a rubber catsuit for me. It was skin-tight and moulded to my body like a smooth shiny coating with zips where my breasts sat and a crotch zip that went from my waist at the front to my waist at the back, virtually dissecting me. She made me come out into the shop to show her; already I was obeying her commands.

Becky went into the other section of the shop and told me to go and try some things on in the changing room while I waited – something to surprise her with, she said, but I knew she was being devious.

All I could think of as I tried on garment after garment was what Becky might be buying. We had seen gadgets for torturing breasts and genitals. Weights to hang from the gadgets and blindfolds and hoods to block the sight of the poor person having the gadgets used on them.

The thought of Becky using any of them on me appalled me but I couldn't stop thinking about each and every item. The racks of whips stuck in my mind and I tried to imagine how it would feel to be strapped to the frame we had bought and whipped. I couldn't even begin to imagine. Yes, Mr King had used a strap on me but only one blow at a time, and then he had instantly given me the pleasure I craved. So it wasn't the same, surely.

I decided on a very cute maid's dress that showed off most of my breasts and, if I bent over more than one inch, it showed most of my arse, too. It was made of taffeta and rustled delightfully when I moved, with its pert little white petticoat that just peeped from below the hem and the crisp white apron tied around my waist to accentuate it.

The other garment I chose needed the help of the assistant, so I checked that Becky wasn't in sight and asked the very punk-looking girl with her orange hair and nose ring to bring me some corsets. I wanted it to be a complete surprise for her. I had always longed for an old Victorian-type corset with bones down the front and back, a cord or ribbon that wrapped round and round the waist with eyelets at the back to draw it tighter. I imagined myself as a character in the old Southern belle films, hanging on to the bedpost while Becky pulled the laces as tight as I could bear, then tying them off with a pretty bow at the front.

The corset I chose was coal-black satin. It nestled under my bust with just a hint of lace cups to cradle my breasts. It was cinched in at the waist and flared out to incorporate my hips in a very sexy fashion then finished at the top rise of my bottom with a line of lace around the bottom edge that framed my buttocks perfectly. The complete picture was of a time gone by when the sort of thoughts that Becky and I shared had not been dreamed of. Maybe.

'Oh, Christ, that looks funky on you. Look how it cups your tits,' the girl said as she turned me around to look at the finished product. 'You've got the perfect figure for this, with your round bottom and your slim waist. I think that with a bit of training someone could get your waist measurement down to twenty-four inches.'

I was stunned at the way she spoke to me but when I feel submissive it's as if I were someone else and I can't control my thoughts properly, and what she said made me feel very submissive. 'Do you think so? Thank you,' I whispered.

That was the only opening she needed. She brushed the backs of her hands across my breasts, trembling on their lace cups. When I didn't stop her she stared at my nipples and dragged her thumbs over the ends, causing a shiver down my spine and a little spasm in my crotch. I leaned weakly against the wall of the cubicle for support as I submitted to her ministrations. My head was arguing that I shouldn't be letting her do this to me, but my pussy, which wanted attention every minute of the day lately, was telling a different story.

I purred with pleasure as her thigh pushed its way between my thighs and ground hard up into my crotch. My head was thrown back against the wall and my eyes were closed, and I assume she took that as acquiescence because she leaned forward and, taking my breast firmly in her hand, forced it up to her mouth and devoured it. She bit and nipped and squeezed quite brutally, tugging on the nipples in turn with her sharp little teeth and continuing the onslaught with her knee between my legs. She was becoming quite frantic in her arousal when reality snapped me back.

'Cassandra, have you nearly finished?' Becky called out from the shop floor, and the girl pulled away from me and, without a pause, took out a tube of black lipstick from her jacket pocket and renewed her warpaint. I glanced down at my breast to find teeth marks mixed with the dirty grey of her lipstick smudged all over my nipples. I rubbed hard at them and between us we quickly undid my corset.

We both left the changing room a little flustered and as I walked away with Becky to leave the girl to wrap up my purchases Becky grabbed hold of my arm and drew me to her. 'I hope you weren't behaving like a dirty little slut in there, Cassandra. I think you'd better tell me all about it when we get home, don't you?'

My heart pounded at the thought.

We made a pact that we would play no naughty games until our playroom was ready and, even though it was very difficult, we stuck to it, apart from the promise, which Becky had no intention of forgetting. We sat as usual talking over the adventures of the day, laughing about Pete's eagerness and marvelling at just how much we could have spent if we had had the resources. Just as I was relaxing into the conversation and had totally forgotten the incident in the changing room with the punk girl, Becky shocked me out of my complacency.

'Oh, yes, you naughty little slut. I think you'd better tell me what you were getting up to with Miss Gothic in the clothes shop, don't you?'

I had regretted it deeply as soon as my pulse rate had slowed and I desperately hoped that Becky wouldn't be too cross with me. I explained what had happened without telling her about the corset I had been trying on and tried my best to make it sound casual, but I don't think I was very convincing.

'It wasn't very nice, actually,' I tried to explain. 'She was very rough and brutal with me. She squeezed my breasts really hard and bit me all over.'

'Did she now? Perhaps you should show me, Cassandra.'

I knew from the way that she used my full name that she meant business, so I stood up and pulled my T-shirt up over my head. As I reached behind me to unclasp my bra I looked down, hoping there would be no lingering signs of my infidelity, but I was disappointed.

'Look at that, you disgusting creature!' she growled as she gazed at the many tiny red teeth marks that were still blatantly obvious against the pale skin of my breasts. 'I leave you alone for five minutes and you let any silly little girl that wants you have their way with you. So, tell me, Cassandra, what was it that persuaded you to let her carry on even though it wasn't very nice?'

'Oh, I don't know, Becky,' I wailed. 'It seems that as soon as anyone attempts to take control of me, if they're forceful enough I give in. There's a very scary aspect of my submissive nature that I'm only just discovering that'll accept any violation imposed on me. As long as the perpetrator's dominant enough and just the fact that I'm submitting to another's will, whatever that may be, turns me on. And she called them tits. It was so basic.'

'And that's it, is it? She called your breasts tits and she was dominant so you let her. It sounds a little pathetic, don't you think?'

It was strange how Becky managed to sound almost jovial, but the way she talked also combined mother, matron, lover and best of all – dare I say it? – mistress.

'I want you to pull that chair into the middle of the room and kneel up on the seat facing backwards,' she ordered. 'Put your hands on the top of your head and wait for me.'

My heart started pounding rapidly as I dragged the hard-backed kitchen chair into the middle of the room as she had instructed and knelt on the seat. Becky had left the room and it was a minute or two before she returned, and already my knees were becoming uncomfortable. I wriggled, trying to ease the pressure, but before I had a chance Becky had returned with a strap that she wrapped around my calves and the chair seat and buckled tightly. I flinched as she pulled it as tight as it would go almost in anger, but she ignored me.

'Do you agree, Cassandra, that you deserve to be punished?'

I didn't know how to answer. I was damned if I said yes and damned if I said no, so I stayed silent.

'You must be getting uncomfortable by now. If you don't answer me we will stay here until you do.' And with that she sat down at the table and started drinking her tea.

'OK, OK, yes, I think I deserve to be punished.' As soon as the words were out of my mouth I wanted her to punish me. I did feel awful for letting the punk girl touch me and I felt guilty that my submission was so available. And, of course, it excited the hell out of me.

She stood up, walked over to the kitchen drawer and took out a spatula, turned it over in her hands and walked slowly over to me. She stood behind me and tucked my skirt up into its waistband and pulled my knickers down around my thighs, exposing my bottom. I felt like a naughty schoolgirl. Wonderful.

'Right, Cassandra, I'm going to teach you that at any time in the future it will be *me* who decides who can play their games on your body. Is that clear?'

My heart skipped somersaults then. So ... she didn't mind my playing with other people as long as she decided who it was to be with. The prospect of her 'giving' me to someone for their games thrilled me to the core, so I knelt up straight and nodded.

She started on my already marked breasts.

The sting as the spatula slapped my breasts was intense but the litany that Becky almost chanted while she punished me took the edge off the pain and burned warm through my body.

'Let's see how much this naughty slut's tits can take, shall we?'

'Your tits are getting very red now, Cassandra. Does it hurt?

'Come on now, Cassandra, push your dirty slut's tits out for me.

'Isn't it a good thing that your tits are so big, Cassandra, or all this attention would be centred on an area much smaller? Then it would hurt more, wouldn't it?'

Becky warmed to her task and punctuated every sentence with a sharp whack of the spatula across my breasts, which by now were very tender and red. She systematically lifted each one by the nipple and stung the soft underneath area and very carefully covered every inch until my breasts glowed and throbbed.

I was so predictable. I clenched my thighs together tightly and wriggled to get the maximum contact on my clitoris as the punishment of my 'tits' was carried out. I groaned every time she slapped the spatula down and moaned helplessly with each delicious insult she threw at me.

Just as my arousal grew to fever pitch she stopped what she was doing and walked behind me. She was even harder on my buttocks and pounded away until the erotic glow in my breasts had subsided and all my attention was on the blows raining down on my bum. Eventually that pain too turned warm and horny and again I wriggled my pleasure, but she hadn't finished with me yet.

She returned to the front of me and stood looking from one breast to the other as if she were making a decision. She chose the right one and started a repetitive direct tap of the spatula right on my erect, aroused nipple, gently at first but then increasing in severity until I brought my elbows in and hunched over to ease the pain.

'Oh no you don't. Kneel up straight or I'll do it harder.' She demonstrated her intentions, so I knelt up as straight as I could and forced my elbows back to offer my breasts for further torment, just as she instructed.

She started again with the slow repetitive flicks but this time took pity on me and slid her hand between my thighs and delved among my wet sticky hair to find the hot entrance to my sex and explored until she found the hard bud of my clitoris. She didn't rub it quite hard enough to make me come but just tantalised it with her fingertip as the blows of the spatula got harder and faster, never moving from its position. The increasing assault on my nipple burrowed deep inside my guts and became a new entity. My pain threshold was rapidly left behind as the intensity I was experiencing grew into a raging monster and consumed me in an almost catatonic bliss. I can only describe the feeling as euphoria – pain-induced euphoria.

The magnitude of the throbbing waves of pleasure that completely wasted me clinched any doubts that I still had about my submission. This was me! I was born for this, this exquisite moment of total submission.

Did I learn my lesson? Probably, but I couldn't wait to have to learn it all over again.

Almost daily, parcels arrived in brown-paper wrapping bearing Becky's name. I had no idea she had bought so much but the excitement built in me. I was desperate not only to see her purchases but also to experience them. I imagined all sorts of delicious torments and tortures. My nipples were constantly erect and my knickers permanently damp.

We were both very horny by the time the van arrived with our furniture. Becky initially went upstairs with the two men who had come to set it up and wouldn't let me near the top floor at all. It took the whole day to install and I paced up and down like a pregnant father waiting for a chance to test it out, and when we were finally left alone we walked up and stood looking in awe at the finished room.

I couldn't believe how just standing in a room could be so devastating. I felt the sweat prickle down my spine and my pussy quickened at the sight before us. The furniture looked so imposing against the black walls, all the shiny bolts and buckles catching the light from the candles we had lit. It was a minute or two before I could catch my breath enough to speak, and even then I only squeaked.

'Wow, Becky, it's amazing! I had no idea it would have such an effect on me. I feel like doing something totally submissive but I don't know what.'

'Oh, good. I know exactly what you should do, Cassandra. Take your clothes off.'

Without a second thought or even a question passing through my brain I responded to her command. I stood before Becky and stripped off all my clothes as she had instructed, still unable to take my eyes from the room.

'Now put your hands on your head, Cassandra, and come over here.'

With that, Becky walked across the room and pulled out an item of furniture that I hadn't seen and we certainly hadn't ordered. It was a tall, imposing, regal-looking chair with the whole frame made of thick, rigid, silver-linked chain. It had a high back, no arms and a deep red velvet seat. Becky placed it right in the middle of the room and sat on it looking every inch a mistress. I was hovering, waiting for her to tell me what to do, when she looked me straight in the eyes and beckoned me closer with one finger.

'A few rules, Cassandra. When we're in this room, I am in control,' she said in what I thought was mock severity. 'You will obey my orders at all times and not hesitate to carry them out whatever they may be. Do you agree?'

'Yes, I agree,' I stated, getting right in the mood of the game, but nearly giggling.

'Good. This is your first instruction. If I tell you to go to the playroom and get ready for me, I want you to take your clothes off, fold them neatly and place them on the floor outside the door. Then I want you to come and stand here in the middle of the room just where you are now and get into the following position.' She then blew me away with her description. 'You will kneel on the floor with your knees at least two feet apart, so that your horny sex is available to me at all times. Then you will put your hands on top of your head like they are now and kneel up straight. Is that clear?'

'Er, yes, I suppose so.'

Even though the bit about being available to her at all times sent a thrill down my naked spine, I stammered a little, confused by her demeanour. OK, so we had agreed that she would be the dominant one, but I felt she was going a bit over the top for a first game.

'I know you don't understand at the moment, Cassandra, and I'm not sure I do completely,' she explained, her voice a little softer. 'But I promise you that if you obey me in all things when we're in this room I'll show you a side of yourself, of *our*selves, that we haven't even touched on yet. I had no idea of the level your submission could take you to until the other day when I punished your breasts. You went into a kind of subspace that now I want to explore. Neither did I realise how the dominant in me would be encouraged by your submission.

'Also when you invaded my bottom and made me cringe with embarrassment in Wales I wanted to make you feel that delicious humiliation and acceptance. I am convinced I can give you pleasure that you've only dreamed about. I know I can make you accept and do things that even Mr King probably hasn't thought of. Every time I touch you my brain fills with a million disgusting, rude and totally diabolical acts that I want to perform on your sexy body. Ever since you shared with me how you felt when Mr King was in total control of you I've wanted to have free rein on your sexuality to test your limits as he did, for days at a time if you'll let me.'

I thought about what she said for a few moments but I didn't think she would like my answer.

'But what if I don't want to do something that you tell me to do? Like anal sex, for instance? That's an area that I don't really think I want tested. Like I said the other night, I know that I enjoyed what I did to you but I've never really fancied anyone messing about with my bum. And I haven't got a clue what other ideas you have in that perverted little mind of yours, have I?'

'You love the unknown. Remember Mr King? Give me a week, Cassandra, and if I can't persuade you to agree to my every whim by then we'll think again. And don't forget: there's always the bell to protect you. I promise I'll never start a heavy game without giving you the bell first. Will you at least agree on those terms?'

I mulled it over and realised that I was still kneeling up straight with my hands on my head. My breasts were thrust out provocatively and my knees were the regulation two feet apart. My sex was as Becky had said, available to her. I so wanted to play but this was heavy stuff. Then I remembered Mr King. I had gone to him, not knowing who he was or what he was like. I loved Becky and trusted her with my life. I remembered the new feelings I had experienced when I knelt on the stool in the kitchen and longed to feel that acceptance again, and my sex wanted some attention. My immediate need answered for me.

'OK, you win, but only in this room, eh?'

'Good girl. First I have a present for you.'

And with that she walked across to the cupboard and pulled out a black carrier bag. As she closed the door I could see piles of black. I tried to make out any individual items but it was impossible: the cupboard was just like Pandora's box.

She walked behind me as she searched among the contents and it wasn't until she slipped her arms around my neck that I realised she was buckling a black leather collar around my neck. It was about six inches deep and the soft leather covered a rigid boning that held my head at a very proud angle and also had the effect of not allowing me to look down.

I could hear a tinkling noise and I knew then that the bell would always have two totally separate purposes. Yes, it would protect me if I wanted out and couldn't speak for some reason, but also it warned me that a new or heavy game was Becky's intention. My pulse quickened.

'More than anything I want to see your argumentative mouth stuffed full with a gag so you'll be unable to tell me if you've had enough of what I'm doing. Hold the bell and if I push you past your limit drop the bell and I'll stop what I'm doing and release you immediately as we agreed. OK? When we don't need it, it will be here to remind you.' She clipped the bell on to a ring on the front of my collar.

I nodded and the little bell tinkled. She then delved again into the bag and drew out a black leather gag like the one we had laughed over in a magazine, convinced no one would ever be able to get it in their mouth. It had a rubber dildo like the one Mr King had put in my mouth but the penis bit looked about twice the length. I was just about to protest when Becky stood over me and without any ceremony pushed the gag between my jaws and buckled it behind my head. When the rubber hit the back of my throat I gagged a little. Becky unclipped the bell from my neck, put it in the palm of my hand and wrapped my fingers around it, all the while staring into my eyes and crooning softly to me.

'Go with it, baby. Take deep breaths and imagine it's the biggest cock you've ever had the pleasure to suck. Then imagine it's mine and suck it to please me.'

She stroked my hair and I calmed a little. She was right: if I persuaded myself that I was sucking her cock it felt quite good. I tried to tell her that and found out just how effective it was. My jaws were so stretched I couldn't even grunt properly. My head spun at the knowledge that only the bell stood between me and whatever diabolical plans Becky had for me.

My eyes darted about following her every move like a scared rabbit. Having no idea of the toys she had bought I imagined all the instruments of torture we had laughed over in the magazines and the wicked devices for pain, humiliation and endurance that had amazed us in the Soho sex shops.

Becky moved around behind me, making my pulse race with fear and anticipation. For at least five minutes I could hear rustling and shuffling that fuelled my imagination.

Sexual submission is such a strange, inexplicable condition to be in. My overriding feeling was fear, and as the seconds ticked by I really wanted to get up and run away from what was ahead of me. I had no doubt that Becky meant it when she said she would test my limits. I only had to remember the car park on the way home from the cottage and the punishment I received for letting the girl in the shop play a game with me to believe in her sincerity. But – and it is a very big but – running alongside the overwhelming fear was an almost heart-stopping anticipation. Becky hadn't even touched me yet and my chest was heaving with arousal, my thighs trembled and as usual my very brazen cunt was seeping its secretions copiously.

Becky returned to stand in front of me. I gasped. Well, I did a gagged interpretation of a gasp when I saw Becky's outfit. I had no idea even after all the time I had spent with her naked body just how voluptuous she was.

She had on skin-tight, black PVC trousers that stretched over her bottom and hips like a second skin. They stopped halfway down her calves with a tiny one-inch slit up the side. Then there was about six inches of naked ankle, which showed to perfection her black patent shoes. The shoes were at least as high as the ones I had worn for Mr King and had two thin straps that encircled her slim ankles and buckled at the sides. She didn't even wobble but seemed to glide on them as if she had been wearing them all her life. Perhaps she had.

My eyes travelled upwards revelling in the sight of her. Her midriff was bare and she wore a PVC bustier that completely covered her beautiful breasts and thrust them out in front of her in a most formidable manner. The top finished in a high polo-neck that gave her a haughty, very dominant look and the whole ensemble was topped with the most fabulous hood imaginable. It encased her head in black and all I could see of my wonderful Becky was her soft full mouth and her navy-blue eyes through purpose-made holes. The last hole was at the very top and Becky had obviously scraped her hair up and pushed it through the hole until it hung down her back like a thick luscious tail, rising first to give it an arrogant swish when she moved. Just like the plume on the pony girl.

'Right. Just this first time I think I'll be kind to you and just get to know your pleasure limits. There'll be time enough to explore pain and humiliation another day, won't there?'

Becky obviously loved my stunned reaction to her outfit and had no need for me to answer her, so I just nodded, in complete awe of her. At that stage I had no idea how painful extended pleasure could become.

Leaving me kneeling naked and vulnerable in my place on the floor, she moved about, in front of me this time. She must have known the effect she was having on me because she kept turning quickly so her hair swept in a circle of gold around her, then bent over in front of me, feigning the need to adjust her ankle straps.

I delighted in the temptation of her. At that stage I still felt the odd rush of the dominant in me wanting to put her down and ravage her. But not being able to do the things you want is part of the attraction of being a submissive. Don't ask me why.

That all changed as she brought over a small table and placed it next to the bondage frame. On it she ceremoniously placed a soft rubber whip with tails about two foot long. The tails hung over the edge of the table tormenting me with their blackness.

Next to them she laid a pair of nipple clamps – we hadn't even known what they were in the shop, but the assistant had explained as if he had beginners in every day.

My heart started to beat double time then. Next to the clamps, all laid in a neat row, was a series of black forbidding weights. What happened to the 'pleasure-only' decision? my head screamed. Already I was clutching the gold bell hard in my hand.

'Come over here, Cassandra,' Becky enticed. When I reached her she moved me about until I was standing with my back to the cold frame. She hunkered down on the floor in front of me and pushed my legs apart until the sinews in my thighs were tight and standing out. Then she buckled the straps that were attached to the frame around me, first my ankles, then just above my knees and lastly the tops of my thighs. As she closed the last buckle she dragged her nails gently up the inside of my thigh, right up to the lips of my sex, just to tease. I groaned with pleasure.

Next came my arms, which were spread across the cross bar and, like my legs, buckled in three places until I felt tight, open and helpless.

Becky then found some long straps and fastened them, one around my hips and the upright post, just above my pubic hair, and one just below my breasts and the post. I twitched and wriggled, trying to see how much movement I had, and was surprisingly delighted to find that I could only flex my muscles. I had no actual movement available to me. I tried to look down at my bound torso but the stiff collar wouldn't allow it. I could only look straight ahead.

'I was going to blindfold you,' Becky said as she stood in front of me in all her glory. 'But I think I might let you see what I intend to do to you. It all adds to the anticipation, doesn't it, Cassandra?' I nodded the best I could.

She stepped in close to me until I could smell her perfume mixed with the smell of the PVC and the combined smells of our arousal and the leather furniture. It made a heady cocktail. I could only stare straight ahead as she bent down to my breasts, which waited, thrust forward and at her mercy, and then she took each nipple in her mouth and sucked hard. I whimpered my response to her attentions and that spurred her on further. When my nipples were hard Becky picked up the wicked-looking clamps and dangled them in front of my eyes. I snorted through my nose and I could feel my nostrils flare at the fear that threatened to erupt in my chest.

She rubbed the ends of my nipples one at a time with the jaw end of the clamps, to prepare them, I suppose; then I felt a sharp tightness, first in one breast, then the other. I panted fast, trying to absorb the intensity, until

Becky bent again and kissed and fondled the breasts surrounding my squashed nipples. The pain of the clamps and the exquisite pleasure of Becky's caresses combined to create the mixture that is my downfall.

My hand relaxed on the bell.

Within a few seconds the pain in my nipples abated and Becky, reading this, lifted up the first weight to show me. It swung like a pendulum from her fingers as she taunted me. When the weight was clipped on to the clamp it dragged my nipple downwards, and then she added the second one. I again sank into submission, and the extra pull from the weights was delicious.

Becky dropped from view then and again the fear washed over me, not knowing what was coming next. I felt a sharp pull on the puffy outer lips of my cunt. I couldn't believe it: she had clamped my lips but I had to acknowledge that the gentle tug was like nothing I had felt before. Again she stood before me and dangled a second pair of weights in front of my eyes and then kept looking down towards my sex. I realise what she had in mind with a jolt and shook my head vigorously, grunting my disapproval. Again I prepared to forfeit the bell.

As the weights were clipped on to the clamps and my lips were dragged down, just as my nipples had been a minute or two earlier, I felt the weight pull the hood of my clitoris down over its throbbing head. It was like nothing on earth. The fabulous tugging sensation sent sparks of electricity zigzagging up through my guts to my breasts and my breasts throbbed in response. My thighs trembled and shook as they tried to shut out the intensity. I had expected to feel pain and to have to learn to accept whatever level Becky decided, but this was perfect pleasure. It wasn't like the pleasure you feel while having normal sex, the sweet fluttering pleasure of a hard cock entering or a knowing caress of a hungry breast. This was like the difference between the pleasure you experience watching a good movie and the pleasure you experience sky diving. Both are pleasure but one is an incredible, mind-exploding experience.

Becky gently knocked the weights hanging from my sex until they swayed, stretching and pulling my lips and clitoris until I was finding it very hard to breathe. I felt one of Becky's fingers slide between my lips and she dragged it between them in a sawing motion that sent me wild. Each time she pushed the finger forward it brushed against the tortured bud of my clitoris and also moved the clamps that bit into my lips. I didn't know what I was feeling by then, only that this was what I had longed for, this was my fantasy. The flooding pleasure from Becky's finger on my clit and the pain, already dulled to a throb, sent me into a new level of heat. She slipped the finger that explored my channel up into my depths as far as she could and I ground down on to her hand trying to regain the pulsing that she had created in my clit. I grunted and moaned, writhing against my restraints and sucking the gag for all I was worth. Becky kept her finger deep inside me and very delicately brushed her thumb across the hard lump. I came and came, flooding her hand with my secretions. My muscles spasmed, gripping her finger for dear life. The violent contractions racked my helpless body, shaking me in the straps, and I jerked and twitched and marvelled at this new experience.

Oh, yes, this was my fantasy.

12

After our first game in the playroom I can't say that I stopped thinking about Mr King completely because, quite often, I found myself comparing him to Becky. I would weigh up the love I had for Becky added to the wonderful games we played and the totally mind-blowing treatment I 'suffered' at the hands of Mr King. I even found myself longing for the simplicity of straight sex with a man. The penis gag that Becky had surprised me with reminded me how I used to love a hard cock.

The life I was leading was so exciting that thought of our games filled far too many of my thoughts each day. I knew I didn't want to lose Becky and the dynamic power relationship we shared, but I felt it would be good to once again have a good hard fuck. As usual I shared my feelings with Becky; we talked about it and she agreed that I should go with my feelings. We had reached the stage where we were going to be tied together for a long time to come, not only by our bizarre sexual partnership but also our love and friendship. We agreed that there is something very special about being able to call your sexual partner your best friend.

At Becky's suggestion I called Ruth. Even Becky at that stage drew the line at coming with me while I went on the pull. I was feeling a little guilty at having almost dropped Ruth as a friend, anyway. It had never been intentional that we drift apart, but Becky had taken up all my time. Ruth was just as pleased to hear from me as I was to talk to her. I had really missed her.

I asked if she felt like a night on the razzle with me, and she agreed without hesitation. We agreed to go to our favourite local wine bar the following night. Becky and I both knew I was going out to find a man, and as she suggested what I wore and helped me get ready, she even managed to turn it into a game between us.

I had my shower as Becky laid out what she wanted me to wear, but when I returned to the bedroom I noticed there was no underwear. All she had put out was a very short leather skirt that I would normally consider wearing only in the playroom, and a red, glittery halter neck, that accentuated my breasts. On the floor next to the bed were my very provocative black leather thigh boots.

'I can't wear them to go out with Ruth,' I begged.

'Oh, yes you can. If I'm going to let you go then I have to call the shots. And I want every man in the place to be ogling you. I want you to pick the horniest one you can find and shag him senseless. But you had better remember everything that happens because, before you go to bed tonight, I want every sordid detail,' she explained. I couldn't tell what the inflection in her voice meant. I think she was as excited as I was.

'Oh, and by the way, I want you to follow my instructions to the letter. If I find you did this any other way I will punish you in a manner that you cannot even imagine.'

I felt a little bit like Cinderella, but it was exciting. I asked what my instructions were.

'I want you to see how quickly you can get a man to take you outside for a shag. You must do it in a reasonably public place, either the car park or somewhere with equal exposure. As soon as you are finished you will phone me and leave a message on the answerphone to say that you have completed my instructions. Do you agree?'

'Of course I do. You know how exquisite I find our games. I am raring to go already.'

'Well, you had probably better get dressed first. I know I'm not letting you wear much, but you should at least make the effort to cover up that disgustingly rude body of yours,' she said, grinning broadly. She slapped me on the bum and watched closely as I wriggled into the skirt and pulled on the top. As I sat on the edge of the bed to pull on the boots, her gaze never left my crotch. She licked her lips suggestively as, with each boot, my pussy was open to her view.

At that moment I actually longed to stay at home but Ruth saved the day by ringing the doorbell at just the moment I let my booted thighs fall apart.

Ruth looked rather shocked at the change in me, and especially in the clothes I was wearing, but she didn't say anything. I didn't know how to begin to tell her my plans for the evening. Luckily she was wearing a rather provocative outfit herself, so I didn't feel too out of place.

When we walked in the bar, literally every head turned to look at us. On the way in the taxi I had decided that Ruth wasn't really up to my confessions, so I had no idea how to begin to arrange to slip outside with a man.

Already I could see the perfect contender, however. He was standing at the bar staring at my boots as if he would start wanking any second. He grinned manically at me and licked his lips when I smiled tentatively back. I was dying to go to the loo and look in the long mirror to see just how short my skirt was. Becky had refused me permission to look before I came away, and I felt very self-conscious. I was very sexually charged, but part of me was petrified that everyone was staring because they could see I had no knickers on. The other problem I had was that the more I thought about it, the more wet

I got, and I was even more scared that my juices would trickle into sight.

I asked Ruth to get the drinks. She agreed readily as she had spotted someone she knew. I walked past Mr hard-on to go to the toilets. He leaned casually against the bar and blatantly ogled me. I looked him up and down just as daringly, pausing at his crotch. I took in his tight pale jeans, that showed his bulge, and the white T-shirt that showed not only his muscles but also his very sexy strong forearms. He looked a bit of an animal. He had a black leather belt that held up his jeans and I imagined being whipped with it and thought of Becky. What a perfect contrast between this hard hunk of man and my soft beautiful lover! I made a mental note to work on him when I had been to the loo.

I walked down the corridor to the ladies'. My spike heels clicked on the stone tiles. I pushed open the door and breathed a sigh of relief to find it empty. Just as I stood at the mirror staring at the hem of my skirt, the door opened and I met the gaze of Mr hard-on standing behind me. Without a word he walked up behind me and whispered in my ear.

'You are the most amazingly sexy woman I have ever seen in this place. I know what your clothes are saying. You want to be fucked, don't you?'

All I could do was nod helplessly.

His slightly rough hands gripped the bottom of my skirt and dragged it upward, over my hips to my waist, exposing my wet pussy. I groaned loudly but his moan of sheer approval drowned mine as he stared in disbelief at my nakedness.

'Fuck ... you dirty little tart. You're gagging for it, aren't you?'

I was deeply shocked by his words but disgustingly turned on. He was right. At that moment I was a very dirty little tart and I revelled in it.

Without another word he scooped me up in his arms and forced his mouth down hard on mine. His long brutal tongue stabbed its way between my lips and almost choked me in his enthusiasm. He strode into the nearest stall and kicked the door shut behind him. There were no preliminaries apart from the kiss. He stood me on the floor just long enough to unzip his trousers and get out his cock out, before he shoved me against the stone wall. I braced my hands in front of me as he forced my legs apart with his feet and, without a pause to aim, he rammed his hard cock into my soaking pussy.

He must have been quite uncomfortable, his body curled underneath me to gain entry. So he picked me up, still impaled on his cock, turned around then plonked himself on the toilet seat with me on his lap. God, it was amazingly horny. I couldn't even see him. It was as if I was just sitting on a cock, and that was just what I had wanted. His thick hairy forearms wrapped around my torso and groped for my breasts. I grabbed the hem of my T-shirt, whipped it over my head and, immediately, his hands found their goal. With no finesse whatsoever he squeezed hard, one swollen breast tightly held in each grabbing hand.

'Christ, you've got lovely tits, girl. Are they real?' he grunted as he ground them into my chest.

I realised that if I leaned as far forward as I could, I could brace myself against the door, and that made me more capable of running the show and getting what I wanted – but he had other ideas.

We were pumping against each other with the sweat running all over us when he obviously thought he needed another ingredient. He picked me up bodily as if I were a doll and turned me to face him. His cock slipped back into me as if he had never been away and, however much I loved Becky and our games, it felt wonderful. Let's face it, all the dildos and vibrators in the world can never compete with the hard heat of a horny cock and the pressure of a man's groin forcing his way in. Forcing it in so far that his body at the base of it grinds into your cunt and mashes your lips and clit.

The hardness filled me to stretching point as I wrapped my naked legs around his back. He stood up and again slammed me against the wall. This time his cock jabbed its way deeper inside me and I braced my boots against the far wall. He fucked me exactly the way I had fantasised about – hard and deep.

I was right with my first instinct – he was an animal. And he was right: I was a tart. We suited each other perfectly for those few minutes. The sheer force of his thrusts kept me up against the wall. I braced my legs either side of him and ground down on to his cock as hard as I could. I wanted to swallow his maleness. His hands wrenched away at my now-tender breasts, as mine wrapped themselves into his hair and forced him to face me.

We devoured each other totally and completely, with not one thought for each other's pleasure, only our own. The smell of our frantic coupling filled the cubicle. We were individually selfish, but in our complete selfishness we fed each other's need to the point of perfect pleasure. Absolute primeval obscenity!

Somehow, even in our selfishness, we managed to explode into exhausting orgasms at almost the same time, even though it had only been a few minutes since I had clapped eyes on him. My climax bore no resemblance to the exquisite, drawn-out, almost painful climaxes Becky forced out of me, but it was great in its simplicity. Mr hard-on had provided just what I had longed for, and he laughed delightfully when I told him just that. He sat on the loo seat again, still breathing hard, still with his sticky cock sticking out of his jeans, still with a hard-on, and watched me straighten my hair and my skirt and struggle into my top. I ran some lipstick around my still-tingling mouth and left him where he was. I had a phone call to make.

'Becky. I have just had the biggest, hardest, dirtiest fuck of my life. And I can't wait to tell you all about it.'

When I returned to the bar Ruth looked at me a bit strangely and I realised that I would never be able to tell her about my new life. Even though we had a great night catching up on old times, I knew that in a subtle way we had grown apart. As I walked out of the bar and grinned red-faced at Mr hard-on, I was a little sad. He leaned backward on the bar with his groin thrust out toward me and his elbows behind him, reminding me of what I had done. His eyes twinkled in a very knowing way as he leaned forward and chuckled, 'Thanks for coming, gorgeous.'

When I got home I told Becky every tiny detail and she loved it. Then *she* became the dirty tart as she manoeuvred us into the classic sixty-nine position, with my head buried between her thighs and her tongue working on my tingling clitoris.

As the weeks passed I found my fantasies turning to Mr King more and more often. My debauchery in the bar had been fun, but had changed nothing, and, to be honest, I never gave Mr hard-on another thought. In hindsight I know that Becky guessed I was twitching again, but at the time I had no inkling of her diabolical plans.

Becky and I still spent every spare minute in the playroom, experimenting with our toys and making up games that would make your toes curl, so I should have been able to have put Mr King out of my mind. But he hovered on the edges of my fantasies, with his spanking technique and his candles. Occasionally Becky sensed my restlessness and usually responded admirably.

One day as I sat in the garden waiting for Becky to come home from work and musing over our relationship, wondering if what we had would be enough for me, the phone rang. I hurried inside and managed to catch it before the answer machine picked up.

'Hi, Cassie. It's me, Becky.'

'Hello, lover,' I responded, but my heart sank at the knowledge that she usually called only if she was going to be held up on the ward.

'I'm afraid it's the usual. We've got a visiting Australian doctor here and I've been given the dubious pleasure of showing him round. I really ought to at least offer to take him for a drink or something. Only he lives in digs and it would be a bit rude if I just left him and came home. I'm sorry, love. I had something rather exciting planned for tonight as well.'

'Oh, well,' I whined. 'If you must, you must. I just wish you didn't wear such a devastatingly horny uniform. Just keep your hands off him.'

'Don't be silly, Cassie. I'll see you later, and let's hope he doesn't keep me too late. Bye.'

'Bye.'

She blew me a kiss and the phone went dead. I was so pissed off. Like Becky, I had had high hopes of playing a game later after a meal. My thoughts were drawn to her job and the demands that being a nurse put on her. What with my job, which often stretched into late hours, and her shifts, the precious time we had together when neither of us had to get up in the morning was to be treasured.

I picked up a book, curled up on the sofa and lost myself in a power struggle between a group of detectives and a serial killer who tied up his victims and then raped them. The descriptions of the murders all started off really exciting, then each time I would get involved in the sexual side of things only to be repulsed when the victim was torn limb from limb. I had probably been reading for an hour or so, lost in the tale, when the phone at my elbow rang again. I picked it up absent-mindedly and, while still reading my book, casually said, 'Hello?'

'Hi, is that Cassandra?'

I was instantly alert at the gorgeous male drawl whispering huskily in my ear. The hairs on the back of my neck tickled and my crotch prickled shamelessly.

'Speaking. What can I do for you?'

'Rebecca asked me to call you because she's been held up even longer than she thought and she wondered if you'd like me to come around and keep you company until she gets there. This is a little embarrassing but she's invited me to dinner and asked me to come ahead of her to help you prepare. What do you think? Is that OK?'

What the hell was he talking about? Prepare? Prepare for what, for God's sake?

I asked that very same question of him, and, when he answered that the suggestion was that he help me prepare dinner, I am not sure if I was relieved or disappointed.

'How in hell's name do I know you are who you say you are?' I asked him, knowing already that it didn't really matter because my pussy was flooding just at the sound of his voice.

'Oh, sorry. I did say to Rebecca that you wouldn't believe who I was so she said to mention the bell.'

I was dumbstruck. Totally speechless!

Did I detect suggestion in his voice? I stuttered and swallowed hard to compose myself. What on earth was Becky up to? We played some wild games but I had no idea if this was one of them.

'Cassie, I had quite a long chat with Rebecca and she

assured me that you would enjoy my company. Especially with what she was telling me about your loft. I think you should open the front door for me. I am in a taxi outside.'

The purring quality of his sexy voice caused me to shiver with anticipation as I mumbled into the phone. Already Becky was forgotten and only for one brief moment did I wonder if I was doing the right thing.

'OK.'

The phone went dead but it wasn't until I heard a light tap on the front door that I realised I was still sitting in exactly the same position with the phone against my sweating cheek, conflicting thoughts tumbling for supremacy in my brain.

I returned the handset to its cradle and almost like a robot moved through the lounge into the hall to stand behind the front door. I couldn't bring myself actually to open it, though, and memories of standing outside Mr King's front door were rife, sending shooting darts of pleasure through my belly. I stepped forward and released the catch.

'G'day, Cassie. I'm Greg, a friend of Rebecca's. And I'm pleased to be meeting you under such interesting circumstances. I think our meeting's going to be very interesting, don't you?'

He stood in front of me in an immaculate dark business suit, tall and bronzed, with sun-bleached hair and a grin that melted any resolve I had – not that I had much at that stage: I was still in shock. He resembled a tawny predatory animal as his gaze devoured me.

His voice took on a slightly more serious tone as he added, 'I asked you a question, Cassandra. Do you agree that our meeting's going to prove interesting? Please answer when I ask you a question, then I'm sure we will get on admirably.'

'Y-yes,' I stuttered, devastated by his use of my full first name. He was so dominant and in complete control that my knees turned to jelly. I followed meekly as he led me into the lounge as if he had been there before.

He took control of the whole situation immediately. He towered over me as he pushed me gently down into the soft cushions of the sofa. I was helpless, hypnotised by his looks and eyes that seared through my soul as if he knew my innermost thoughts.

I watched in stunned awe as Greg very casually moved about the room as if he lived there, placing his jacket over the back of a chair and loosening his dark tie. He slowly, calmly removed gold cufflinks and rolled up the cuffs of his white shirt precisely and carefully so that each cuff matched the other. He removed his wrist-watch and laid it over the end of the sofa, then turned to me for the first time since I had sat down.

'I think we should just get this out of the way first, then you'll hopefully have no doubts that what I intend to do to you is at the request of Rebecca.' With that he hunkered down in front of me and, reaching into his trouser pocket, brought out, and dangled before my eyes, my tiny bell. I knew then that Becky must have planned it all. I was amazingly excited at that thought. If I wasn't already under his spell, that clinched it. I was a wreck, utterly in awe of him and the power he seemed to have over my senses.

I groaned at that point. My submission in response to his dominance was absolute. This was nothing like the scary unseen Mr King or my games with Becky: this was control in its purest form. I would have done anything requested of me and he instinctively knew it. My thoughts strayed for a tiny moment as I wondered how anyone could read me so well, but I snapped back to the present as I clutched the bell in my hand.

'I'd like to dispense with the bell if you'll trust me, Cassandra. Will you do that for me?'

I nodded frantically, mute.

Greg had to prise my fist apart to remove the bell, not because I didn't want to give it up but because I was unable to move. Reluctantly I released it and tried to relax. I was unable to take my eyes from his. My gaze followed his every movement like a cornered rabbit scared that it's about to be attacked but with no idea where the attack is going to come from.

I clenched my knees together trying to stifle the trembling that threatened to consume me as he whispered in a calm but controlled voice, 'Do you have panties on, Cassandra?' I nodded. 'Would you remove them and give them to me, please?'

I delved up underneath my skirt and wriggled and writhed to remove my shamefully damp knickers without actually opening my legs so much as a centimetre. He smiled, obviously amused by either my embarrassment or my contortions, then took the proffered garment and held it to his nose, breathing deeply.

'Oh, God,' I groaned under my breath, the sweet humiliation washing over me in hot waves.

'You smell very aroused, Cassandra. Are you?' I nodded with my chin tight into my chest. 'Look at me, please, when I talk to you.'

I raised my head and met his eyes. The flood of juice from my now naked sex was instantaneous. I knew the sofa would have a very wet patch when I moved.

'Now, listen carefully, Cassandra. I want you to pull your skirt up until it's around your hips but without removing your eyes from mine. Do it now, Cassandra.'

I followed his instruction, still clenching my legs tightly together. I drowned in his eyes with no option but obedience. His pupils were dilated and smouldering with what I could only read as amusement. How help-less I felt. His deep brown eyes held me in bonds that were stronger than any ropes as I floundered in his control.

He tucked my knickers into his trouser pocket and placed his still cool hands on my bare knees. His eyes burned into mine, daring me to disobey and break the contact. My chest was heaving dramatically, my skin alive and tingling as his hands slowly started to spread my knees apart. For one fleeting second I was reminded of my naughty encounter on the train, the one that had in effect started all this. But the thought lasted for only a second, because my thighs were separating.

Sweat began to trickle through my hair as every blink I took left me frantic at leaving his gaze, but, each time I opened my eyes again, his were burning into my psyche. I am slightly ashamed to admit that all thoughts of Becky had left when I shut the front door: there were just him and me, his eyes in my soul, his power in my head and his hands on my knees. Oh yes, and my crotch being exposed more and more each second. Not once did his eyes leave mine to look at what he was doing. His only interest was how what he was doing affected me – and, God, how it affected me!

I experienced so many conflicting emotions during those minutes. The deliberate way he was slowly spreading my legs apart was humiliating, shameful but completely thrilling. I got to know him just by looking into his eyes. I could tell that his control of the situation was very exciting to him by the glow deep in his eyes. He was definitely amused by just how excited I was becoming, but that was also part of the mind game he was playing with me.

I felt the sticky lips of my sex cling, then separate in a most disgraceful manner, exposing bits that I would have preferred not to expose, but for the moment it was all right because he wasn't even attempting to look.

When my legs were stretched tightly apart Greg smiled a knowing sort of smile and I knew whatever came next would be just as devastating as the other things he had done.

'I'm going to look at you now, Cassandra. I'm going to look at your cunt and when I've done that you're going to do something for me. Is that clear?'

We both knew by that stage that I would do absolutely anything for him. I nodded. Sublimely acquiescent!

I actually felt a trickle of creamy juice ooze from my spread lips and run down to the crease of my bum the second I knew he was looking at me. My stomach lurched in a spasm of pure arousal. I dared to look down at the top of his bowed head as he almost devoured me with his eyes and I longed for it to dip and taste me, but he was much too subtle. This was to be a mind fuck.

'I want to look inside you, Cassandra. You see, I'm going to fuck you in a minute and I would like to see where my hard cock will be going. I want to be sure you're ready and open for me. I have a very hungry cock and I need to be sure that you can accommodate it. Do you think you can accommodate a big, very thick, hard, hungry cock for me, Cassandra? Well, do you?'

The groan in my throat filled the room; my hands clenched by my sides and my cunt gaped like a fish's mouth, hungry and desperate now for his cock.

'Go on, then, Cassandra. Take hold of your pretty wings for me and spread them apart. I want to see you.'

I couldn't do it. It was far too degrading. However much I longed for him to fuck me, I couldn't do that and I shook my head.

'I caaan't,' I whined.' Please no. It's too disgusting. I really can't.'

'You know the nature of my dominance and your

165

submission, Cassandra. The more you feel humiliated and disgusted the more I want you to do it for me. The more I want you to, the more you want to please me. Will you do it, just for me?'

His eyes were burning into mine again; his arousal was like a beacon destroying my shame and resolve.

At that moment I heard a noise from the hall behind my right shoulder and I started to turn, but Greg snapped kindly, 'Oh, no you don't. You keep your eyes right where they are, young lady. If your eyes leave mine even for just one second I will stop what I'm doing and you'll sit there for the rest of the evening just as you are, with your very rude thighs spread apart and your brazen cunt shamelessly advertising what a dirty girl you are.'

I knew it was Becky instantly because I could smell her perfume. I heard the creak of her rocking chair in the corner by the window and I could see the dark outline of her in the periphery of my vision. My sex twitched and jerked in response to her presence.

'Do it now, Cassandra.'

My hands trembled as they fluttered between my legs, unable to control themselves enough to do anything as dextrous as take hold of my lips, but eventually the encouragement in his eyes spurred me on. I took hold of each inner lip and delicately held them slightly apart, my submission entering the depths of depravity. I was mortified but almost delirious with arousal.

Greg chuckled out loud. 'You can do better than that. I can't get my massive cock in there now, can I, Cassandra? Or have you been having girl sex for so long you've forgotten just how big a cock is?'

My groans and moans became punctuation for his every sentence and again Becky was forgotten.

'Let me show you why you need to be much more

available than that, Cassandra.' And with that he stood up in front of me, between my spread knees and close to my exposed sex, and slowly pulled down his zip, his eyes still clamped on to mine. He stepped out of his trousers and footwear, then undid his shirt and removed that, too. I longed to look at him but I was so afraid I would break the incredibly horny spell that held all three of us in its grip.

'Open wider for me now, Cassandra.'

I didn't need to be told again. I gripped the tips of my inner lips harder; they were slimy and slippery and I stretched them as far apart as I could. I didn't care how disgusting it looked because it felt very exciting to be exposing my insides for him. Of course, knowing Becky was watching helped, especially when I heard her emit a low, almost inaudible groan herself.

He glanced down for a second and the breath caught in his throat. The words he spoke then came out as a croak.

'Perfect, baby. Exquisite! It wasn't that difficult, was it? I can see just how much you want me now. Now, I want you to scoot forward until your bottom is on the edge of the settee, and then I can get to you, can't I?'

I obeyed instantly, wriggling without the use of my hands. I was too scared that if I let go I wouldn't get the cock I had been promised.

'Now, stay exactly like you are and open your mouth wide for me, Cassie. I need a little extra lubrication.'

Groan.

He stepped forward and leaned over my head, his hands on the back of the sofa, and I dared to look down at his cock. God, it really was beautiful. It throbbed and danced to the tune of his erratic pulse inches in front of my eyes. First he teased my lips with the soft hot tip until my mouth was gaping and lunging for him like a baby bird in a nest salivating unashamedly. Finally I managed to lick the end and he was hooked. He grunted then and thrust his beautiful cock into my mouth, filling and stretching my jaw. I longed to touch him but through the fog of my heat I heard him warn me not to let go of my lips because he would be there in a minute. He fucked my mouth as if it were a sensitive pussy, thrusting gently, then withdrawing until just the shiny tip was still between my wet lips. The interior of my mouth suddenly had erogenous zones as the velvet rod of hard flesh nudged and prodded me to a height of need I had never experienced before. A need to be fucked. I dribbled copiously from both orifices, no longer caring what I looked like.

I became aware of Becky standing behind the sofa and wondered for a moment what she was going to do. Just as I thought I was going to come, the magnificent beast was removed, leaving my mouth hanging open, feeling bruised and swollen.

'Guide me in, Cassandra,' he croaked.

As I felt his slippery cock prod my exposed hole there was no need of my help. It found its own way in on the slick tide of my juices and he rammed it home hard, right to the hilt, in one smooth thrust.

'Oh yes, fuck me, please. Harder.'

I removed my hands from their squashed position between my legs and began to touch him, but Becky from behind the sofa grabbed my arms and manoeuvred them until they were underneath my body, restrained, just how I always longed for them to be.

She quickly pulled up my T-shirt and wrenched my bra upwards until my breasts were squashed out of the bottom, and then she grasped them in a vicelike grip.

Greg was pounding away inside me, filling me to

capacity and thundering down on the mound of my sex with every prolonged thrust. The size of him was painful in a delicious sort of way and, added to Becky's hands gripping my breasts, was creating a perfect blend of pain and pleasure. The exquisite combination of man and woman threatened to send me crazy. Becky changed to cupping my breasts and pushed them forward until Greg took the message and sank his teeth into first one, then the other, biting at my hard nipples and teasing the engorged flesh until I wailed.

'Please make me come. I need to come now. *Pleeese!*'

They must have believed my need because Becky leaned over the back of the sofa and kissed me long and hard. Her mouth ground down where only moments before a warm cock had thrust. Greg bit harder on my nipple and took up a sort of rocking motion in my sex that filled me to bursting point and nudged my raging clitoris.

I exploded, shouting obscenities. Or was it *im*ploded? I'm not sure. But fuck, it felt good.

Within seconds, Greg pulled out of me and I was manhandled on to the floor. Becky got into the position she loved most, kneeling astride my face with her head buried between my thighs, and Greg sat beside us on the sofa, watching. I'm not sure when she had got naked but she was, and her horny fragrant pussy filled my hungry mouth and made up for the loss of Greg's cock. I wrapped my arms around her back and dragged her down to me, covering my face with her. While I slurped unceremoniously on her clit she gently nuzzled my exhausted pussy and Greg pushed his fingers inside her. Between us we assailed her senses and brought her to a shattering orgasm that covered my face with her wetness and shuddered through her taut body.

Greg begged Becky to stay right where she was and,

with her still kneeling above me on all fours, he thrust into her from behind and fucked her just as hard as he had fucked me minutes earlier. I lay on the floor totally entranced by her bobbing breasts, which dangled over my belly, and the magical sight of Greg's powerful cock driving into her body right above my eyes. His balls swung just out of reach of my mouth, so I stretched up and caught them, sucking deeply. Almost immediately I felt his scrotum tighten as he pumped his come deep inside my beautiful, manipulative, scheming lover.

'You were far too wrapped up in your own thoughts, Cassie,' she said later as she explained that something in Greg had sparked the knowledge in her that he enjoyed the same games as we did. She had actually known him for months but had been sounding him out recently with a view to just the scenario she had instigated. Greg had gone back to his digs after sharing a bottle of wine with us, thanking me so politely for 'having' him. They both laughed when I blushed, joking that it was a bit late to feel embarrassed.

The next morning over breakfast Becky kept looking at me until I said, 'What?'

'I know we've got to go shopping, but as soon as we get back I intend to send you to the playroom and teach you just what happens to dirty sluts who let just any old passing stranger fuck them.'

We did the supermarket bit as quickly as possible, chucking everything and anything in the trolley just to get it over with, then, laughing about the night before, we piled the back seat of the car with enough food for a month. Then we hit the high street shops, so comfortable with each other that I felt a very warm glow in my stomach. We tried on clothes for at least two hours until we were tired out and hungry.

'Come on, I'll treat you to lunch at that new pub on Princes Street. You never know, we might pick up a playmate for tonight,' Becky teased.

We sat on tables outside in the sunshine and ate delicious hot baguettes filled with melted cheese that dripped on the plates and we watched the world go by, happy in our thoughts. Mine as usual were very rude.

'Hi, girls, mind if we join you?' came a voice from behind us. I turned to see two rather charming-looking men already confident that we would welcome them to eat with us, but Becky in a very innocent voice answered, 'Sorry, boys, but we're together, if you know what I mean.' With that she took hold of my hand on the table and glared at them until they turned, muttering, and left us in peace.

'Becky, how could you? You really upset that one in the leather jacket. Did you see his face? They really thought they were in with a chance, didn't they?' Secretly I was pleased that she had openly acknowledged our relationship as not just to be kept to the playroom. I squeezed her hand and remembered what she had said before we left home. I anticipated a good game.

'I think you've had quite enough cock for a while, don't you? You greedy little tart. You'll just have to make do with me, won't you?'

We sat a while and watched the same couple of men try their luck at another table, amused when they sat down and immediately took over the conversation with two other unsuspecting women.

We browsed the antique shops next, thrilled when we found an old leather riding crop in a dusty corner. Becky made me stand near the shop assistant and hold out my hand while she tested the sharpness of the sting. She asked me to rate it on a scale of one to ten and I whispered, 'Three', hoping the girl didn't hear. The girl let out a loud huff and went to the other side of the shop, busying herself.

We were giggling like a couple of teenagers when we left the shop, knowing without a doubt that we had been charged over the odds. But also knowing, like the girl in the shop, that we would have paid almost anything for our new toy. It wasn't even wrapped, so, all the way home, Becky kept slapping it across the palm of her hand, sending shivers down my spine.

I knelt naked in the middle of the room as instructed and, putting my hands on my head, waited for her to join me. The images of Mr King and Greg were swept away as I tried to imagine what new horror she had planned for me. I hoped it would be wicked, because I knew that that would have the effect she hoped, to redress the balance.

The first thing she did was buckle on my collar, unclip the bell and pass it to me. My stomach churned. She helped me to my feet and brought out the rubber catsuit that we had bought in London. It took us a while to pull it on me but the effort was worth it. I turned about, looking at myself in the mirror, admiring the smooth black body that strutted before me. We were both thrilled with the way it looked as if I had been poured into it. Already I could feel the heat building up inside and the sweat started trickling down between my shoulder blades.

Becky helped me to my feet and led me to the frame, then went again to the cupboard and returned with a long pole that totally confused me. She screwed on to the bottom of the pole a platform about a foot square, then, on to the other end, she screwed a rather large black rubber dildo.

'OK, sweetheart, I want you to stand on this piece,'

she said, indicating the platform, 'but first open your legs.' I opened them hesitantly and she unzipped the crotch from the top of the crease of my bum round to the top of my pubic hair.

'Oh, that's horny,' she whispered, and she stroked my sex as it bulged out of the split in the rubber. 'Now stand on it.'

I stood on the wood with my feet placed either side of the pole and marvelled at the invention of it as realisation swept over me. Becky grasped the middle section and started twisting it. Slowly the dildo moved higher and higher, closer to my exposed bulge. When it reached the point where it was brushing the lips of my sex as they were forced out of the slit in the suit I bent my knees, desperate to gain access to it. It slid between my slick lips with a little help from Becky, who spread my lips apart and gradually stretched me wide open. Within a minute or two it had screwed its way deep inside me until I was standing on tiptoe. When I was stretched up as far as possible with just the balls of my feet and my toes on the floor she stopped and stepped back.

'Mmm, very nice. How full do you feel, Cassandra?'

I wriggled about to gain maximum penetration and murmured my pleasure. Becky took hold of my wrists and added handcuffs, then pulled my arms up to the crossbar above me and clipped me in place. She turned around and walked out of the door.

As she left she turned and grinned.

'I'll be back to let you go in about half an hour, Cassandra. Try not to think about men too much, won't you?'

It took a minute or so for it to sink in what a diabolical situation she had contrived. I couldn't step off the platform because of the dildo and I couldn't relax and ease the tension in my legs because the dildo was in me too deeply. I just had to wait there, shuffling from foot to foot, trying to stop the cramps that threatened to reduce me to a sobbing wreck.

'Right, Cassandra, let's turn this to your advantage,' I said to myself, trying to jolly myself along. I gripped the dildo with my vaginal muscles and tried to manoeuvre myself slightly so the edge of the intrusion rubbed on my clitoris, and it worked. The pressure was ever so slight but it had the desired effect of making me want an orgasm. I knew I was on the right track when I felt the first drops of my juice trickle down the inside of the tight rubber casing.

I ran through my mind every sexy thing that we had done since we moved in together, trying to experience again each touch and indignity I had suffered at the hands of Becky. Slowly but surely my arousal heightened until I was grunting with the effort of riding the dildo. My thighs, which were under an incredible strain from having to stay on tiptoe, ached abominably; my legs shook with the strain. The strange mixture of sensations – the dildo, the tight rubber, slippery now with sweat and my secretions, the helplessness and of course my submission – created in me the catalyst I needed. I experienced a shaky little orgasm that left me breathless and aching even more, but did nothing to ease my frustration.

The cramps in my calves were beginning to cause me pain by the time Becky returned, so she took pity on me and released me immediately. She helped me up on to the bondage bed and did all the things she was good at. She stroked and sucked and licked and nibbled my hot, horny, sweaty sex as it bulged even further through the gap left by the zip in my suit and took me to a shattering climax.

13

Becky took to phoning me at work and instructing me to be prepared for her when she got home. She never bothered asking if I was alone in the office, just ploughed straight in with orders like, 'I'll be home at six and I want you to be ready in the playroom for me.' Just the thought that within an hour or two I would be kneeling on the floor in our playroom, with my breasts aching for her attention and my knees spread wide to make myself accessible, would finish me for the day. I would have to cancel any appointments I had and I would sit for hours, sometimes, daydreaming about what devious plan she had prepared for me that night.

I know that everyone at work saw me as the same independent, powerful career woman, but I knew the real Cassandra now. Just like before Becky and I got together, I again would find myself sitting at one of the endless meetings staring at each individual person to see if I could tell what sort of games they played in their own home.

It was impossible. After all, how could anyone tell that Cassandra Paige, who always power-dressed, would actually prefer to be in a maid's dress taking orders? For work I always chose to wear the severe suits in dark colours and coupled them with quite plain blouses, sheer stockings and court shoes. I always scraped my hair back into a French pleat to avoid the bimbo look and it was obvious that at least the staff underneath me believed in the image I portrayed.

At Becky's insistence I had taken to wearing either

very rude underwear or none at all and I loved the naughty feeling it gave me, especially when I had to take a phone call from her and she would ask me to tell her what I was wearing.

'Come on, baby, tell me how your dirty little pussy is packaged for me today,' she would say down the phone, enunciating every syllable to make the maximum impact. I would shiver with delight as I explained in careful detail for her that I was wearing perhaps a crotchless pair of rubber knickers or a tiny lace thong. She would fail, then, to keep up her dominant persona and would give herself away with comments like, 'Oh, yes, baby! I wish I was there with you.'

Once when I played the same trick on her and rang her at work to tell her that I had a surprise for her that evening, she turned up at my office an hour later and insisted to Amanda, my secretary, that she be let in to wait for me to return from the meeting I was in. I walked through my office door and sank into my chair, dropping my briefcase on the floor beside me, and before I could even draw breath she was behind me. She grabbed my hair and dragged me over the desk, forcing my face hard down on to the wood and with her other hand dragged my skirt up over my hips.

'I should grip the desk hard if I were you, Cassie, because you can't afford to cry out, can you? I intend to punish you here and now for teasing me like that. I intend to spank your very rude bottom until you share your surprise with me.'

'But I wanted to tempt you ready for tonight,' I mumbled into my blotter.

The slap sounded like a gunshot and resounded through the office. I felt sure they could hear what was going on down the corridor.

'For Christ's sake, Becky, pack it in. Someone'll come

in,' I whispered. Just at that moment we heard a soft tap on the door and my secretary's voice enquiring, 'Are you all right in there, Ms Paige?'

I struggled to get to my feet but Becky held me fast and, bending close, whispered in my ear. 'Tell her to go away, Cassandra, or I will slap you again with her out there listening. You've got to the count of three. One ... Two ...'

'I'm fine, thanks, Amanda, I'll call you if I need you,' I croaked.

I was furious that she had put me in that in compromising position but found myself responding instantly. I whimpered and spread my legs as Becky pushed her knee between them, grinding her hard thigh between mine. She forced it into my crotch and almost lifted me off the floor with it. My head was squashed against the desk and hurting. My breasts too were squashed beneath me under the pressure of her weight, but I pushed as hard as I could back against her knee, grinding just as hard as she was. I moaned deeply my response.

'Tell me now, Cassie.' And with that she picked up the ruler off my desk and whacked me hard with it, right across the tops of my thighs. Tears stung my eyes and I gasped with outrage but I didn't dare risk her doing it again, so I gave in.

'All right, I'll tell you. I bought an outfit when we were in London and I wanted to surprise you with a role-play tonight. It was going to be a surprise for you but if you really want to know every detail ...' I drew it out, hoping she would change her mind and let me surprise her.

Within two seconds Becky had removed her leg, and walked away leaving me flustered, frustrated and as horny as hell. She straightened her uniform skirt as she walked out of the door and she called back, 'Make it good.'

That evening when she got home I had the dinner ready for her and had laid the table with candles, flowers and napkins. The wine was chilling and the smell of the roast filled the house.

As she came in through the front door I made my entrance. I was wearing the taffeta maid's dress I had bought in London with black, fishnet, seamed stockings and the high heels that I had brought to wear to Mr King's. The assistant in the shop, who had nearly turned my head, had insisted that I buy a frilly pair of white knickers to go underneath. I felt very silly in them but when I saw the effect that they had on Becky I knew she had been right.

She just gawked at me. She stood with her mouth open and stared at my breasts. The structure of the dress forced them upwards until the swell of them spilled out over the top. I felt like a wicked harlot and I loved it. I held the pretty lace apron out as I bobbed a curtsey. 'Good evening, Madam Rebecca. May I take your coat?' I asked in the most innocent voice I could muster. 'I will be your maid for this evening and I am yours to command. Anything you want is yours. I will obey you in all things.'

Becky was mesmerised. She reached out and pinched my nipples, pulling them free of the neck of the dress, and I didn't even move, so she pushed her hand into my crotch and fondled me until I made little snuffling noises, but then I controlled myself. She made me turn around and bend over and, as I did so, she lifted the ruffled hem and patted my frilled bottom.

She took the crop we had bought from the hallstand and whacked it across my frilled bottom.

'How many on a scale of one to ten now, Cassandra?' she cajoled.

'Five,' I squeaked.

She whacked me harder and I shouted, 'Ten, ten, Becky.'

'Oh, good, very nice. Did you say you would do anything, maid?

'Yes, madam,' I replied. Already my hormones were leaping, wondering what she would instruct me to do. I wanted her to do nice things to me but I also wanted her to want to do horrible things to me, and to force me to accept them.

The game she came up with was bizarre to say the least. Within ten minutes I was sitting on the end of the dining table with my legs spread wide apart. Between my legs was Becky's dinner and she sat in front of me on the chair. I had removed the pretty knickers on her instructions and my crotch was open to her gaze. I could feel the steam from her dinner tickling my nether lips as I fed her. She tormented my body every minute that I was feeding her. Every time I leaned forward to put a forkful into her mouth she squeezed one of my nipples, gripping on to them as I tried to sit upright again. As I scooped more food ready to pass it to her mouth she slid her finger between my lips and delved into my depths, wiggling it about and sending me into frenzy.

That wasn't even the game. The game went like this: if I dropped so much as one drip of gravy down her clothes, or my clothes or the tablecloth, I would be punished, but every time I tried to steady my hand she increased the titillation. I became quite worried when, after I had spilled at least six drops of food, she started saying how pretty the candles looked. She was a devious woman. I remembered Mr King's mind-blowing candle game and shook even more.

Finally she finished and I knew I was in for a hard time when she revelled in counting the spots on the cloth, even inventing one so that the total came to ten.

'Right, maid, now for the punishment. After you've cleared the table and washed up I want you to come back in here.'

As I washed up I became more and more nervous. I remembered only too clearly how painful the wax had been on my genitals and this time I was expected to walk right into it. At least then I hadn't known what was coming. Becky had become far too fond of devising wicked new ways of punishing me and testing my limits.

By the time I returned I was quite agitated and, as soon as I walked in the room, I knew why. Everything had been cleared from the middle of the room and a dining chair sat in the space. Tied to the four legs were lengths of rope.

'OK, now, I want you to come round the back here and bend over this chair and grasp the seat with your hands.' I had assumed I was to sit on it, so this instruction threw me, but I walked behind it as instructed.

Becky and I had had numerous conversations about anal sex and although she loved it I had always refused to have anything to do with it, and until now she had respected my wishes. I suppose I knew that one day she would use her power over me to force my acceptance of this ultimate humiliation, but I at least thought we would have discussed it first.

I hesitated and looked at Becky, seeking her recognition of my fear, but it wasn't there.

'Come on, maid, snap to it. I thought you said you'd do anything for me and I want you to bend over this chair. Now!'

She's obviously going to spank me, I decided as I

obeyed her command. And, after all, a promise was a promise and I had committed myself to doing anything.

The back of the chair was slightly too high for comfort, so I had to stretch up on tiptoe so that I could bend over it properly and I wobbled for a moment or two but gripped the seat to steady myself. Becky tied my hands to the seat and my ankles to the back legs of the chair. My head hung down almost on to the cushioned seat and my arse stuck up. I felt the most vulnerable exposure possible.

Even though I could feel my cheeks part as she pulled my ankles over to the chair legs to secure them – and again I feared the prospect of anything to do with my bum – I was still very horny. What a traitorous libido I have. I knew that just having my naked buttocks thrust up into the air like that would tempt Becky to torment me.

First she ran her nails over the spread cheeks of my bottom and I flinched and tried helplessly to clench my buttocks together. It was bad enough that she could see my most secret place but the thought of her touching it sent waves of shame down my spine.

'No, don't do that,' I cried out as she ran her finger down the open cleft, over the screwed tight sphincter muscle and into my wet pussy.

Becky came around the front of the chair, pulled my breasts out of the bodice of my dress and clamped very tight clips on to them. On to the clips she attached delicate chains that she then pulled forward and fastened on to the front chair legs. My poor breasts were stretched tight, and if I just relaxed the tug on them was exquisitely painful.

Next she became even more diabolical. She clamped more clips on to my sex lips and more chains on to them, then stretched them tight out to the chair legs. I knew my pussy was gaping open and I could feel the cold air on the sensitive inside of my stretched lips.

My head screamed with breathless suspicion but the walls deep within my cunt seeped their nectar, telling a different story. I couldn't even flinch without the clamps pulling painfully somewhere, so I stayed rigid and still, waiting for her next move.

When it came I knew why she had immobilised me so completely. She parted the cheeks of my bottom with the fingers of one hand and pressed the tip of her finger on to the tight screwed-up hole. I tried to wriggle away but any slight movement tugged at my most tender places. I was completely at her mercy.

I was wondering what had happened to the timid Becky who only a few weeks before had, like me, been ignorant of the joys to be had from S&M games, when she moved to the front of me and stood a large black rubber dildo on the carpet.

I begged her, 'Please, Becky, I know I said you could do anything, but please, not that. Please don't do that to me.'

Becky left the room then and returned a minute later to push the tiny gold bell into my hand. I groaned, knowing that from that moment the choice was mine and not hers. That always made games more difficult for me because it's easier for me to trust her to know when I have reached my limit and, if she chooses, to push me past it. That's what I enjoy most, my limits being tested. But if *I* have to make the choice of when to stop I can never seem to do so. I couldn't imagine myself ever dropping the bell and admitting defeat.

She ignored my pleas and, moving around behind me again, warned me that if I said one more word or protested at anything she did in the next half-hour she would shove the dildo so far up my arse I would choke on it and if I didn't like it I should drop the bell. I was shocked to hear my beautiful lover use such language but I have to admit that it excited the hell out of me. I had only to raise my head slightly and the dildo was right in my line of vision, and I swear it was at least eight inches in length with the girth of a cucumber. A large one!

I was very aroused at this stage, what with the fear and the restraint and the forbidding sight of the monster dildo. The sweat trickled down my spine into my hairline and my eyes watered with the strain of trying to look at how horrible the dildo was.

That inquisitive finger was doing the business again. Pushing itself just inside my bum and then, just as I gripped my hole and clenched my cheeks – which didn't stop her at all – she would remove it.

The helpless feeling when my legs are stretched to open my sex is heaven but this sort of availability was awful. I truly couldn't even squeeze my cheeks together so when she said her next words my control was destroyed – what there was of it.

'This is your punishment, my sweet little maid. You said you'd do anything for me but I'm even going to give you the chance to refuse this one. Isn't that just perfect torment? Either accept my wicked punishment or take the chance on disappointing me. The best bit is that I'm not even going to tell you what the punishment is to be, only that it will test your limits to the full. Which is it to be, Casssandra? Will you take your punishment ten times, one for each drop of food you spilled, or will I untie you and we will go to bed and say no more about it? But if you refuse to do this for me I will be very, very disappointed in your service as a maid and we might as well throw your uniform away. Well, what is it to be?'

I stared at the dildo, trying to imagine how it would feel buried in my anus, and I knew it would be awful, but would it be as bad as upsetting all our future games by refusing?

I almost imperceptibly nodded my head, but that wasn't good enough for this strictest of mistresses. 'Is that a yes, miss?' she questioned me.

'Yes!' I almost shouted.

She slapped me hard across the bum and the resulting jerk pulled at my nipples and stretched my lips. I instantly regretted my outburst and lay over the chair without moving a hair waiting for her to start.

Becky squirted something ice cold on to the ring of my anus and again I jumped, unable to stop myself. I shuddered uncontrollably and the goose pimples popped out all over my body. But then the cold gave way to her warm sensual massaging of my whole bottom. The cream or whatever it was had spread across my cheeks and trickled down the crease, sending a delicious shiver through me. My anus relaxed a little as Becky ran her creamy hand over and round my whole bottom, but it was just a trick.

As soon as I responded to her caresses my sphincter obviously softened, so she slipped just the tip of her finger in and then removed it, carrying out this procedure over and over again until I couldn't stop myself from responding. Every time she moved it away I pushed my buttocks as much as I could upwards, but then she would explore the rim again, not giving in to my gyrations. After a few minutes of this I really did want more and I groaned out my willingness to experiment further. She obliged by inserting the tip of her finger and not removing it, and I again panicked and tried to pull in my muscles even tighter, and it wasn't until I started wriggling against it that she took it away.

It was a sexual game of cat and mouse we played, with her tormenting me until I wanted more and then refusing me.

'We just need to help my entrance a little,' she crooned as if she were talking about anything but invading that devastating place. She showed me what she intended to do and I gulped with horror. She was holding a large tube of cold cream and unscrewing the top as she left my vision and returned to her position behind my spread cheeks. 'This should help.'

Again she pushed the tip of her finger in and I clenched my internal muscles to inhibit her progress.

'Relax, honey. All you have to do is trust me and relax those tight little muscles and you will love it, I promise. Come on, do it for me. Push out as if you're trying to get my finger out. Do it, Cassandra. Do it now and I promise I will make you feel good,' she bribed as she continued the soft caresses down the channel of my bum, swirling her fingers deliciously just inside the tender dip.

I decided that I might as well get it over with so I did as she asked and pushed outwards. Her slippery finger slid out and was replaced by what proved to be the end of a tube. I squeezed my sphincter muscles sharply but it was too late: I felt the coolness of the cream squirt deep inside my hot anus, slowly filling me until I felt as if I would burst.

'Oh ... Oh ... Oh no, Becky, no more. I can't take any more or it's all going to come squirting out. Please stop. Please.' I was howling my distress, but that only seemed to spur her on. She kept squeezing the tube until I heard the horrible toilet noise that tubes make when they are empty. My stomach felt bloated and crampy but the pressure must have been pushing on one of my arousal organs because the sensation was very erotic. The noise of the tube reminded me of what could happen to me at any moment and I clenched even harder, increasing the pressure and the cramping sensation.

Then the need to expel it gripped my abdomen and again I wailed.

'Becky, stop! Please stop or I'm going to make a mess all over the carpet. I'm begging you, Becky. *Stop!*'

Becky walked around the chair, bent down until she was level with my face and whispered, 'Then drop the bell, sweetheart. All you have to do is drop the bell and all of this will stop.' The only problem was that while she crooned her powerful words her hands were titillating my breasts, pulling them until the chains tugged in a most seductive way, taking my mind completely from my other end.

She picked up the dildo from the floor in front of me and I nearly choked; I wasn't ready for that yet.

Again I clenched my buttocks tight but her finger and the cream she had filled me with must have paved the way, so to speak. Before I knew it the bulbous end was pushing relentlessly against my hole and the slipperiness created by the cream was assisting its entrance against my will.

I was far too scared to relax. Scared of having that monstrosity inside me but even more scared of what would happen to all the cream she had pumped in me. Would it explode all over everything?

But I liked it when Becky persuaded me to accept her will. And she did. She crooned the same mantra that had worked for her finger and of course it worked again. I like pleasing her!

As I relaxed she pushed inwards and slowly I felt the enormous rubber cock fill my bottom.

I panted and tried to shrink my insides away from the tight gripping fear that filled me. My abdomen went into spasm and contracted around the intruder, but it stayed fast. I couldn't get away from it. I tried to pull away but the clamps and clips held me fast and I wasn't about to risk ripping them off. The thing she had forced in me felt like a tree trunk and I could feel the tears prick my eyes as I swallowed hard, trying not to cry. I did so want to please my lady.

For a minute or two I was aware only of the invasion that threatened to take control of me and the all-consuming need to go to the toilet, but gradually I heard Becky's voice come through the haze.

'Oh, my darling, you've done it. There's a clever girl. I knew you could do it for me. I wish you could see how horny you look bent over there with your bum stuffed full of rubber and all that white frothy cream oozing out around the black rubber and trickling down your thighs. One of theses days I'll get a strap-on dildo, and I will fuck you in your beautiful virgin arse with it so hard you'll never want a man again.'

At that she leaned on the dildo and pushed against me, forcing it deeper still. I cried out with the intensity of the feeling but realised that it wasn't quite pain any more. It was just the most intense experience ever and I warmed to it. Once it was in as far as it could go the fear left me. I tried to go with the feeling – and it worked.

When I automatically tried to shut my bottom the held-open sensation sent waves of sweet humiliation washing over me at the realisation that I was stuck in an open position.

Becky was stroking my back and thighs and still crooning to me, telling me how fabulous I was and how rude I looked. I am not sure which compliment I enjoyed the more.

Once Becky was convinced that I liked what was happening to me she dropped the bombshell. For some reason I had forgotten about the punishment being ten of something, so when she explained that she intended to drip ten drops of wax on to my forced-open bottom I forgot our pact and I shouted at her, 'No, you can't. You really can't, Becky. I don't care if I displease you, I can't let you do that to me.'

I was genuinely scared now and frustrated that I couldn't get up. It is not easy to conduct a convincing argument when you are staked out so thoroughly with a large dildo churning up your insides. I continued pleading with Becky to let me go but I couldn't persuade myself to relinquish the bell.

'I need to take our relationship one step further, Cassie. I want to control you completely. You know that when I take you past your limits you actually get even hornier. You like pain. You orgasmed when Mr King used wax on you and that was on your clitoris, for God's sake.'

While she talked she played with my stretched lips and scooped up the dribbling mix of my juices and cream, then worked them into my anus around my packed hole.

I still kept protesting but in a quieter tone and in a less convincing way. She read me well and kept up the secondary arousal. When she slipped her finger into my sex to run alongside the plug in my anus and gently rubbed, my complaints tapered to nothing. Her other hand slipped between my thighs, too, and stroked my burgeoning clitoris. I hadn't realised just how much it had been screaming for attention. It throbbed and danced, pulling on the clips that held my most sensitive, vulnerable places wide open.

'Oh, you are a very dirty girl, Cassandra. You're dripping all over my hands and I can see your sphincter contracting around that cock stuffed in your arse. What'll happen when I take it out, I wonder?' She knew that any hint of my making a mess would fill me with the terrifying humiliation that for some totally unknown reason horrified me but took me up to the next step on the arousal ladder. That delicious state where pain becomes pleasure and humiliation floods over my nerve endings like a river of hot syrup.

'I'm going to do it now, Cassandra, my horny little bum slut.' And she took up the candle from the table and the acrid smell of the wax burning seared my nostrils and enflamed my fear. The first drips were exquisite torture. They dripped on to my spread cheeks and scorched the skin for a very brief moment, sending my arousal to a new level. I sucked in breath through my clenched teeth and the drips moved closer to my tender groove, stretched open to its limit.

One or two missed their mark and dropped on to my sex and the pain zipped down my thighs as I tried to close my legs to get away from the burning heat.

I am sure Becky lost count. I know I did. After twenty, I didn't bother trying: I just rode the sweet pain and let it sweep through my whole body. Each drip still caused the roots of my hair to prickle and my anus desperately to attempt a retreat, but it was impossible. My submission was taking over.

I felt the dildo being moved in and out and that took my mind off the wax as it continued to drip relentlessly, but my arousal was still at such a level that I didn't want to lose the dildo – I was enjoying being fucked by proxy. I rode up and down on the cock, ignoring the tugging at my lips and nipples, and craved the next drip of wax.

'More, Becky,' I screamed. 'Give me more.'

She let go then and fucked me deeply with the rod, pounding my hole until I could feel it rasping against the tight entrance. On each up stroke she dripped one solitary drop of hot wax on to the stretched ring that held the dildo and then pushed it in hard again. I was yelling at her by then to make me come. The combination of the clips, clamps, chains and dildo all grew in my belly and consumed the burning wax until all the sensations joined forces to crash through my senses and force a monumental gripping eruption to rip me apart, racking my body with spasms of relief.

When I had started to come down, Becky very gently released my nipples and lips. Now the hunger had gone, the pain, as the blood flooded back into the squashed flesh, was excruciating, but, as soon as she took the ropes from my limbs, I collapsed on the floor, squeezing hard on to the dildo, scared of the mess that was inevitable. Becky helped me up and I waddled to the loo with my knees clamped hard together and my hand firmly holding the dildo in place. I was totally drained but as I left the room Becky shouted, 'Next time we'll do it on the commode chair and I'll take the dildo out.'

A delicious shiver of terror washed over me.

'I can't believe we just did that,' I said as I snuggled afterwards in her arms. I was beginning to be confused and a little scared by my need to be abused and punished. The hunger for more and harder punishments grew in intensity almost daily. I tried repeatedly to analyse why it was exciting for me to be forced into painful and humiliating games.

'Does it matter? I don't really hurt you,' Becky said. 'The most I might do is leave a red mark for an hour or two on your fleshy bits. You'd get worse than that if you went mountain biking or played football. Don't try to put everything you feel into little boxes and then you'll just be able to enjoy it. Anyway, maid, it's about time you showed your mistress just how sorry you are for spilling the gravy and making me forget how to count.'

I chuckled, my concerns pushed again to the back of my mind as I wriggled down in her arms until my head was between her knees. I couldn't believe that after all that exercise my lovely Becky still had on her very horny nurse's uniform and she still looked immaculate with not a hair out of place, and even her red lipstick was only slightly smudged from dinner.

There was I with rope marks around my wrists and ankles, a very tender bum covered in hard, cold wax that dragged at the tiny hairs around my anus, and thighs that were covered in a mixture of love juice and cold wax and cream. I knew I looked totally ravaged as Becky took my face between her hands, gazed into my eyes tenderly and groaned, 'God, we're disgusting, aren't we?'

'Mmm,' I replied, my mouth already working its way up her stockinged thighs to find the soft warm flesh that slightly bulged over the welt at the top and led to that most fragrant place imaginable: my lover's sex.

Her hands still cupped my head and she gently pushed my face into her crotch. As I sucked at the wet silk covering her mound she whimpered and leaned back against the chair behind her, relaxed and purring. I drew her knickers off and pushed her thighs apart. The petals of her pussy opened, soft and glistening with moisture. The tiny pink bud of her clitoris peeped tentatively from the folds that protected it, proud and erect.

I devoured her with my eyes, my hands and my mouth, teasing and arousing her, sliding my tongue into her depths, then slurping on her hard clitoris until she wriggled desperately under my attentions. Her pink interior was like a beacon drawing me in, titillating my senses and starting a heavy pulsating deep within my belly.

I experienced an overwhelming emotion akin to adoration then. I wanted nothing more than to worship this amazing woman who had taken me beyond my limits. She had shown me that it is OK to have the submissive craving that had been a part of my life for so long. It was OK for me to want pain and humiliation – after all, it was just a game we played.

I pushed my face as deeply as I could into her sex and drank of her juices, thanking her for my punishment and breathing her heady smell, revelling in her beauty. Her thighs clasped my head in a vice until I thought I would drown in her depths, but I didn't care: I was entranced by her body and its smells. I blew cool air on her wetness, then opened my mouth until it all but covered her whole sex and lowered its burning heat down into place. Becky's body arched up to meet me, urgent and needy, her throat emitting an earthy moan. I grazed my teeth softly across her clit, nipped the fleshy outer lips, then ran my tongue from her clit to the crease of her bum.

My need surged through me as urgent as hers did then. I wanted to devour her completely. I pulled her flat on the floor and pushed her legs up until her tight pink anus was available to me so I could get at that too. And devour her I did, forcing my tongue into her bum, then fucking her hard with it until she could stand it no longer. I was caught up in a sort of frenzy, still linked to my worship of her and my humiliation, creating a need in me to engulf her completely. I kept up a constant barrage of feelings in her sex and her anus and on her clitoris, sucking, biting, fucking and adoring her.

Her orgasm when it came filled my mouth with throbbing swollen flesh that quivered and wept.

14

It was a Friday morning that his letter arrived and our world was turned upside down. We had been together three months exactly and our lives blended together perfectly.

Cassandra

It has been three months now since we met.

During your first visit I attempted to show you that your sexual destiny is to be submissive. You learned that lesson well and left here with, I believe, a clearer understanding of your needs, and an acceptance of your hunger to obey.

On my visit to you, I attempted to show you that I will always be in complete control. Hopefully this has also showed you just how you crave that control.

You have had sufficient time now to reflect on your first and second lesson, and should be sufficiently prepared for lesson three.

I intend to teach you that it is your lot in life as a submissive to experience anything that your controlling dominant wishes you to experience. I would not presume to call myself your Master, but I do believe that I am qualified to explore your submission further with a view to that position being reached in the future.

Send the usual postcard and I will in turn send your instructions.

Submit to me, Cassandra.

Mr King

The letter changed all our plans. I opened it and read it in silence, my wicked thoughts racing ahead. It wasn't until I realised that Becky had stopped what she was doing and was watching me like a hawk that I dragged my eyes away from it, my heart hammering in my chest, my blood pounding in my ears.

'It's from him, isn't it?' Becky questioned, a flicker of hurt in her voice.

'Yes, but it's rubbish. You know I'm not interested in him any more. What more could I ask for?' I argued feebly. 'I have the most beautiful sensual lover in the world. She's my best friend and best of all she shares my fantasies and my love of sexy games.'

'Let me look, Cassie.'

Like me she read it in silence. I was terrified that it would change things but I knew that there was a part of me – the part that loves sexual danger, the part that took me to him before – that was already trying to remember whether I had kept the pack of postcards.

'So, what do you think?' I asked her as casually as I could when she placed the letter on the table between us.

But then she picked it up again and read it out loud, slowly and with purpose, pausing at the end of every sentence to monitor my reaction. She looked into my eyes, memorising each line before looking up at me to speak it.

There was no way I could control my arousal, so, by the time she had got to the sentence about experiencing anything my controlling dominant chose for me to experience, I knew I had blown it. My nostrils were flaring, my pupils dilated and my breathing left a lot to be desired.

The way that Becky was reading it excited me greatly but I knew deep down that the real desperation I felt came from the unknown. How could I ever feel that with Becky, that forbidden delicious shiver eating away at my insides? That feeling instigated by the prospect of being at the mercy of an unknown person? It was impossible.

'Do you love me, Cassie?'

'Of course I do. Why? What's that got to do with anything?'

'Well, I love you too and I love our games. I'm not the sort of lover who feels the need to keep you to myself. Perhaps it would be horny to share you for a night. After all, it worked with Greg, didn't it? And ... if I were to tell you the truth I'd have to admit that one of the most horny experiences of my life was to listen to you recount your adventures at the hands of Mr King to me. Sharing all that with you and knowing that I was going to have you later was mind-blowing. All the time you were telling me I could feel the juices oozing through my knickers to soak into the car seat. It was so horrifying but delicious that I was hypnotised by your spell. It was then that I fell in love with you. Up until then I'd fancied you like mad but that really did it for me.'

'What are you saying? Do you want me to go to him?'

'If you put it cold-bloodedly like that, no, I don't, but if we turned it round then I think it could be a very, very exciting game for us. But only if we're sure that it won't change us.'

I was a little apprehensive that she was tricking me into admitting that I wanted to see Mr King again, so I trod carefully for a while, letting her make all the suggestions.

'Mmm?' I questioned noncommittally.

'Well, what if we incorporate it into one of our games?' As she spoke I could see that her brain was already making plans and that the plans were definitely arousing her. I could see her erect nipples poking through her thin white T-shirt. 'If I agreed and approved, would you want to go?' She looked at me then, and with a wicked glint in her eye she added purposefully, 'Would you do it for me, Cassandra?'

I bent across the table and grabbed her face in my hands and plonked a kiss on her nose. 'You are priceless, Becky. Yes, yes, yes, I'd go like a shot.'

'Right, you'd better get the postcards, hadn't you? Then we can get this reply in the post before we change our minds.'

Fat chance of that, I thought to myself as I pulled out the drawer to search. While I was rummaging through the papers that spilled out, I asked Becky how we were going to incorporate it into one of our games. She amazed me with her answer. In just three short months she completely understood my complex sexuality.

'Never you mind. This is my game and you know how you love to be kept in suspense. Anyway, you're supposed to be the submissive. Remember the lesson you learned with Mr King: you're submissive and your lot in life is to experience anything your dominant wants you to experience,' she recited with a chuckle in her voice. 'Whatever games we let Mr King play with us, I call all the shots. You won't need to know what the arrangements are because I will make all the plans; you just make the appointment. Enjoy the anticipation, Cassie, it's what you do best.'

Mr King must have enjoyed the last time as much as I did because he was just a little impatient. We received the card with the instructions after only four days and the date was set for a week after that. I was so glad because I didn't think I could wait much more. Becky refused even to talk about her plans and I was left to imagine all sorts of diabolical deeds. I was in a constant state of arousal and naturally Becky took full advantage of it. Practically every time she passed me she would grab my crotch through my jeans or slip an unexpected hand up my skirt to test for 'the dirty-girl syndrome', as she called it. I just called it horny.

Becky had to go away on a nursing course for a few days that week and I'm not sure which was worse, her constant teasing when she was at home or her absence.

'Have you been thinking about our new adventure, Cassie?' she asked when she got back. 'I haven't been able to think of anything else. I know to begin with we were a bit worried that your seeing Mr King again might affect our relationship, but I'm convinced now that this will just enhance our love of experimenting with new ideas.'

'What made you change your mind, then?' I queried. But she was very noncommittal, just adding that she had done a lot of thinking while she had been away. I knew she must have been thinking about our games because she was positively rampant and, I found later, feeling very pervy.

'You're obviously going to explode if you have to wait as long as last time for your instructions from Mr King. How would you like to play a little game while we wait?' she cajoled as we faced each other across the kitchen table. She had just shocked me by asking if there was anything that was taboo for my visit to Mr King. I knew she was scheming and she knew I was as horny as hell. I guessed immediately there was a catch. Her voice had taken on an almost syrupy note and I shivered with fear and expectation of the game to come.

I answered yes on the first count – I would like to play a game – and no on the second count: luckily, I hadn't grown up with any baggage and as far as I was concerned nothing was taboo, not now I was anally friendly, anyway. I had decided long ago that, the more deviant or rude the game was, the more it excited me. I had developed a voracious appetite: the more bizarre the games the better.

As soon as she had asked the question I searched my brain to think of what depraved idea she had in mind. The casualness of her question didn't fool me for a second. I knew she had a specific act in mind and was covering herself. If I had known the extent of her perversity, would I have still agreed to the game that day, or to the game with Mr King?

I expect I would have done, I thought to myself.

It was obviously the answer she was waiting for and probably just the right time for her to ask the question – when I was champing at the bit and desperate for attention.

'Go and wait for me in the playroom, Cassandra. I'll be up in ten minutes and I want you to think about what's going to happen to you while you wait. Decide before we start if you really are prepared to experience anything that your dominant wants you to experience.'

I climbed the stairs to the attic with my chest pounding. I had a feeling that this game would really test my submission.

As I knelt on the floor in the middle of the room with my naked knees spread apart and my hands on my head, I knew a perfect moment of acceptance. This was what I wanted for ever; I wasn't playing at being submissive; this was no longer a game. This was my reality.

My thoughts ran away with me as the helpless feelings swamped me and it felt like only seconds later that Becky walked into the room and again took my breath away. She was dressed exquisitely in a rubber corset that cupped her breasts and buckled down the front to her hips. The corset had six wide suspenders dropping from it on to her gorgeous thighs, clasping her shiny deep black stockings, which shimmered in the light from the candles. I groaned as I looked at her legs. I could see only about three or four inches of stocking because she towered over me in the most amazing pair of black leather thigh boots I had ever seen. Mind you, the fact that they were on Becky helped. Again she had captured my fantasies. A veritable Amazon of power, she strutted about pretending to be busy but was just showing off her fantastic body. So dominant but alluring as she stood in front of me with her legs spread apart to reveal her lacy G-string exactly on a level with my eyes. I could smell her musk and longed to touch her but knew it was against the rules.

'Are you ready, Cassandra?'

My adoration of her overwhelmed me then and I dropped forward to hug her thighs. I buried my head in her smell but she pushed me away and, in a very stern playroom sort of voice, she ordered me to get up and sit on the edge of the bondage bed.

She went to the cupboard that filled me with dread – I wasn't allowed to look in it – and carefully picked out numerous items. She had a definite agenda in mind as she piled her selection in a heap and brought them over to the bed.

The items she brought shocked even my new-found sexuality. Becky laid them out on the bondage bed in all their gleaming black, aromatic, sensuous glory. The first piece I picked up seemed like a strange shape to begin with. I thought it was a pair of knickers or something like that, but Becky chuckled and, taking them from me, turned them up the other way. She pushed a clenched fist up into the shiny rubber shape like a puppet and a definite face took shape. It was a hood, and the image of it and the thought of wearing it created heat pulses deep in my crotch, but I was also terrified.

My hands were shaking as I took it back and Becky

watched as I turned it over and over in my hands, bringing it up to smell its heady scent, and she smiled to herself. The front of the hood, even though its face shape was obvious, had no holes for eyes or nose and instead of a mouth hole there was a tube sticking out about two inches long. I tried again to imagine how it would feel to wear it and the nearest guess I could conjure was the harness I had worn for Mr King.

I put the tube to my lips and, gripping it with my teeth, breathed through it deeply. It was surprisingly easy.

Next she picked up what I thought was a sheet, until she shook it out and I saw the body shape. The garment she held was like a bag of rubber with a zip from bottom to top. The top ended in a collar shape with a locking padlock. I tried to imagine how it would feel to be trussed up in that bag like a cocoon, but could liken it to nothing I had ever experienced, so the adventurer in me was aroused. The side of me that braved all to go to Mr King to explore my sexuality now prowled again in my veins.

'I decided it was time to initiate you into the depths of my secret fantasies, Cassie, now you've shared yours with me. I've loved rubber ever since I had a rubber sheet on my bed as a child. I probably wet my bed long after I needed to just to keep the rubber sheet that had become part of my dreams. I only hope you take to my fantasy as completely as I took to yours.'

Before I had a chance to examine the other items on the bed, my beautiful lover took my hands and stood me up. I stood totally naked before her trembling at what was to come. But by that stage I wanted to experience every sexual act known to man – or should I say woman?

'Put this on for me, baby,' she cajoled as she held the mouth tube up to my face. 'It won't be so scary for you if you do it yourself. Once it's on I'll help you adjust it until it's comfortable. I really want you to wear this, Cassandra. I want to see your whole body clothed in slinky rubber and under my control, for my pleasure. That includes your limbs, your whole body from top to toe, your sight, sound and genitals. The catsuit we bought you is beautiful but this is the ultimate rubber bondage.'

It was the use of my full name, Cassandra, and her plea of 'put this on for me, baby', plus the huskiness of her voice that clinched it. All the ingredients swam through my senses until I felt powerless to resist.

I took the hood in my hands and gripped the back as I placed the tube in my mouth and breathed a few times to get used to it. Becky's hands stroked my breasts the whole time and her murmured endearments spurred me on. 'Come on, honey, you can do it. I know you can. You'll look so beautiful. Please, baby, do it for me.'

I took a deep breath, gritted my teeth and tugged it over my head, pulling it down until my whole head was encased. I hyperventilated for a moment or two but Becky helped me struggle with it, continuing her whispered endearments. Gradually my nerves calmed and I cautiously felt the hood; its almost skinlike quality was already warm from my body heat. My mane of hair held tightly in place by the hood cascaded out of the lower opening and fell soft on my back.

I felt Becky's hands caress my head encased in its bondage and gasp as she looked at me. I felt beautiful and surprisingly serene in the knowledge that I was a siren to her fantasy.

Becky leaned close to my hooded ear and asked if I was ready for the rest, and I nodded my consent.

I felt Becky's attempt to pick up my left foot and I lifted it to oblige her. She slipped something cool and slinky on to my foot and then did the same with the other foot, and, as she raised the garment up, I realised I was now wearing a pair of rubber knickers. They were tight and clung to my thighs on the way up but Becky persevered and I helped the best I could by writhing. I had become very good at writhing lately.

Eventually, between us we managed to get this unforgiving item to the tops of my thighs and I knew by then they would be tight. I liked that idea. Before pulling the pants up to my waist I felt Becky fumbling around in the gap between the waistband of the rubber knickers and my very damp crotch.

'Ooh, who's a dirty little girl, then?' she teased as she felt my arousal and slipped what felt like a slim dildo into my sopping pussy. I clutched gratefully on to this piece of stimulation and wriggled about to gain the best position, but before I could really enjoy it Becky slipped it out again and laughed at my frustration. 'Sorry, love, I only wanted the lubrication. Now bend over for me and touch your toes, please.'

My stomach somersaulted at the knowledge of what she planned to do but of course I obeyed her. She held apart the cheeks of my bottom unceremoniously and slipped the dildo into my anus surprisingly easily. I grunted into the tube clenched between my teeth and felt the cold dribble from the end drip for the first time. Why was that more humiliating than what Becky was doing to my very vulnerable rear end? I wondered.

'You might as well stay where you are for the next bit,' she added, and, without a pause to allow me to accommodate the existing intrusion, I felt another invasion into my already hot pussy. I was completely stuffed. The sensation of both my orifices being stuffed full at the same time was exquisite. I clenched and released my muscles to appreciate fully how completely packed I was. I could feel the complete hole that was my vagina and a sweet pressure pushing into the walls of my very full anus. I can't describe fully how that felt. It was as if my lower half were in bondage, but internally. That portion of my anatomy no longer belonged to me. It was Becky's, it was full, and she controlled it.

The sensation in my bum felt different, not as if it were full but as if it were held open, leaving my insides exposed to the elements. As soon as that image crossed my thoughts I was petrified at the fears that that conjured up. I was terrified that I would be unable to hold my waste. I immediately felt a cool sensation deep within me. I collapsed on to the floor, mumbling, trying hard to express to Becky how cruel it was to leave me open like that, but of course I couldn't speak or even mumble coherently because of the hood and the tube holding my mouth conveniently open and helpless. Perhaps I was imagining it, perhaps it was a dildo and the lubrication from my sex or my uncontrollable arousal made it feel like a tube, but I couldn't convince myself.

She sat next to me on the floor and cradled me in her arms breathing soft words in my ear as she calmed me down ready to accept the next stage of her diabolical bondage. I tried desperately to loosen my arms from her embrace to feel what she had put inside me but she would not allow it. She held my hands tightly and whispered, 'Oh, no you don't. The not knowing is what makes the game so exquisite for you, isn't it, Cassandra?'

She drew me to my feet again and tugged the pants up to my waist, holding in place the plugs that tormented me so deliciously. My hands were held one at a time as firm leather cuffs were buckled on to my wrists and then pulled behind me and caught together with a clasp of some sort. I was beginning to feel completely captive.

Next, as I stood in front of her helpless and horny as hell, Becky flicked and squeezed my nipples, pulling them and tugging at them until I tried to pull away from the onslaught, but she just waited until I relaxed and then flicked some more. The aim was obviously to get me highly excited for the next bit and to tenderise my poor nipples and, as usual, my breasts betrayed me and responded on cue.

I snorted my need into the tight rubber hood as my treacherous secretions flooded around the dildo that was held tight in my body by the rubber knickers. My anus spasmed around its intruder and contracted rhythmically. In fact most of the rubber in contact with my treacherous body was already slick with my secretions.

Eventually, Becky was happy with the turgid state of my now tender nipples and, leaning me over, attached soft leather straps around my dangling breasts so when I stood up they jutted out proudly, thrusting forward, the nipples already aching for more attention. I moved forward so my breasts contacted with Becky's body and I rubbed the very sensitive, tightly strapped mounds against her, shamelessly begging for more, but Becky moved away and tutted at me.

'Come, now, Cassandra. You know better than that, don't you? I decide when and what part of your anatomy gets the pleasure, don't I?'

I groaned loudly but Becky took no notice.

Next she moved me closer to the bondage bed and helped me up so I could sit on it. I felt her manoeuvre my feet into what I assumed was the bag, but then I thought I was wrong as she buckled straps around my ankles. After clipping my feet together, allowing only an inch or two of movement, she buckled another strap around my knees and stood me up again to put another around the tops of my thighs. I could still move around a little, just enough to fidget and wriggle, so I could feel the dildos move and rub against each other deep in my belly.

Then the most exquisite experience of all: I felt the

coolness of the rubber bag slither and slide up over my burning aroused body and turn to liquid heat as it settled on me.

The musky smell of the rubber already filling my nostrils heightened as the bag was drawn up, over my breasts, capturing my bound arms and my shoulders until it closed snugly around me. By this time the mixed smells of the hot rubber and my desire were a heady aphrodisiac and I thought I would explode.

Becky oh so slowly zipped it up, tormenting me on the way. I felt first my legs, then my hips being drawn in and tightened as the zip was pulled upwards towards my thrusting breasts. I felt the firmness of the rubber skin squeeze my thighs on to the twin plugs of rubber that filled me and squished inside the already very sweaty pants. It moved upwards and captured my breasts. Before Becky finally drew the zip to the top, she again squeezed my nipples, eliciting another drawn-out groan from my throat. My breasts felt enormous and my nipples huge as she pushed and tugged to get them safely encased in their rubber coating.

Then, just as the zip finally made it to the top, I shuddered as a stream of ice-cold dribble trickled from the tube clenched between my teeth to the deep channel between my rock-hard breasts. I cringed with shame at the embarrassing liquids that my traitorous body managed to produce when I was aroused.

I felt slightly unsteady as I stood there trying to imagine how I looked. I could feel Becky's hands shimmering over my tightly enclosed flesh, from my ankles up to my neck. Over and over again she stroked and caressed me through the now warm rubber until I was panting and whimpering through the tight hood, sure I would fall over if she didn't stop soon. I came so dangerously close to orgasm as she raked her nails across my rubber-clad nipples that I stumbled. Becky steadied me and stopped tormenting me, which helped my composure but sent me crazy for her touch again.

When she was obviously satisfied that I was screaming for more and every nerve in my poor trapped body was jangling with arousal, she arranged the bottom of my hood so it lay smoothly against my neck. Then my sweet tormentor buckled the top of the bag around the outside, then, grasping my head, moved it backwards and forwards to check I had plenty of movement.

I began to cool down a little and found myself briefly wondering how she would get to my sexy places now that she had trussed me up so sublimely. I needn't have worried: she had no intention of getting to me at all.

Very carefully, Becky guided me backwards until I was leaning against the bondage bed, then hoisted me up until I was perched on the edge. She lifted my feet and swung them around, laying me carefully backwards. It was a little scary at first, so, as before, Becky held me and stroked me while she whispered how horny I looked and how aroused she was just looking at me and touching me through my rubber cocoon.

She tormented me cruelly by explaining in perfect detail how wet her crotch was and how she was going to have to masturbate if she wasn't careful. I got really frustrated then and shouted at her the best I could and thrashed about a bit to show my disapproval, but it all fell on deaf ears. The best I could manage was an animal grunt and very, very slight movement, probably indistinguishable from a 'please touch me' type of wriggle to my wicked captor.

I felt Becky lean over me then and I wriggled to show that I wanted her to touch me, but she just said, 'I'm going to leave you now, Cassandra. I'm going to leave you for one hour. You won't know if I'm in the room or not. Sometimes I'll be sitting here watching and enjoying you struggle and sometimes I won't. I'm hoping I've given you enough stimulation to keep you on the boil. What with your tender bound breasts and your naughty, greedy holes packed to the full you might even be able to bring yourself to orgasm. I'll probably help you along once or twice just to keep you on the boil and I might even give you the option of release; but if you want out before the hour's up you don't get my attentions at the end, so the choice is ultimately yours.'

She completed my torment by strapping me on to the bed in two places, across my hips and my chest, which I must admit did make me feel a little safer, and then I heard her move away and listened intently for movement. For some reason I desperately wanted to know if she stayed in the room but, however hard I strained my ears, the hood just about kept me in the dark, so to speak. For a few minutes I just lay there unsure of myself. I was so completely helpless. Even when I had been at Mr King's mercy, I hadn't felt this intense sense of deprivation.

An indescribable rush of love for Becky filled my thoughts for a minute or two, but I'm not sure why. Of course I did love her, but this overwhelming feeling was all tied up in the fact that she held the strings and, until she chose different, I was hers to do with as she liked. Although that thought scared the hell out of me I also felt such a wave of pleasure wash over me that I clenched my thighs tightly together to grasp as much stimulation as I could. The only problem with that was that each time I gripped my thighs together it started a chain reaction. First the rush of pleasure would engulf me but no sooner had my arousal started to escalate than I could feel the gaping hole that was my bottom. I was so petrified that I was going to lose control that a new torment took me over. The fear of messing myself counteracted any pleasure I had previously felt and humiliation engulfed me, but that in itself was exquisite torture.

Within what seemed like hours, but was probably only a few minutes, I was a wreck. I worked my breasts against the slippery inner of the rubber to gain a little friction and rubbed my thighs as effectively I could to push the dildos deeper into my orifices, but that only served to arouse me further. That in turn again set off that despicable chain reaction and I found myself wondering whether I would even *know* if I had lost control.

I knew from other times that humiliation excited me; I just wasn't sure why. When I am not aroused I have no desire whatsoever to be humiliated and I avoid it at all costs, but if it is forced upon me then I immediately take on another persona.

It's as if something inside me relaxes, allowing me to accept my fate and enjoy it. It gives me the permission I need to defy convention and feel however I want to feel.

This unique variety of emotions filled my head as I writhed on the bed and I became totally absorbed by my own thoughts. The tight rubber case I was encapsulated in became sweaty and slick as I became more needy. I tried to imagine what Becky would do to make me come when my hour was up but then another unbidden thought filled my head. What if she was teasing and when my hour was up she made me wait longer for my release? What if she kept me like this for ever?

Just as the new panic welled up in my throat I heard a sound next to the bed and kept as still as I could to try to distinguish what had made it. The panic fled instantly. My excitement at the thought that I was going to at last get some direct stimulation distorted my breathing until I could hear nothing but my own sounds in my head, so when I felt Becky touch me I jumped. My wicked captor unbuckled the straps that held me and, turning me on my side, strapped me fast again.

When I was lying in this new position, my breasts heaving with tension and my thighs clutching at the orgasm that was still way beyond my reach, Becky slapped my bottom. I felt the jolt of the dildo as it buried itself deeper inside me and the breath whooshed from my lungs with surprise. It was not at all what I had been expecting but the sharp sensation woke me up and again all my pulses and erotic places twitched their response. Then she left me again.

This time I had no idea whether she stayed in the room because I was too busy trying to bring myself off. I tossed and turned, wriggled and struggled until the sweat pooled cool in the bottom of the bag where it wasn't in constant contact with my skin. It was useless. I calmed down again and dissected my thoughts.

I was so totally trussed up that if Becky chose to keep me there I would be able to do absolutely nothing. Would I enjoy it if she kept me prisoner for days? I thought so. But then a moment later I knew that, if she didn't come in soon and put me out of my misery, I would indeed go crazy.

Long, long minutes later I felt her hands on me again. She opened the buckle and the top few inches of the zip and squirmed her hand down inside my steamy bag to slide her palm over my straining breasts. Again my arousal leaped at this tiny offering and I moaned my response. I hoped that this time she would take pity on me and make me come, but my inner clock lied to me and once more, after arousing me to fever pitch, she just zipped me up and left.

My mind drifted this time. I thought of other games we had played and those thoughts alone kept me at boiling point until I felt Becky lean over me and put her arm around my restrained body.

'You look so amazing, Cassandra,' she purred. 'You are all mine – all black and shiny and smooth. There isn't one single inch of you that isn't under my control.' Then I felt her lean nearer as she added, 'Even your bowels.'

My stomach contracted as I clenched my internal muscles, trying to keep any unwanted emissions where they should be, but that just caused my other parts to pound rapidly in response. I was a lost cause. I mumbled and groaned, hoping she would know I was begging her to allow me relief before my body let me down, but she took no notice.

Becky again released my straps and turned me on to my back, then introduced me to the joys of double-ended zips. I felt cool air on my lower regions as she unzipped me from the bottom and then her hand wriggled its way between my clamped-shut thighs and just about managed to touch my sex. I didn't need more than that.

I slithered against her hand like a snake trying to gain purchase of anything that would take me further on my journey, and she finally responded by pressing the heel of her hand against my mound, which in turn pushed the dildos slightly deeper.

I groaned again and ground my hips forward to press against her and so relieve the pressure building up inside me. I was gasping hard through the tube and the sweat was running into my eyes as Becky returned the pressure. She forced the apex of my thighs as far apart as she could and pulled my clitoris hood free of its bondage, and then I knew I was nearly there as she slipped it back, uncovering the centre of my arousal. My exposed clitoris felt raw as it braved the outside world, and tried its hardest to retract when Becky ran a finger covered in my juices over its nerve endings, round and round mercilessly, until I was rolling about and thrusting my groin up to her hand.

I felt the tears well up in my eyes with frustration and mix with the sweat that filled my hood. I squeezed my eyes tight and concentrated as hard as I could – on the tube in my straining anus, the plug filling my spasming sex to bursting point, the straps around my aching breasts and the rubber teasing my straining nipples. I gripped the breathing tube with my teeth and let my body feel every swirl of Becky's slick fingertip as it resolutely pushed me to my limits.

'I want you to come now, Cassandra, but don't forget to clench your bottom – we don't want any accidents, do we?' Becky's words thundered through my brain and I gripped my bowel muscles as hard as I could, imagining my insides pouring out. The waves of humiliation and shame, spurred on by the constant manipulation of my clit, sparked the orgasm that ripped through me. I twitched and jerked until the spasms had ceased, my whole body throbbing around the dildo and my anus clenched tightly in fear.

15

Cassandra

I was pleased to hear that you are ready and I hope eager for your third lesson. This lesson will be a big step forward for you; I hope you are mentally prepared for it.

I will pick you up on Friday at 7 o'clock and take you to my place in the country. Please be waiting behind your front door, blindfolded and prepared. Don't bring anything. All that you need will be provided for you.

Mr King

We pored over the card at breakfast, trying to think of what he might have in mind. I can't remember ever being so excited but I think I say that quite often. Becky was a little quiet at first but as we talked it over I guessed that she was just as aroused by it all as I was.

'It does sound a little challenging, Cassie. Are you sure you want to go through with it? It's not too late to change your mind, you know. What if you get there and he starts doing something you hate? What will you do?'

'I don't want to shock you, Becky, but if he did try to persuade me into a situation that I wasn't comfortable with I know that just the fact that I wasn't comfortable with it would make it even more exhilarating. Even thinking about it now, I don't know how I'll wait until Friday. I'm so horny, Becky. The image of you knowing what I'm doing and getting off on it will be the icing on the cake.'

'We need to ring your office and tell them you're sick, or I'm going to have to ravish you,' Becky said. I quickly grabbed a piece of toast off the table and shouting that I would see her later, I left for work.

There is something very exciting about being a submissive woman in a powerful dominant job. As I parked my car in my space in the company car park I noticed Kevin, a young lad from the post room, watching my arrival. I played to the gallery and failed to pull my skirt down as I swung my legs out of my seat. I called him over but the poor thing trembled as he walked towards me.

I put on my sultry voice, looked him up and down, smoothed down my tight skirt and asked him if he would be kind enough to carry my briefcase and laptop up to my office for me.

'Yes, Ms Paige . . . er, right away, Ms Paige,' he stammered as he took the pile I handed him and preceded me to the building. As usual the outer office to mine was a hive of activity. The clerks rattled away on their keyboards and my own secretary grinned very knowingly at Kevin, my packhorse, and then looked questioningly at me.

'I know,' I said, shrugging, after he had put my things on the desk and grovelled out of the door. 'I just have to bait him. Let's face it, Amanda, he does rather ask for it, doesn't he?'

'Well, I think he's rather sweet. Don't you just want to mother him?' she asked.

As I walked into my office and sat at my desk, Amanda followed me in with the day's post, plonked it down in front of me and hovered.

I looked up at her, tearing my thoughts away from the image in my mind of Greg with his balls bashing

Becky's crotch and his hard prick driving its way into her and the difference between him and the post boy. I decided I had never wanted to mother anyone.

'Sorry, was there something else?'

'Mmm, your friend Becky rang just before you got here and asked if you could go straight home tonight because she has plans. She said you'd know what she meant.'

I blushed as I thanked her. She turned and glanced back for a second with raised eyebrows.

Just you mind your business, Amanda, I thought as I prepared for my first appointment. The rest of the day was spoiled already. I never could concentrate once a single rude thought entered my head. I knew I would be on tenterhooks now until I got home and she put me out of my misery.

When I got home that night, before I even said hello, Becky dominated the scene.

'Right. Up to the playroom,' she laughed before I even had a chance to take off my jacket.

We ran upstairs giggling and pushing each other until we stumbled through the door and Becky as usual took charge.

'I brought you a present. Let's see how you like it.'

She went to the Pandora's cupboard and took out a bundle of black leather. 'Take your knickers off, Cassie. I think you're going to like this.'

As I slipped my briefs off she came and stood closer to me and held up the toy for me to see. I was speechless.

'Come on, Cassandra. You'll get used to it, and it's only for three days.'

'What?' I exclaimed as I moved slightly away from her.

As usual I capitulated and she carefully buckled me

into the soft leather chastity belt. First there was a rather imposing-looking dildo, which she slid far too easily into my vagina; again my insatiable hunger for experience gave me away by lubricating me copiously.

As the soft bendable intruder settled itself inside me she arranged a spider's web of straps around my hips and waist. As with the last few pieces of a jigsaw puzzle, she interlocked them and drew them around me until they all came together in a hasp and padlock at the front of my torso. This she fastened with glee, letting out a sigh of pure, satisfied pleasure.

I reached down and explored my new garment and found to my dismay that, not only was the dildo locked inside me until she chose to let me go, but I couldn't get to my clitoris. I tried to wriggle my finger into the gaps around the edges but it was impossible. I tried pushing hard on to the leather that covered it but the sensation was so dulled that it wasn't worth the effort. There was a tiny oval slit that would allow me to pee but it was so small it was no help at all. The wide strap that held my plug in place ran down from my waist at the front, squashing my clitoris on the way, then split slightly in the little oval hole. Just behind the dildo held in my vagina it divided and encircled my cheeks to meet again at the waist strap.

'But what about now?' I wailed, secretly revelling in the feeling of being so captured.

'Patience, Cassandra. You'll have your chance on Friday. Until then I think it would be nice to keep you in a state of helpless excitement. Now come with me.'

She led me by the hand into the bedroom still in my suit and lay down on the bed with her thighs bare and inviting.

'I want you to pleasure me, Cassie. Lie between my legs and show me what a good little submissive you are. You're going to make love to me every day between now and Friday and that naughty pussy of yours is going to be so desperate by then you'll probably be begging for attention.'

But I am now, I thought.

I longed to refuse because I knew how hard it would be for me to take Becky to orgasm and have to remain frustrated myself, but the sight of her on the bed inviting me to help myself clinched the deal. I climbed between her legs and did the two things that I do best: obeyed her order and devoured her sex with my obedient and willing mouth. When Becky was writhing on the bed in the throes of coming I thought I would explode. I didn't know whether I could stand to wait until Friday.

Each morning she would release me long enough for me to shower, and then, without taking her eyes from me, she would replace the chastity belt. She actually made me go to work like that. For three days I sat on a dildo in a constant rage of need. The dildo became a part of me and my juices poured into my knickers continuously. If I had thought work was becoming merely difficult before that week, concentration was now totally impossible. Every time I tried to stem the flow it meant squeezing my muscles tight, and that just accentuated the effect of the plug inside me and aroused me further until I truly thought I would go mad.

I became paranoid that everyone was looking at me and noticing my aroused state and my continuously flushed face, but nobody said anything, so I just kept a low profile and stayed out of the office as much as possible.

Eventually Friday morning came and, as we had both taken the day off work, we lay in bed until lunchtime talking about the possibilities of what was going to happen that evening. All we did was succeed in making Becky horny enough to want another dose of my fingers and tongue and me to reach the stage where I was climbing the walls. She tantalised me further by constantly playing with my breasts, which always made me believe it would take me to orgasm but never quite did. She loved my desperation because it increased my dependency on her and probably convinced her that whatever happened while I was with Mr King would make no difference to us.

When we did finally get up we spent hours trying to decide what I would wear. We wanted to combine the need for me to look sexy to Becky, feel sexy myself and look appropriate for my date. Just as we reached despair and the bed was piled high with clothes, pervy and not, I remembered the corset I had bought in London. I hadn't had a chance to surprise Becky with it, so I suggested it as a possibility and Becky urged me to go and get it, obviously aroused by my description.

We agreed that it would be perfect and if I teamed it with the thigh boots that Becky had worn in the playroom the overall image would be just what was required.

At about five o'clock Becky said it was time she got me ready. I was thrilled that she was going to help me. I knew it would make the coming adventure even more exciting, if that were possible.

We went into the playroom, where Becky gently removed the chastity belt, leaving me with a gaping hole desperate to be refilled. My hand instinctively flew to my sex, but Becky slapped it away crossly and dragged me over to the bondage bed. She laid me back on it and told me to open my legs. I was grateful that at last I was to get my relief, but again Becky surprised me; she was doing that a lot at that stage.

She went to the bathroom, leaving me with instructions not to touch myself in her absence, and returned with a bowl of warm water, some soap and a razor. My stomach lurched crazily when I took in what she intended to do.

She spread my thighs and laid out a towel under my hips before lathering a great deal of warm soap over my dark pubic hair until it was soft and pliable. Then she started scraping away at the growth.

The massaging of her hands, the coolness of the soap and the scraping of the razor fuelled my desperate hunger, but I responded as little as possible, because I knew that Becky would stop if she thought I was going to come.

I couldn't help the occasional tiny whimper or shiver that ran down my spine when she pushed aside my clitoris or pulled my inner lips to one side to shave me smooth. But, when she slipped her wet slippery finger between my lips and touched my hard clitoris – accidentally, she assured me – I groaned out loud, all thoughts of the night ahead of me forgotten. I pushed my hips up to her wantonly, but she just pushed them down again and carried on with her task. It wasn't too frustrating until she was nearly finished and with every stroke of the razor she began smoothing her hand after it to see if she had missed anywhere.

There is something in my make-up that becomes increasingly turned on if the person I am playing a game with stays calm and unconcerned by my arousal, and that was what was happening here. Becky was treating the exercise as if she were peeling potatoes and her total disregard for my mounting frustration just sent me on an upward spiral until I was ready to push her away and relieve myself furiously.

I tried hard to control myself but remembered how my passion had increased at an alarming rate when Mr King treated me like an object, and that again multiplied my wanting.

Becky managed to stun me yet again with her next

instruction. 'OK, Cassandra, I'm finished here. Turn over on to your hands and knees for me.' I don't know why I was still so bum-shy but I turned over very reluctantly and breathed deeply as she carried out the same procedure on the crease of my bottom. My whole body ached for relief as she carried out her task of removing every stray hair from my anal area, even the soft fluff that surrounded the puckered hole. I was being prepared well for my encounter.

'I need to get in further, Cassandra. Hold your cheeks apart for me, would you?' She was so casual, so controlled.

'I can't,' I pleaded. 'Please, don't make me do that. I really can't.'

She just stopped what she was doing and left the water to cool on my skin. She knew I would give in eventually. She didn't tell me to turn back over; she didn't get angry or try to persuade me. She just stopped and waited.

'Becky, please, you know I hate it,' I argued. But I was arguing with myself: Becky had nothing to do with the inner agony that I had to control. The argument buzzed back and forth in my head. If I do it the ultimate feeling will be pleasure but I would have to suffer the crushing humiliation first. Was it worth it?'

I reluctantly lowered my shoulders to the bed to release my hands. This action played havoc with my resolve because it had the effect of pushing my rear end even further into the air. My bottom clenched furiously as I placed my spread hands on my cheeks and tried hard to obey her order but I couldn't finish the deed. I couldn't bring myself to pull the cheeks apart and willingly expose my core to her gaze.

I collapsed on the bed and implored her not to insist, but she was hardened to my pleas. She at least knew how much I really wanted to debase myself before her.

She took pity on me and gave me permission to obey by becoming even sterner with her next order.

'If you can't even carry out a simple instruction like that there's not much point in your going tonight, is there?' Her disdain wounded me into obeying.

I returned to the position she required and hardened my resolve. My hands again clutched my cheeks and I drew them apart shamelessly, as waves of humiliation engulfed me.

I gripped hard and held them apart as she carried out her task of lathering and removing the offending fluff until I was as smooth as a baby. She slapped my naked bottom playfully and told me to turn back over, then pulled me over to the mirrored wall.

'Look, isn't it exquisite?' Becky teased. 'All baby pink and naked. Look at your rude lips, how they protrude unashamedly, and I can actually see your clitoris. Look, Cassie, look.'

I was astonished at how exposed I felt as I looked, as instructed, at my naked sex. Sex wasn't the right word for it in this condition. It looked very, very rude, all open and available with the darkness of my inner lips protruding in quite a disgusting fashion. There was nothing secret or hidden: everything was on display, leaving nothing to the imagination. I loved it. It expressed my new feelings of submission in that everything was disclosed, my sex needs and my submission.

I touched the deliciously naked flesh and was thrilled at the smoothness. I caught Becky's gaze in the mirror, surprised that she hadn't stopped me, and was delighted when she made no move to do so. I leaned back into her arms and massaged my mound – lips, slit and clitoris – rubbing in the plentiful juices while Becky caressed my shoulders and breasts. I was petrified that she was just tormenting me, but as I rapidly neared my goal I relaxed and enjoyed the show I was putting on for her.

All the pent-up frustration of the preceding three days gathered in my guts and wrenched me apart in a wild explosion, flooding my hand as my insides grabbed hungrily for the dildo that was no longer there, and I slipped to the floor, sated and exhausted.

'What about you?' I asked as she sat on the floor beside me and gathered me into her arms. 'Can I please you now?'

'I'll wait, darling. I really enjoy being in a state of arousal for long periods of time. Thanks anyway.'

'But you might have to wait for ages,' I urged, longing to taste her and feel her thighs tight around my head.

'Don't you worry about that, Cassie. I'm sure I'll manage somehow,' she added, amused by my continued hunger.

I went to take my bath with visions of Becky masturbating filling my head and setting off delicate little tremors in my belly.

'Let's see how pretty we can make you for your adventure, shall we?'

Becky sat me in front of the dressing table and applied subtle make-up to my eyes. She took a crimson lip stain and outlined my lips with it, then filled in the rest, leaving my mouth with a very horny pout.

'That gives me an idea,' she said, and proceeded to stain the areolae around my nipples the same deep crimson of my mouth. Just to complete the look, she sat me down, spread my thighs apart and did the same to my inner lips.

She stood me against the bedpost, just like in my fantasy, and after hooking the pretty corset around me she laced the back and told me to hang on. As she drew the laces tighter and I hung on for dear life holding my breath, she kept telling me how beautiful I would look and how proud of me she was.

The horny girl in the shop had been right. My waist

at the end of the tug of war was a tiny 23 inches and, just as predicted, the corset swelled over my hips, accentuating my curves.

Becky sat me down again and brushed my long hair until it shone – a waterfall of red highlights – then caught up the sides with pieces of ribbon that matched the black of the corset. I moved towards the door and was delighted to catch a glimpse of myself in the mirror. My hair hung in soft curls to the top of the corset and my figure was reminiscent of a Victorian picture I had once seen. My breasts spilled over the top of the lace cups, pushed up by the tightness of the cords, and my hips flared out into voluptuous proportions. My waist was cinched with the cord that ran around my middle four or five times, then tied with a pretty bow, the ends dangling tantalisingly on to my bottom.

My eyes travelled further, down to the bottom of the corset, where my crimson lips peeked from between my legs, below the lace of the corset. I knew I looked delicious and I felt so ready for my adventure that I looked at the clock, wishing away the time until 7 o'clock.

I paced up and down for the remaining forty minutes while Becky sat calmly watching my agitation. We had spent a few minutes putting the stockings and the boots on that would complete my outfit of submission, but once they were on I couldn't settle. I pranced about trying to get used to the height of the boots, remembering the pony girl in the magazine and my excitement at reading her story.

Nothing calmed my nerves or the fear that collected in the outer reaches of my brain, waiting to pounce and threatening to destroy me.

When it was 6.45 p.m. Becky in her wisdom decided that I should be ready and waiting when he arrived, so she got the leather blindfold that we had chosen and, taking one last look in my eyes, asked, 'Are you sure you want to do this, Cassandra? You aren't doing it just for me, are you?'

I took a very deep, shaky breath and kissed her hard on the lips before taking the blindfold from her and placing it over my head and settling it into a comfy position.

This was it: I was on my own in the hall waiting for Mr King to come for me. I knew that Becky was behind the scenes somewhere but it was as if I had already left her behind. I knew that whatever happened to me over the next few hours would be a part of my relationship with her and not removed from it. I also knew that, as Mr King did the diabolical things to me that I was sure he would do, I would be thinking about Becky and remembering every detail so I could tell her the full sordid story. I felt a heat burn inside me as I imagined the telling of that story.

By the time I heard the front door open I was chewing my lip in fear. My feet ached and my legs were becoming cramped, but all that disappeared when I heard his breathing next to me and felt a cool pair of hands on my shoulders, propelling me towards the door.

16

The cool rush of the night air caused shivers to shroud my whole body, but his hands stayed firm and grew warm on my flesh as he steered me out of my house and over the two or three metres to his car.

I was so glad we lived in a detached house and only one property overlooked our drive. I imagined Susan, my neighbour, with her accountant husband and her 2.4 children, watching me from her kitchen window.

It didn't matter any more. I was already sinking in to that realm of total acceptance.

One of the hands that guided me left my shoulder and sat gently on my head, pushing me into a crouching position and propelling me forward into the car. I complied with these silent instructions and clambered into the seat. The door was shut firmly behind me. Within seconds I heard the other door slam, and the car moved away.

As the fear of the unknown flooded my thoughts I longed to speak to him and ask where we were going and what he intended to do with me, but I remembered just in time that he was very strict about being obeyed. I remembered that he didn't like me to make any decision on my own but only to be guided by his instructions, be they silent or otherwise. I was hardly in a position to argue, so I sat on the seat and waited.

We travelled for what seemed like hours. There was some very soothing music being piped around the car. Twice we stopped, and my heart thumped, as I thought we had arrived. But Mr King just leaned over and pushed a straw between my lips. I drank deeply, pleased to find that I wasn't going to be fed on bread and water. The wine that poured down my parched throat was heady and good.

The third time we stopped I assumed that again he was going to ply me with drink but I felt the cold air rush in as he opened the door beside me and helped me out. I wobbled a little on my heeled boots but managed to steady myself in time and stretched to get the cricks out of my body.

I could hear faint music and conversation from a radio somewhere and turned my head to try to home in on it, but lost my bearings.

Mr King stood in front of me, right out there in the open, and showed his appreciation of the way I looked by caressing my body, from my face and arms down to my thighs. He didn't at that stage touch my erogenous zones, which are many and, as you have probably guessed by now, very closely spaced.

He finished the tour by turning me round and titillating the lace and cords of the corset, then, turning me back, he took my face in his hands and gently placed a kiss on my mouth. I murmured encouragement but he ignored it.

'Listen to me, Cassandra, and listen carefully,' he said, still cupping my face. His voice was cultured and gentle, just as I had imagined, but it was strange to hear him talk for the first time. 'You are here by choice, but if that choice changes in any way during your time with us, or if at any time you feel you would like time out, then all you have to do is drop this.' And with those words he took my tightly clenched fist and, prising it open, placed a small bell in my palm and closed my fingers around it. I found myself wondering just how many he had and whether he sent all his conquests away with one.

'Just be careful that you don't become so excited that

you drop it inadvertently, because anyone you're likely to come into contact with in the time you spend here will have their ears tuned to the tinkle of your bell. You have my word that the slightest ring will halt all proceedings. Just one other thing: we're all game players here and all games have rules. If you do ring the bell be sure that you want everything to stop. Because you can be assured that if, even by accident, you cause the bell to ring, you will be sent home immediately and will not be invited to return.' He chuckled in a slightly embarrassed manner as he added, 'Let's hope we're clever enough to make you forget its existence.'

He linked my arm through his and led me forward, up six or seven steps into a building, with his hand cupped around mine, which clutched the small bell like a lifeline.

The smells and noises that assailed my nostrils as soon as we entered the hall gripped me with alarm. My head screamed for Becky, wondering what she was doing.

It wasn't a radio I had heard: it was people. Slightly removed from us, at least three or four men's voices were laughing and chatting amiably as if they didn't have a care in the world.

The smell of old leather and cigar smoke, mixed with muffled voices and the soft chink of glasses, managed to create an image of an old house where the men stand around in the library drinking brandy, and the women have retired to the lounge – the sort of situation you see in old films. I could tell by the resonance of the voices that the rooms had high ceilings and were large and spacious.

The voices were at least happy ones. I did bristle at the occasional laugh in case I was the subject of the mirth, and I clutched my bell tightly.

Mr King again calmed me down by gripping my

shoulders firmly and, just as he had done twice before, he placed one finger under my chin and raised it to a jaunty angle. He didn't have to tell me twice: I had come a long way since then and was now proud of my submission.

I stood as tall as I could, thrust my rouged breasts out as far as I was able, sucked in my breath and squeezed his arm to let him know I was ready, and we moved forward.

As we moved into the room every sound stopped dead. You could have heard a pin drop in the silence, then a stifled appreciative moan started the cacophony of sound that erupted. Everyone in the room started at once.

'Oh, good choice, King, she is exquisite.'

'Look at those tits.'

'Shaved pussy, too, perfect.'

'Jesus, I want to fuck her now. Can I be first, King?'

'Her arse is begging for the paddle, just wait until it's my turn.'

I had never felt so desirable but detached. As far as I knew they had no idea who I was or whether I had even chosen to be there, and all they wanted was to ravish me. I started to cringe away from the continued onslaught of sounds until I felt Mr King take hold of me firmly again and move me to another position in the room.

Again silence fell as Mr King gagged me with the harness he had introduced me to months before, and I took to it like a baby with a dummy. I was now able to let myself enjoy. All they had to do now was restrain me and my submission would be complete – after all, I thought by way of convincing myself, if I am tied and gagged I just have to accept my fate, don't I?

Mr King led me further into the room towards the voices and I felt lots of hands on me. They stroked and explored, pinched and probed all my intimate places as I wriggled my pleasure. I spread my legs to allow them further access and they obliged by holding my legs apart and delving into my sex. Already I felt my knees go weak but a loud voice and a banged gavel from across the room put a stop to my enjoyment.

'Come on, gentlemen. If you are all finished shall we get started? Let's get Cassandra up here into position and deal, shall we?'

What the hell were they talking about? I wondered, but before I could think too hard I was grabbed from all sides and lifted up and placed face down on to what I presume was a table. The surface felt cool on my belly and I could smell the wax as they started on me.

They all appeared to have a prearranged role in my restraint. As one held my arms behind me, another pulled what felt like a large leather glove over my drawn-together arms, then pulled and tugged it up until it reached my shoulders. One of the others buckled wide straps around my ankles and fastened them together. I was very glad at that stage that I am supple because the glove squeezing my arms together was then pulled in somehow until my elbows nearly touched each other. The only part left free was my clenched fists at the bottom. Straps were passed around my shoulders and buckled tightly. This new garment forced my shoulders close and thrust my breasts out from the top of my pretty corset. The sensation this produced was of having no arms at all and I felt even more helpless than usual.

I felt someone jump up on to the table beside me, and then another in front of me and before I knew what was happening I was helped into a standing position and the tip of my arm sleeve was pulled up towards the ceiling. The strain made me bend over into a very uncomfortable, hunched position. I didn't feel quite so desirable then. Gone was the pride I had in the way I looked and that feeling was replaced by an overwhelming feeling of being just an object – a toy, a plaything, a body for them to do what they wanted with.

My head was hanging forward and the strain on the backs of my legs in the ridiculously high heels was quite painful. My shoulders ached already, my bottom was thrust out and my arms were being wrenched from their sockets.

I grunted my disapproval and tried to show how uncomfortable I was, but it really was impossible.

I was beginning to feel very sorry for myself when I felt a gentle warm hand run up the tight stretched muscles in the back of my right thigh, hover there for a moment or two and then push its way between my thighs and worm its way into my pussy.

'Deal quickly, King. I don't think I can wait much longer. I want to get my hands on this lass, now,' a deep sexy voice said from my left.

I could hear the noise of a card game being played, bids being placed and cursing when someone lost, but I could only concentrate on the finger that still probed me. I moved about as much as I could, trying to gain purchase on it, but its owner was far too clever. Every time I gyrated enough to force the finger in further, it moved away, tantalising me.

As soon as it moved from my sex it would take hold of one of my breasts, which hung over the top of my corset and dangled, completely unprotected, and caress it, stroking it and pulling on the nipple just as Becky did.

All these attentions took my mind off my discomfort and of course off the card game until I heard a whoop of joy and the voice that I had picked out earlier cheer with delight.

'Congratulations, Bishop, the pawn is yours. Choose

your game,' I heard Mr King say, with a slight tinge of regret, I like to think.

I had no idea what he was talking about but I knew that it was me he had won and my heart pounded in my chest, wondering exactly what rights were now his and what game he would choose. I also wondered what they meant by a pawn and what the choice of games was.

The hand stopped its manipulation of my nipple and there was a minute or so of silence as they waited for something. I strained my ears, wondering what the hold-up was, but then they all chorused, 'Yes.'

I sucked hard on the gag, trying to produce a little saliva to wet my throat, but the fear that coursed through my veins had effectively dried it up and the rubber mouthpiece had stuck to the roof of my mouth. My fist clutched and squeezed the bell in my palm.

The atmosphere in the room was electric. Other voices excitedly asked the voice that had whooped with delight a moment ago what he chose to do with his pawn, but for ages he didn't answer. Then, after another long pause, he explained, gushing with anticipation. 'Apparently she loves to be humiliated, and the most exquisite humiliation I can think of is to watch her piss for us.' My heart sank. 'I intend to ply her with drink until her bladder is so full she's bursting, then hold her until she can control it no longer, then watch her urinate. I want to watch the humiliation destroy her. I want her to be so full that it gushes out of her in a torrent.'

'Bloody hell, Bishop, that's a brilliant idea, I couldn't have thought of a better one to warm us all up myself. Let's do it.'

I was so disappointed. I had so wanted them to spank me or something, or at least do something that tested my limits. But this? There was no way I was going to pee for anyone. I wouldn't have even done that for my Becky.

I heard a chuckle so soft that I wasn't sure I *had* heard it, and imagined it was Becky, reading my mind and knowing just how I was hating this. I wouldn't even let her in the bathroom when I took a pee.

I was released from the ceiling and sat on the edge of the table while my gag was unstrapped and the dildo removed from my mouth. I immediately spewed out a tirade of abuse.

'I am not doing that. I absolutely refuse. You can't make me drink if I don't want to. Speak to me, you bastards,' I screamed when nobody confirmed that I wouldn't have to carry out their wishes.

I was picked up again by many hands and held down on the table on my back. My arms were crushed underneath me, my legs, still tied, were held down.

I heard a lot of movement and someone leaving the room and returning as I tried to protest more, but it was useless. It was abundantly clear that I would have no say in my fate. This alone sent a surge of arousal through me, which quickly turned to raw need when a pair of hands held my head steady and another hand tried to open my mouth. I clamped my lips together in a grimace and flatly refused to open them, but they were not to be thwarted. My nose was pinched and when I ended up gasping for breath a cup was forced between my teeth.

I tried my hardest to spit it out but I couldn't and almost immediately I felt a trickle of cool water dribble into my throat.

I choked a little at first, spluttering and gagging, but they didn't stop. I had either to get into the rhythm or end up choking, so I gulped furiously to keep up with the stream that was now steadily pouring down my open throat.

I thought they would never stop. I could feel my bladder fill up and then start expanding until I was sure I would pee, there on the table. Perhaps that would satisfy them, I thought.

There was one hand that sat on my belly monitoring its capacity, gently squeezing and releasing my distended abdomen. When it was removed, the force-feeding stopped. I was bursting to go but as they lifted me off the table and untied my legs the feeling eased and I knew a moment of arrogance. I wasn't going to pee for anyone.

They stood me on what felt like sheeted rubber and spread my legs wide apart and urged me to relax and let it all go. I tried to do what they wanted but I couldn't. My pride just would not allow me willingly to do such a humiliating, disgusting, personal thing in front of these unknown men.

I sobbed my distress. 'I just can't. Whatever you do I won't be able to relax enough to do it.' And then in a moment of sheer anger I shouted, 'Anyway, I don't *want* to!'

'We shall see about that, lass,' said a voice. And with that I was hoisted again on to the table and before I could draw breath or gather my thoughts the cup was again held in my mouth.

'This time we won't stop until you beg us to let you go.'

Again I gave in to their strength and gulped at the liquid as it invaded my helpless throat. I became so full I kept trying to twist my head away from them but they held me fast and kept pouring.

At least a hundred times I nearly gave in and released the bell but eventually all my resolve vanished. All I was aware of was my bursting bladder. I knew that if they didn't stop soon the whole thing would become involuntary anyway. I knew that another ten seconds and I would pee on the table and that would be even more shameful. So I nodded furiously to let them know I was ready to give in. I really thought I had reached my limit and I would have to do it now, that I had no choice, but, as soon as they stood me up again, the desperate need to go receded.

Again they stood me on the crinkly rubber and again I mumbled, 'I can't.'

The voices around me were taking on a different tone. No longer were they playfully bantering with me: they were tinged with determination.

'Right, my lass, you've asked for it. We've given you ample opportunity to do this the easy way. Now it's my turn. But believe me: pee for me you will.'

I was at the end of my tether and had just opened my mouth to shout that I wanted to leave when I felt the plug of the gag again forced into my mouth and instantly buckled around my head.

They left me standing where I was, my distended belly hard and tender and all moved away to whisper. I tried to hear what they had in mind for me but the voices all mingled into each other and I caught only snatches of the conversation.

I tried to walk towards the door to show I was unhappy but as soon as I bumped into the first chair I stopped in my tracks, petrified.

I felt like a puppet as I was picked up from either side by two very strong pairs of hands and held like that. They each held one hand under my back and one under my knees and they pulled my legs apart. So I sat in midair, held up by two men I didn't know with my legs stretched apart. My rude sex was stretched open and I could imagine all those pairs of eyes gazing at it with its smooth mound and ruby-red lips.

I felt another pair of hands unceremoniously pull my inner lips apart to expose the pink wet interior and I was engorged with a new hunger.

All my resolve disappeared with just this exposure and I knew that eventually they would persuade me to give in. While I had felt just anger and determination I could probably have held on for ever, but this strange man who called me lass had found my Achilles' heel.

'This little minx is no more wanting to go home than I am. Feel this sweet little pussy, gentlemen. It's dripping all over my hand.' His booming laugh filled the room and became infectious for the others until they were all laughing at my puny attempt to disobey.

Without any warning he pushed two or three fingers up into me and, curling them forward, rubbed on to my bladder through the delicate divider. From that moment on I didn't have a hope in holding on to the water that was now threatening to burst forth all over his hand. Again I grunted my complaint but he repeated his sentence from earlier.

'As I said before, sweetie, you *will* pee for me. Tip her back, lads. I can't get at her.' I was pushed backward until my sex was tipped up and totally available to him. He removed his fingers, creating a very wet sucking noise that mortified me but encouraged a round of cheers from his friends. Then he spread my lips wide apart with one hand, exposing everything, even my erect clitoris, and ran his finger down the length of the cleft. Up and down his finger went, searching around and arousing each spot it passed until I was panting and no longer concerned about his intentions.

When he reached my tiny hole hidden in the folds he stopped his searching and rubbed the tiny opening with the very tip of his finger. I struggled in my human seat, trying to hold back the now urgent need to let go, but he was relentless. His partners in crime held me still and he carried on, forcing the very tip of his finger slightly into the hole and stimulating all the nerves that ended there. I could feel my bladder muscles start to relax and I grabbed them back again, desperately attempting to retain the fluid that now threatened to humiliate me. His abuse of me was persistent and distressingly effective. It loosened my bladder and my resolve until I felt the liquid bursting to be released, pushing at the weakened muscles that held it.

I panicked then and struggled as hard as I could when I realised that I could hold on for only another second or two. The hands on my thighs opened me further and clutched me tighter as my bladder throbbed and struggled to hold on.

'Come on, lass, pee for Daddy,' he purred, convinced he had won even before I gave in and rubbing my pee hole in soft little circles.

That did it. All I needed to break my resolve was that persuasive 'pee for Daddy' bit.

My bladder opened until a hot stream gushed from my overstimulated hole, exploding and sparking a tight little ripple of orgasm that gripped my stomach. I heard 'Daddy' groan too as I felt burning spurts of his come splash on to my thighs to join the torrent that still rained down, dripping off my puffy lips and running through the groove of my bum.

I was laid on the floor to recover and again felt soft warm hands stroking my body and smoothing the damp hair away from my eyes. I felt a hot wet cloth, mop up the sperm and pee that dribbled down my legs, then the same hands gently released my arms from the glove. Mr King, I assumed.

'Can you believe that?'

'Fuck, that was intense!'

'I've never seen anything so exciting in all my time at the club. What about you?' There was a chorus of agreement and approval that filled my chest to bursting point with a strange erotic pride.

The satisfied chatter that followed those specific exclamations sparked off mixed reactions in me. Part of me was still dying with shame but the part of me that loved to please bloomed with pleasure at their rude, intimate remarks and longed for the next game.

I didn't have to wait long: my captors were just as keen as I was.

This time I was stood upright against a pillar and wrapped tightly with rope while the next leg of the game was played out. After what seemed like only a minute or two of banter and laughter I heard 'So, Rook, the pawn is yours for the taking and we all know what game you want. Isn't it about time you had a change?'

'If it ain't broken don't fix it – that's my motto,' a slightly rougher voice than I had heard so far answered, to the amusement of everyone. Everyone apart from me, that is. I was untied and lifted up as if I weighed only a pound or two and was laid on the table on my back.

I was pushed to one end until my head hung over the edge while many unseen hands cuffed and spread my limbs to the four corners of the long table. My head was supported as the large dildo gag was removed from my mouth. I worked my jaws gratefully, allowing the feeling to creep back in. But my gratitude didn't last long. Before I even had a chance to mutter a single word and just as I was stretching my cramped jaw a new gag was thrust into my mouth. This one was different: it comprised a hard ring that tucked in behind my teeth, holding my mouth wide open, with straps that were quickly buckled behind my head. My tongue flailed about helplessly, flicking out of my mouth and trying to keep the interior of my mouth lubricated.

There was something very exciting about the way this new gag held yet another of my orifices open for attention of and possible use by the men who now sat around the table silently.

I felt at least six hands begin their wanderings over my stretched body. First a soft gentle hand caressed my right breast, kneading and manipulating the rolling flesh. A rough and scratchy hand gripped the other breast with no finesse, pulling and tugging it until I didn't know which one to concentrate on.

My smooth naked sex was being explored by a very sensuous pair of hands that delved and probed my constantly dripping hole, separating the tender lips and gently squeezing my clitoris and pulling on the hood in a rhythmical motion that sent me crazy.

I couldn't believe my luck. This game involved no pain or humiliation and was so far aimed only at my pleasure.

The feeling of having my mouth stretched open to tearing point had the strange effect of transferring that experience to my lower regions, and I felt as if that too were open and available.

My arousal rose willingly as I felt all my horniest places being titillated. I groaned my pleasure and wriggled my need when I felt the first soft touch of velvet on my tongue, invading the space made by the ring gag and probing my stretched mouth. I longed to respond but was unable to close my jaw even one centimetre, so, as the cock head pushed its way into my open space, all I could do was touch it with my tongue. I gathered what lubrication I could find in the corners of my mouth, then forced my tongue out as far as I could to meet the hot velvet that probed its way in and I frantically licked my welcome.

A pair of hands grabbed my head and the cock filled my gaping mouth, hitting the back of my throat and making me retch. So much for all my subtle tantalising. Tears filled my eyes and soaked into the backing of my blindfold, making it cold and soggy, but what did he care? He became incensed with need and pushed his penis in and out of my face, holding my head in position as it hung upside down from the edge of the table. His warm hairy balls knocked into my forehead with every thrust and blocked my nose until I thought I would burst for a breath. I dragged a ragged breath around the edge of his swollen cock and took it deep in my lungs.

An insistent finger pushed its way inside my pussy and twisted and wriggled until my mind was taken off the cock violating my mouth and concentrated on what was happening to my body. I gripped my internal muscles hard to convey my pleasure and gurgled in the back of my throat as the finger was withdrawn and replaced by something much larger. The new invader was warm and knobbly, so I assumed it was a cluster of fingers that now forced their way into me. I tried to raise my hips off the table but could manage only an inch or two. That was enough: his fingertips nudged deep within me, sending a thrill though my body, but I wanted more.

Again there was something about my wrenched-open mouth that transferred to my sex and I tried to show the person filling me that it was not enough. I jerked my hips up and down frantically, gripping his hand with my muscles and trying to grip with my thighs. The cock was still pounding away at my mouth.

The hand inside me withdrew, then I jumped with shock as a cool liquid was sprayed over my open crotch. At first I thought someone had peed on me but the hands returned and spread the viscous fluid all over my sex and my thighs, right down into the cleft of my buttocks and into my already wet sex.

Fingers entered, then left, each of my holes, invading and exploring, taking the smooth oil with them until my whole lower area was awash with lubrication and yearning for more.

The bunched fingers again pushed their way into my entrance, stretching my lips around the intrusion and flattening my clitoris with the sheer force that opened me wide. I gasped and then swallowed hard as the throbbing cock continued its now steady assault on my tonsils.

The slick intrusion in my nether regions twisted gently, reaching further inside me with each movement and forcing my already tight lips further and further apart. I realised what he was trying to do with horror as his knuckles attempted to follow his fingers into my body. My flesh contracted with fear as the fist inched its way further and further in, but I realised that my fear was hindering the process and making the intended progress impossible.

The same gentle hands that had helped me before stroked my spread thighs and caressed closer to my ravished cunt, softly touching my hard clitoris and slipping a gentle finger in beside the unforgiving knuckles to release the trapped flesh. My insides responded as we all knew they would and my body relaxed, flooding outward, letting the hand in further. With almost a popping sensation the widest part of his hand slipped in on the oil and rested while I panted hard, trying to absorb the size of the violation that stuffed me and stretched my internal walls to their limit.

I experienced every minute movement as he carefully curled his fingers inwards to make a fist that threatened to split me apart. I no longer had the ability to tighten my muscles, so I just had to relax the best I could and ride the waves of violation that increased my pleasure tenfold.

Unseen hands untied my feet and pushed my legs up

against my chest, keeping them stretched apart. The fist inside me moved and pulled away slightly until it felt as if it were trying to exit, still in its bunched condition, but then moved inwards again in a gentle fucking motion.

I knew the cock in my mouth was close to shooting its load, and the fist inside me, which forced my sexual orifice as wide as the cock was stretching my mouth, was fucking me harder with each stroke. How many times would this group of debauched men be able to take me to this place where I was ready to explode? I wondered.

Being fisted and mouth-fucked at the same time had to be the ultimate deviation. The man who gripped my head didn't even need my assistance: I was just a hole for his cock. The fist that thundered its message inside me didn't care if I was enjoying the experience. I was a pawn in their game and they were oblivious to my wants and hungry needs.

Or were they reading me perfectly? Didn't I *want* to be that pawn? Wasn't that the helpless state that I craved?

As realisation washed over me my arousal hovered at fever pitch and the cock in my mouth pumped its bitter spurts deep into my throat. I choked and heaved, trying desperately to swallow before I needed to take another breath. The final thrust of his cock had dropped his balls over my face, restricting my breathing, making me panic until I felt the tingles of light-headedness threaten to take over.

As I gulped furiously at his semen, fingers gripped my nipples and thumbed them roughly, rolling and pulling them until the feelings of sweet pain joined forces with the now soft, twitching cock, which refused to relinquish its home and forced the walls of my sex to grip the fist harder. With each thrust of the fist inside me one of the knuckles nudged my stretched clitoris, building my excitement to a mind-blowing crescendo.

I came then, the explosion ripping through me until my chest was heaving desperately and my thighs twitched and jerked against their human restraints.

Eventually the softened cock plopped out of my mouth and my legs were returned to their relaxed position. The fist was uncurled and to the noise of my grunts and groans removed from my depths.

I was dragged back down the table and retied with the gag still forcing my mouth open and I listened in awe as the game continued across my naked spread-eagled body.

While the game progressed a finger played with my tongue, tormenting it and grasping hold of it. A spasm of pleasure lurched in my belly at this new assault, relishing the added immobility. A clip of some sort was attached to my unprotected tongue, forcing it just to hang helplessly outside my gaping mouth. There was no discomfort involved, just a heavy control. I was amazed at how horny this extra restraint made me feel as the contractions of hunger pulsed so soon in my recently abused sex.

Before too long another cheer went up and my tongue was released. Another winner wanted to claim his prize: me!

A rather deep gruff voice exclaimed that he wanted to hang me and the others cheered again but I had never felt so scared. My throat was constricted and my heart palpitated with fear.

I couldn't imagine how such a horny game could have turned so frightening in such a short time. What sort of animals were they? I curled into a tight foetal position and started rocking, squealing my distress.

All noises stopped and someone came over, scooped me up in strong arms and crooned in my ear. 'It's OK, sweetheart, we're not going to do anything you don't want us to.'

I knew immediately that this was Mr King. His voice was melodious and persuasive with a faint lilt of the accent that I couldn't quite place. The smell was right, the arms were right and then he confirmed it.

'It's me, Cassandra, it's OK. He didn't mean that he wants to hang you like that. Remember that this is a game and you'e a willing participant. This is about pleasure – for all of us.'

He stood me on my feet and I felt myself surrounded by people. They all petted me and stroked me to calm me down and show that I had nothing to be frightened about, apart from my own desires.

No sooner had my breasts stopped heaving with fear than they started all over again, but with anticipation of the next part of the game.

My boots were removed and I felt two very deep straps being buckled around my feet and under my insteps. Then, just like before, I was scooped up in some strong arms, something wide and cold was slipped under my lower back and my feet were hoisted upwards. In one swoop I was horizontal. I heard a slow clicking noise fill the room as my legs gradually moved outwards. Cuffs were buckled around my wrists and my dangling arms were grasped and stretched to test my span. They seemed pleased. Someone took both my arms and spread them apart in a mirror image of my legs, tied rope around them, then fastened them at the limits of my reach.

This left me lying in a star shape, my arms and legs spread wide and my back supported, but leaving my bottom exposed. I guessed I was suspended about three feet from the floor and dangling horizontally from the ceiling, writhing about completely at their mercy.

'Have you ever seen a more delectable sight? I know

I haven't. It's a shame to mark that perfect skin but I'm sure she'll forgive me – afterwards!'

I wriggled about, grunting and becoming increasingly agitated. It looked as if finally I was going to experience the whipping I had wondered about. I was not at all sure about the fact that my legs were stretched apart rendering my sex so available.

There was nowhere I could go; I was absolutely open to anything they chose to do. Mr King's words earlier had eased my fear a little but I remembered the pain when he had thrashed me with his belt and I trembled. I kept trying to curl up but all I could do was raise my head slightly. Quite ineffectual, really.

I was truly helpless. My sex lips were stretched open, my breasts tipped out of the corset and my whole body was solidly held, open and begging.

I felt a pair of hands – the gentle ones that had mopped my face, I think – unlace the cord to my corset and then unhook its fastenings and expose the rest of my body. Unseen hands lifted me from my cradle as it was removed completely. At least I could breathe but I knew they hadn't uncovered me just to look, and my pulse quickened.

I tried hard to close my legs when I felt a hard cock shape being pushed into my pussy, but, as it progressed, my wriggle changed to one of arousal. At least they planned to keep me aroused while they tortured me.

Then, shame of all shames, they did the same with my bottom. If I hadn't known better I would have thought they had been speaking to Becky.

I felt my cheeks being spread and a thinner dildo being inserted deep within my bowels. Long after I thought they would have to stop, it continued wiggling its way inside me until I felt invaded and violated. I knew it was buried further inside me than I thought possible and that thought filled my brain and sent my senses racing on to new planes of arousal.

Again the men gathered around me and poked and prodded and touched until the fury of need threatened to shatter me into a million pieces. I bucked and shook as the dildos were pushed in and pulled out. Devious, unseen hands tugged and wrenched at my nipples, and still the gentle hand was there to help me, taking hold of my clitoris and wanking it slowly, keeping up the pure arousal.

When they all moved away and all the touching stopped, a silence fell over the room. I knew the time had come. At last I would experience the ultimate submissive game.

The first flick of the many-tailed whip warmed my flesh where it reached around my thigh and each successive aim after that managed to cover my spread body exquisitely. Never two in the same place but just close enough to keep the burning glow alive. Up and down my helpless arms and legs, occasionally flicking the inside of my tender thighs – just enough to make me gasp. The pace increased until I was writhing and twisting, panting hard into my gag and snorting through my nostrils. What exquisite torture!

Already I was beginning to wish I had not been quite so keen to trust my sexuality to these men, and as the pressure mounted I clung on to my bell for dear life. I could hear their murmurings of pleasure at the ultimate punishment I was receiving and gasps as each determined blow landed on my delicate flesh.

The nice sensations from the dildos, and the exposure, kept me in a state of semiarousal, only slightly dimmed by the subtle exciting pain.

'Use the carriage whip, King, it makes lovely marks,' I heard a voice suggest, and my fear escalated. What the hell was a carriage whip?

The weapon was changed and I heard the sing of a whip cutting through the silence in the room. The breath was torn from my burning lungs when I felt a sting just above one of my breasts, followed in quick succession by more on my thighs, belly and bottom. I writhed again, responding to the burning that each sting left and racking my imagination for a picture to go with the pain, but I came up with nothing. Helplessly, I attempted to escape that relentless stinging but, truly, I revelled in each and every blow.

When a sting landed between my open legs I snorted again into the gag and panted rapidly, trying to absorb the pain, but the second blow fell before I had a chance to control it. My hands clenched into tighter fists, the nails digging hard into my palms, but it did nothing to ease the intensity that racked my body.

Even though the pain was exhilarating, the level of my excitement rose at an even more alarming pace. Part of me tried desperately to avoid the blows but the submissive in me wanted more and more intensity. I wanted to explode with feelings. I longed to experience it all. As the tip of the whip flicked nearer and nearer to my naked breasts I struggled to feel that exquisite pain on my nipples – but whoever was wielding it knew better. Wanting something is much more erotic than actually getting it, so the whip rained down relentlessly in every place but where I longed for it.

I thrashed about trying desperately to picture Becky and myself playing this game at home. The moment I thought of Becky I imagined that I was doing this for her and the pain dulled to an acceptable level and mingled with the pleasure from all that had gone before and the snippets of arousal that still hovered on the fringes of the game.

I was lifted then by many hands, untied and flipped over unceremoniously. My belly lay in the sling and again my arms and legs were stretched to their limits. My hair was tied in a bunch and fastened way above me, supporting my head but tugging irritatingly at my hairline. Clips were fastened on my nipples and dangled, weighted, gripping the tender buds in a vice, but, every time I moved and the weights swung, a delicious ripple of pleasure washed over me.

The weapon was changed again then and I felt the ends of a many-tailed whip being dragged gently through the channel between my legs, tickling my hot sex. I groped helplessly towards this little offering of pleasure and was surprised when I heard a soft mewling sound coming from my throat. I marvelled at my gagged ability to convey my pleasure.

The experience of this new whip was different, more suffused and spread over a larger area. The game took on a totally new personality; it was definitely pleasure in disguise as it built the pressure in me to fever pitch.

'You are going to orgasm just from the whip, Cassandra. Concentrate on how much you're pleasing everyone in this room and do it for Becky.'

I recognised Mr King's voice immediately and realised that he had taken over with the new whip and I relaxed slightly, safe in the knowledge that he had taken me to orgasm through pain before.

But what was he talking about? Something about that last sentence was wrong, but every time my brain tried to capture it another kiss of the whip would take my breath away and scatter my train of thought.

The pain rained down on my bottom, back and legs, occasionally making me yelp when a particularly well-aimed one landed on the dildo inside me, pushing it deeper and catching my clitoris.

Still my arousal hovered at a tolerable level but made no attempt to climb upwards.

Do it for Becky, just as Mr King said, my head

screamed, when the intensity threatened to overpower me.

Again the nagging question crept into my thoughts. What was it he said?

Becky! Becky? He said Becky. But he doesn't even know her!

The confusion pounded through my brain as the blows from the whip continued. Slowly the pain was changing. The thoughts of Becky cleared and I tried to imagine her watching, proud of my submission, and I was overcome by an overwhelming smell of her perfume. It invaded my concentration and clamoured through my brain screaming a string of questions at me. *What?* my head screamed back.

Again the pain peaked and I thought I would cry if he didn't stop soon. I was thrashing backwards and forwards hoping that they would get the message and stop, but they were too excited to recognise my pleas or were unable or unprepared to read them.

Becky would have known to stop, I cried silently.

The orgasm that had teased me for ages was determined to elude me now when I needed it most. My body, desperate for feelings of pleasure, grasped at the sensation of the dildo buried within my depths and the long alien intruder that buried its way far into my anus.

The second that recognition hit me everything changed. The bell, threatening to drop from my hand, was unnecessary. My Becky was here. It was she who had stroked me and mopped my brow and cradled me while the men gambled for my submission. I felt a small warm hand slip into mine and squeeze.

The overpowering surge of raw adrenaline crashed through my helpless, open body and I writhed in pleasure. I imagined my Becky in that room of dominant men, watching everything they had put me through. I pictured her shock when she saw me pee and the shame washed over me in waves. It was one thing performing disgusting acts for people you didn't know and were never likely to have to face, but I would never have been able to allow myself the inner permission it would have taken to perform that act for Becky.

I thought my thumping heart would burst with the intensity of that moment.

I thrust my legs further apart and pushed my breasts forward, begging for the kiss of the whip. Come on, Mr King, my head screamed, I want it now! I want everything you can give.

He read me perfectly this time and kept up that deliberate knowing pace. The whip fell in random unexpected places across my stretched torso, taking me rapidly to that place I craved. Each stroke of the whip was a new surprise that pushed me onward. Every fourth or fifth stroke would land between my tender inner thighs, causing me to twist and turn and thrash about in my bonds. Occasionally he would catch the perfect angle to wrap my breasts, sharply caressing the tender nipples stretched tightly towards the floor, and I thought my head would explode.

Each of these rushes of pain combined exquisitely with Becky's small hand, which left mine and travelled slowly, avoiding the blows of the whip, until it reached its target to provide the transfusion that I hungered for. One all-knowing finger, gentle and small after the large rough insistent hands of the men, searched for and found my straining pulsating clitoris and gently stroked it rhythmically.

The overwhelming waves of orgasm started in my swollen nipples, stretched by the clips. They gathered force and momentum, rushing to my sex on a flood tide, throbbing and rushing through my tightly strung body until I thought I would pass out from the pleasure my two lovers combined to provide.

Mr King carried on while Becky caressed my elongated breasts just as she had earlier – stretching out my pleasure, revelling in my total submission. I moaned a continuous, guttural, howling sob that was swallowed by the gag but was lost on no one as I wallowed in the last gut-wrenching spasms and collapsed in utter submission.

17

I was dazed and completely confused as I regained my senses. I was still lying in the sling but the clips had been removed from my nipples and blood sizzled through my veins. To help ease the pain from the whipping, I tightened my grip on the bell, just to convince myself that I hadn't imagined its presence.

I felt different inside. A calm acceptance filled me. I could still hear muted voices throughout the room but no longer did I fear what would happen next. I craved it. I knew without a doubt that from that moment on I would be different. Nothing held terror for me any more and I waited for whatever my Becky decided to let them do to me next. I didn't even question how she got there. I just longed for more and new experiences to test my thresholds and my submission. No longer did my head scream with questions, but hummed like a well-tuned car engine in neutral, waiting to see what was required of me.

I snapped to attention when I heard obvious plans being made. I heard Mr King and Becky discussing something that I couldn't quite decipher and a general excited chattering that encouraged the suggestions being weighed up. They must have agreed, because Becky came over to me and sat on the floor by my head and asked me some very scary leading questions.

'You're a dirty little girl, Cassandra. All those rude and embarrassing things they made you do. Do you enjoy them?'

'Mmm.'

'Fancy peeing in front of all these rampant men! You naughty girl! I didn't think they'd be able to persuade you to do that in a million years.'

She didn't seem to require answers and I knew she was getting me all worked up again for a reason, so I kept quiet and let her shameful words consume me.

'Remember when we started all this and you said you trusted me, Cassie? Do you still, even though I tricked you a little?'

There was no hesitation present when I nodded my restrained head. She kissed me at the side of my gag then, just where my lips were stretched, and delicately touched her tongue to the hot flesh. I groaned.

'We want to do something now, Cassandra, that's going to test you beyond your limits, but it's very important to me and to Mr King and the rest of these very admiring gentlemen. Will you let us?'

A cheer went up at her words but then an immediate silence filled the room, deafening, expectant and frightening. I could tell that everyone was holding his or her breath waiting for my agreement. My flesh had cooled and my arousal had quietened for the moment so the decision was harder to make. The fear that I thought had left me for ever bubbled tantalisingly in my loins.

Then a male voice took over: 'Come on, sweetheart, remember what I said in my letter. This is your destiny. Everyone in this room knows it and you know it too if only you can see past the fear.' It was Mr King's voice supporting Becky's plea and persuading me to agree. I heard another round of persuasive arguments in the background:

'We want you to belong, Cassandra.'

'Come on, lass, you've come this far, the rest is easy. Just nod and leave the rest to us.'

'Come on, Cassie, say yes.'

The need to please – especially to please Becky and

Mr King – clinched it. I nodded my head and groaned with acceptance of my fate. 'Good, good girl,' said Mr King. 'We're going to pierce your beautiful, horny sex lips and adorn you with our symbol. All our pawns are recognised this way. You won't feel a thing. It only takes a second or two and you'll already be completely numb. This isn't a pain thing: it's symbolic.'

Within ten seconds of my agreement I felt an unseen pair of hands remove the dildos from my sex and my anus and while this was going on Becky removed my gag. It felt so good to relax my jaw and Becky's soft kiss felt even better. She whispered sweet nothings into my mouth as she cradled my head.

I was so torn. Without my gag I could actually ask questions or refuse, but Becky kept my mouth busy, which was just as effective, so the apprehension was pushed to the back of my mind.

I felt something very cold being sprayed on to my inner sex lips and gradually I felt them going numb. I was petrified but Becky sucked away my fears and questions. A little bit of me rebelled but the new Cassandra, the pawn in their games, wanted to go all the way.

The bitter smell of antiseptic invaded the aroma of leather, sex and tobacco already filling the room and I squealed inside. Becky's mouth still covered mine. I could have pulled away but while she devoured me I knew I could put up with anything.

A lot of fiddling about went on between my legs and I just wished they would get on with it. But then, when I knew that it was about to happen, I held my breath and let Becky drown me with her kiss. Her soft hands played with my breasts and rolled the nipples exactly the way I loved.

An almighty cheer went up through the room and as more fiddling went on between my thighs I was touched and congratulated by many hands as if I had won a prize. I couldn't believe it was over – all I had felt was a tugging sensation.

Becky crooned words of admiration and love into my still hungry mouth, still cradling my head as if it was the thing most precious to her. At that moment I knew I was the most precious thing not only to her, but also to everyone in the room. Unseen hands helped me down and massaged my limbs to help restore the circulation.

I was led into what felt like the middle of the room and lifted back on to the table I had graced earlier with my wantonness, pushed into the submissive position that Becky favoured, kneeling with my legs spread as far apart as possible and surrounded by all the men.

All seemed to take turns to touch and explore my new jewellery and I was sorry that I was still completely numb. Even the idea of their looking at me and the gentle intrusion of their probing hands was enough to start me off again, and I strained towards the hands.

'Are we all agreed, gentlemen? Do we accept this pawn into the games?'

There were choruses of 'Yes, yes, yes' and I swelled with pride. I felt more fingers fumbling between my legs and wriggled my invitation with my head held high and my breasts thrust forward.

'Come on, you rude little trollop, you. Let's go home.'

At that I was lifted down from the table and expected to walk with what felt like a ton of iron between my thighs. They rubbed together numbly so I spread my legs apart and waddled like that, not giving a damn what I looked like. It seemed a bit late to worry about that. I was led out of the room and through the hall to loud catcalls and wolf whistles and the finale.

'Three cheers for our new pawn: hip, hip . . .'

'Hooray!' came the reply.

I don't think they could count because I could still hear them all cheering as Becky helped me into the car.

I was still stark naked apart from the blindfold and whatever was between my thighs, but didn't care as I sat with my legs wide apart, dying to see what they had done to me, but my new sense of submission made me wait for Becky to say something. Becky leaned over me and wound down the window and I waited to see why.

'Goodbye, Cassandra. Thank you for coming. We hope to have you again soon at the Chessmen Club.' Mr King's voice was reassuring and still just as horny.

'Are you mad with me?' Becky asked me. 'I'm afraid I got nearly as carried away as you did but it's so easy to let these games run away with you, isn't it?'

I just turned towards her and smiled broadly. She must have guessed that meant approval because she swept me in her arms and we hugged and rocked together on the back seat, laughing and both talking at once.

'I don't understand, Becky. You can't possibly have known Mr King, if that's his name, before I went to see him the first time, so how did you get there?'

'I tricked you, I'm afraid. When I realised how much you still wanted to go to see him I organised a couple of days away – remember my course that suddenly cropped up? Then I went to see him and had a chat and explained the situation. He was very excited and told me about the Chessmen Club, which he's president of.' She nodded back over her shoulder. 'They're all called after pieces on a chessboard to keep their identities secret. I can assure you there's nothing ominous about them. They're just a group of eight men – only six could make it tonight because some live abroad – who're very dominant and, like us, enjoy playing rather extreme games. Apparently King had you in mind for the club as soon as he met you and was just biding his time until he felt you were ready to be initiated.'

'But where do we come in if it's a men's club?' I queried.

'Well, to put it crudely, they need pawns, not only to complete the chessboard idea but as pawns in their games. They all agreed from the start two years ago that all pawns must be completely consensual because none of them gets their kicks forcing their attentions on women, unless they've *agreed* to being forced, of course. Mmm, that gives me an idea for another game.'

Becky thought for a moment. 'To date they have five pawns and with you that makes six. They meet about once a month and summon the pawn of their choice to attend. Then, on the selected date, they send White Rook, the chauffeur – they made a special case of you and King came because you didn't know where you were going – to pick them up for a night of unbridled debauchery. I've agreed to lend you to them as a pawn, but only when I choose. I'm afraid I won't be allowed to go with you again, so you'll have to relay your experience to me in minute detail.'

Becky had read me so well. All the talk of games and being given to them was already sending a surge of hope through my belly, but as soon as it reached my sex I remembered the new adornment to that portion of my anatomy. I started to take off the blindfold but Becky stopped me.

'Wait until we get home, Cassie, and I'll explain the rest.'

'You mean there's more?' I was astounded and starting to get aroused. I reached over to slip my hand up Becky's skirt but she slapped me away.

'You insatiable slut, you!'

I fell asleep with my head in her lap, breathing in the smell of her arousal mixed with mine, and didn't wake up until we pulled into our drive. Becky helped me out of the car, thanked White Rook and led me indoors. How did she know that I had no will of my own left and I needed her to guide me?

She took me straight up to the playroom and shut the door. She stood me facing the mirror and told me to wait there while she lit the candles. Once the room was bright with the flickering light she came up behind me and removed the blindfold. At first I couldn't see anything, but as soon as I could focus I gasped out loud as I stared transfixed at the pretty gold rings that dangled from my naked sex, clasped together with a tiny gold chess piece. The king.

I sat on the floor in front of the mirror and Becky sat behind me and held me in her arms as I opened my legs for a better look. The dark, hairy, neat pussy of the day before was gone. In its place was a naked, rude, split mound crisscrossed with a pink blush, my lips hung heavy with the gold rings that pierced them through.

That image in itself was devastating, and my mouth hung open in amazement as I carefully reached down to touch my adornments of submission.

'What do you think, Cassie?' Becky asked, obviously totally unsure what my reaction would be. 'Do you like them?'

'*Like* them?' I squeaked in delight. 'I *love* them. Thank you, thank you.'

I stood up and spread my legs so they would dangle free and the tug on my clitoris was exquisite. I played with them gently with my fingertips, shaking in case it hurt, but the sensation was deliciously intoxicating, although it made me wince slightly because the feeling was beginning to return. My lips started swelling with arousal and that did sting but, knowing Becky was watching, I started rubbing my clitoris. She pulled my hand away.

'But I want to come for you,' I whined. I could see she

was aroused by what I was doing and I thought she would oblige straightaway, but she just laughed out loud.

'You are incorrigible, you dirty girl, you! It'll take at least a week to ten days for those piercings to heal, so you'll have to try to contain yourself. Oh, and the best way to heal them, Cassandra, is to pee on them, so we'll have to see what I can think up, won't we?'

She turned me round and led me out of the playroom to my bedroom, helped me on to the bed, then went away and returned with a pair of handcuffs. She cuffed my wrists and attached them with a short chain to the top of the bed, turned me on to my back and told me to spread my legs. I obeyed without a second thought and watched, entranced, as she gently examined my rings, tugging them this way and that, then jiggling them about to hear the tinkle as they touched. She squirmed her finger carefully between my clamped-together lips and tutted in disgust at my dripping wetness. Then she took a chain out of her pocket and fastened it to the rings next to the king between my spread thighs. She ran the chain loosely down to the post at the bottom of the bed with just enough tension so that, when I tested it and moved, the chain tugged temptingly on my sex. Each tiny movement sent a flash of desperation through my brain at the knowledge that I was stuck with the situation until Becky decided to release me and every time I moved I would renew my own desperate arousal. What sweet torture.

Becky climbed on to the bed beside me, leaned over and kissed me hard. Then, covering me up, she got ready to leave.

'Goodnight, Cassandra, king's pawn. Sleep well.'

'Becky, can I ask one question before you go to sleep? Please?'

'Mmm?'

'You don't really mean that you intend to keep me this way for ever, do you?'

'Well, there are only two keys – and the other one's hung over the table with all the others at the Chessmen Club. I've promised that I'll take you back to them as soon as your trophy's healed, and in the meantime they assure me that they'll be thinking of more diabolical games they can play with their newest of pawns. But,' she added as she placed a finger over my mouth, 'you ask far too many questions for a pawn, my love. Now, go to sleep, Cassandra. Tomorrow we'll discuss just how much we want to be involved with the Chessmen Club.'

Visit the Black Lace website at
www.blacklace-books.co.uk

FIND OUT THE LATEST INFORMATION AND TAKE
ADVANTAGE OF OUR FANTASTIC FREE BOOK OFFER!
ALSO VISIT THE SITE FOR . . .

- All Black Lace titles currently available
  and how to order online

- Great new offers

- Writers' guidelines

- Author interviews

- An erotica newsletter

- Features

- Cool links

BLACK LACE — THE LEADING IMPRINT
OF WOMEN'S SEXY FICTION

TAKING YOUR EROTIC READING
PLEASURE TO NEW HORIZONS

LOOK OUT FOR THE ALL-NEW BLACK LACE BOOKS – AVAILABLE NOW!

All books priced £6.99 in the UK. Please note publication dates apply to the UK only. For other territories, please contact your retailer.

TIGER LILY
Kimberley Dean
ISBN 0 352 33685 4

When Federal Agent Shanna McKay – aka Tiger Lily – is assigned to a new case on a tough precinct, her shady past returns to haunt her. She has to bust drug lord Mañuel Santos, who caused her sister's disappearance years previously. The McKay sisters had been wild: Shanna became hooked on sex; her sister hooked on Santos and his drugs. Desperate to even the score, Shanna infiltrates the organisation by using her most powerful weapon – her sexuality. **Hard-hitting erotica mixes with low-life gangsters in a tough American police precinct. Sizzling, sleazy action that will have you on the edge of your seat!**

COOKING UP A STORM
Emma Holly
ISBN 0 352 33686 2

The Coates Inn Restaurant in Cape Cod is about to go belly up when its attractive owner, Abby, jumps at a stranger's offer to help her – both in her kitchen and her bed. The handsome chef claims to have an aphrodisiac menu that her patrons won't be able to resist. Can this playboy chef really save the day when Abby's body means more to him than her feelings? He has charmed the pants off her and she's now behaving like a wild woman. Can Abby tear herself away from her new lover for long enough to realise that he might be trying to steal the restaurant from under her nose? **Beautifully written and evocative story of love, lust and haute cuisine.**

Coming in May 2002

SLAVE TO SUCCESS
Kimberley Raines
ISBN 0 352 33687 0

Eugene, born poor but grown-up handsome, answers an ad to be a sex slave for a year. He assumes his role will be that of a gigolo, and thinks he will easily make the million dollars he needs to break into Hollywood. On arrival at a secret destination he discovers his tasks are somewhat more demanding. He will be a pleasure slave to the mistress Olanthé – a demanding woman with high expectations who will put Eugene through some exacting physical punishments and pleasures. He is in for the shock of his life. **An exotic tale of female domination over a beautiful but arrogant young man.**

FULL EXPOSURE
Robyn Russell
ISBN 0 352 33688 9

Attractive but stern Boston academic Donatella di'Bianchi is in Arezzo, Italy, to investigate the affairs of the *Collegio Toscana*, a school of visual arts. Donatella's probe is hampered by one man, the director, Stewart Temple-Clarke. She is also sexually attracted by an English artist on the faculty, the alluring but mysterious Ian Ramsey. In the course of her inquiry Donatella is attacked, but receives help from two new friends – Kiki Lee and Francesca Antinori. As the trio investigates the menacing mysteries surrounding the college, these two young women open Donatella's eyes to a world of sexual adventure with artists, students and even the local *carabinieri*. **A stylishly sensual erotic thriller set in the languid heat of an Italian summer.**

STRIPPED TO THE BONE
Jasmine Stone
ISBN 0 352 33463 0

Annie has always been a rebel. While her sister settled down in Middle America, Annie blazed a trail of fast living on the West Coast, constantly seeking thrills. She is motivated by a hungry sexuality and a mission to keep changing her life. Her capacity for experimental sex games means she's never short of partners, and she keeps her lovers in a spin of erotic confusion. Every man she encounters is determined to discover what makes her tick, yet no one can get a hold of Annie long enough to find out. Maybe the Russian Ilmar can unlock the secret. However, by succumbing to his charms, is Annie stepping into territory too dangerous even for her? **By popular demand, this is a special reprint of a free-wheeling story of lust and trouble in a fast world.**

Coming in June 2002

WICKED WORDS 6
A Black Lace short story collection
ISBN 0 352 33590 0

Deliciously daring and hugely popular, the *Wicked Words* collections are the freshest and most entertaining volumes of women's erotica to be found anywhere in the world. The diversity of themes and styles reflects the multi-faceted nature of the female sexual imagination. Combining humour, warmth and attitude with fun, filthy, imaginative writing, these stories sizzle with horny action. Only the most arousing fiction makes it into a *Wicked Words* volume. **This is the best in fun, cutting-edge erotica from the UK and USA.**

MANHATTAN PASSION
Antoinette Powell
ISBN 0 352 33691 9

Julia is an art conservator at a prestigious museum in New York. She lives
a life of designer luxury with her Wall Street millionaire husband until,
that is, she discovers the dark and criminal side to his twilight activities –
and storms out, leaving her high-fashion wardrobe behind her. Staying
with her best friends Zoe and Jack, Julia is initiated into a hedonist circle
of New York's most beautiful and sexually interesting people.
Meanwhile, David, her husband, has disappeared with all their wealth.
What transpires is a high-octane man hunt – from loft apartments to
sleazy drinking holes; from the trendiest nightclubs to the criminal
underworld. **A stunning debut from an author who knows how to
entertain her audience.**

HARD CORPS
Claire Thompson
ISBN 0 352 33491 6

This is the story of Remy Harris, a bright young woman starting out as an
army cadet at military college in the US. Enduring all the usual trials of
boot-camp discipline and rigorous exercise, she's ready for any challenge
– that is until she meets Jacob, who recognises her true sexuality.
Initiated into the Hard Corps – a secret society within the barracks –
Remy soon becomes absorbed by this clandestine world of ritual
punishment. It's only when Jacob takes things too far that she rebels,
and begins to plot her revenge. **Strict sergeants and rebellious cadets
come together in this unusual and highly entertaining story of military
discipline with a twist.**

Black Lace Booklist

Information is correct at time of printing. To avoid disappointment check availability before ordering. Go to www.blacklace-books.co.uk. All books are priced £6.99 unless another price is given.

BLACK LACE BOOKS WITH A CONTEMPORARY SETTING

☐ THE TOP OF HER GAME Emma Holly	ISBN 0 352 33337 5	£5.99
☐ IN THE FLESH Emma Holly	ISBN 0 352 34498 3	£5.99
☐ A PRIVATE VIEW Crystalle Valentino	ISBN 0 352 33308 1	£5.99
☐ SHAMELESS Stella Black	ISBN 0 352 33485 1	£5.99
☐ INTENSE BLUE Lyn Wood	ISBN 0 352 34496 7	£5.99
☐ THE NAKED TRUTH Natasha Rostova	ISBN 0 352 34497 5	£5.99
☐ ANIMAL PASSIONS Martine Marquand	ISBN 0 352 34499 1	£5.99
☐ A SPORTING CHANCE Susie Raymond	ISBN 0 352 33501 7	£5.99
☐ TAKING LIBERTIES Susie Raymond	ISBN 0 352 33357 X	£5.99
☐ A SCANDALOUS AFFAIR Holly Graham	ISBN 0 352 33523 8	£5.99
☐ THE NAKED FLAME Crystalle Valentino	ISBN 0 352 33528 9	£5.99
☐ CRASH COURSE Juliet Hastings	ISBN 0 352 33018 X	£5.99
☐ ON THE EDGE Laura Hamilton	ISBN 0 352 33534 3	£5.99
☐ LURED BY LUST Tania Picarda	ISBN 0 352 33533 5	£5.99
☐ THE HOTTEST PLACE Tabitha Flyte	ISBN 0 352 33536 X	£5.99
☐ THE NINETY DAYS OF GENEVIEVE Lucinda Carrington	ISBN 0 352 33070 8	£5.99
☐ EARTHY DELIGHTS Tesni Morgan	ISBN 0 352 33548 3	£5.99
☐ MAN HUNT Cathleen Ross	ISBN 0 352 33583 1	
☐ MÉNAGE Emma Holly	ISBN 0 352 33231 X	
☐ DREAMING SPIRES Juliet Hastings	ISBN 0 352 33584 X	
☐ THE TRANSFORMATION Natasha Rostova	ISBN 0 352 33311 1	
☐ STELLA DOES HOLLYWOOD Stella Black	ISBN 0 352 33588 2	
☐ SIN.NET Helena Ravenscroft	ISBN 0 352 33598 X	
☐ HOTBED Portia Da Costa	ISBN 0 352 33614 5	
☐ TWO WEEKS IN TANGIER Annabel Lee	ISBN 0 352 33599 8	
☐ HIGHLAND FLING Jane Justine	ISBN 0 352 33616 1	

☐ PLEASURE'S DAUGHTER Sedalia Johnson   ISBN O 352 33237 9
☐ JULIET RISING Cleo Cordell   ISBN O 352 32938 6
☐ DEMON'S DARE Melissa MacNeal   ISBN O 352 33683 8
☐ ELENA'S CONQUEST Lisette Allen   ISBN O 352 32950 5

BLACK LACE ANTHOLOGIES
☐ CRUEL ENCHANTMENT Erotic Fairy Stories   ISBN O 352 33483 5   £5.99
    Janine Ashbless
☐ MORE WICKED WORDS Various   ISBN O 352 33487 8   £5.99
☐ WICKED WORDS 4 Various   ISBN O 352 33603 X
☐ WICKED WORDS 5 Various   ISBN O 352 33642 O

BLACK LACE NON-FICTION
☐ THE BLACK LACE BOOK OF WOMEN'S SEXUAL   ISBN O 352 33346 4   £5.99
    FANTASIES Ed. Kerri Sharp

To find out the latest information about Black Lace titles, check out the
website: www.blacklace-books.co.uk or send for a booklist with
complete synopses by writing to:

        Black Lace Booklist, Virgin Books Ltd
        Thames Wharf Studios
        Rainville Road
        London W6 9HA

Please include an SAE of decent size. Please note only British stamps
are valid.

Our privacy policy
We will not disclose information you supply us to any other parties.
We will not disclose any information which identifies you personally to
any person without your express consent.

From time to time we may send out information about Black Lace
books and special offers. Please tick here if you do <u>not</u> wish to
receive Black Lace information.   ☐

Please send me the books I have ticked above.

Name ....

Address ....

....

....

....

Post Code ....

Send to: Cash Sales, Black Lace Books, Thames Wharf Studios, Rainville Road, London W6 9HA.

US customers: for prices and details of how to order books for delivery by mail, call 1-800-343-4499.

Please enclose a cheque or postal order, made payable to Virgin Books Ltd, to the value of the books you have ordered plus postage and packing costs as follows:

UK and BFPO – £1.00 for the first book, 50p for each subsequent book.

Overseas (including Republic of Ireland) – £2.00 for the first book, £1.00 for each subsequent book.

If you would prefer to pay by VISA, ACCESS/MASTERCARD, DINERS CLUB, AMEX or SWITCH, please write your card number and expiry date here:

....

Signature ....

Please allow up to 28 days for delivery.